A New Era Begins

You cannot close what has been opened....

Thomas Franciscus Malick

Prologue

-25 Years Earlier-

"You may want to grab a hold of something," William bellowed sufficiently loud enough to be heard over the strained engine noise of the Cessna he was piloting. Phillip, beside him in the small craft, nervously shifted in his co-pilot's chair.

"What the hell are you doing?" He called out in lamented fear.

"You know that gibberish you just heard on the radio?"

"Yeah," Phillip said, while his eyes widened the faster they descended.

"Well, it's Portuguese and the pilot of the military plane behind us just said he'd open fire if we don't land immediately," William yelled as the small plane was half way through a nose dive toward the jungle tree tops. The small craft continued to lurch downward at an incredible speed as Phillip's hands were vainly about to push through the top of the plane.

"If they capture us, our entire society will be discovered, and I can't let that happen," William said with the brazen confidence his angular face exuded.

"So we're committing suicide?" The engine noise continued to become higher pitched and thousands of images of their lives raced through both the men's minds.

"No, I'm going to try to land," William desperately blurted out with white knuckles grasping the flight stick.

"Where? It's nothing but jungle. There's no clearing!"

"You think I don't know that!?" William momentarily lost his composure and gave into Phillip's hysteria. "We have no choice," he turned and looked his younger brother piercingly in his eyes. "I'm going to put her down in the tree canopy."

"Are you insane? We'll be obliterated!" Phillip reacted in rage.

The radio called out again in a contrastingly calm Portuguese voice, and when it stopped, a few moments of silence passed before Phillip spoke.

"What did he say?" Phillip yelled, his face frozen in panic.

"He's going to open fire in ten seconds if we don't stop our descent, but I doubt he'll do it," William replied confidently. The Brazilian Military plane was now within five hundred yards of the unarmed Cessna while William continued suicidally toward the tree tops. The pair quickly realized the validity of the threat as multiple bullets flew seemingly unimpeded through their plane. Immediately the engine noise shifted from a high pitched whizzing to a low grumble. Both men turned their heads toward each other knowing in some form or fashion, this situation was about to be abruptly met with resolution.

William had planned on quickly performing a barrel roll to evade the pursing craft; however, the loss of a substantial portion of his thrust quickly changed the situation. With both hands on the flight stick he attempted with all his might to pull the plane out of it's treacherous dive and to the surprise of himself and his co-pilot, the Cessna momentarily leveled out just barely brushing the tops of a few soaring Amazonian trees. In reaction to the rustling branches, thousands of vibrantly colored birds exploded out of the canopy directly underneath the craft. By this point the Brazilian military plane had closed the gap to within three hundred yards and was about to use this leveling opportunity to obliterate the brother's attempted escape.

With his finger on the trigger and the Cessna in range, the air force pilot was a hair away from completing his mission, when suddenly he caught glimpse of the birds ascending from the tree tops and had no time to react. The plane met twenty of the sizable fowl, and the first five were deflected harmlessly off the hull. The next fifteen of them all did considerable damage, knocking off propellers and becoming lodged in various critical parts of the twin engines. Still thinking they could at make an emergency landing even if their chances of pursing the Cessna had vanished, the Brazilians had not anticipated one final bird whose beak went directly through the windshield of the military craft, savagely piercing the captain's forehead.

As William was still trying to stabilize their damaged Cessna, in his mirror he caught sight of the struggling pursuer violently entering the jungle below, and watched in awe as a huge fireball arose victoriously from the trees.

"What was that?" Phillip, still panic stricken, called out.

"That brother. . . .was sheer luck, but it's still a little too early to celebrate."

The small plane was now heaving massive puffs of black smoke from its bullet ridden fuselage, and William knew he had to somehow land in the trees. The pungent smell of burning oil singed their nostrils.

With gravity winning the battle against the battered craft, the two brothers turned and gazed at one another, nodding in mutual understanding that their chances of survival were low. As the plane neared one of

William calculatingly looked around for a solution and although it was not perfect by any means, he decided it was their only chance. He wrapped his arm around a strong vine for support and after testing its strength, he *very* carefully inched out on a limb toward his brother. The wreckage shifted and let out another series of noises which Roger began to associate with sudden death. As he neared his target he could make out the expression on his brother's face, and it became clear that Phillip was beginning to understand exactly how close to death he really was.

"William, hurry," he whispered as he looked around in panic.

"Shhhhh, relax, just sit tight, I'm almost there."

Still grasping the vine like a safety rope he was now close enough to reach an arm into the twisted, metal wreckage toward his brother.

"Ok, now, in one fast motion I need you to reach out and grab my hand with all the strength you've got, when I give you the signal. Can you do that for me?" William said methodically and calmingly.

"Yea, I think so," he said and looked around at his wobbly pedestal.

"Hey! Don't do that," his face stiffened in seriousness, "focus on me, I've got ya." William said commandingly.

Phillip pursed his lips, looked squarely in his brother's eyes, and nodded in confirmation that he was ready.

"Alright, NOW!"

Phillip's hand suddenly clasped onto ~~Roger~~ *William*'s with an adrenaline fueled grip. The sudden movement was all the wrecked tail section needed to dislodge itself from the precarious perch and finish its descent forever toward the jungle floor. Within the blink of an eye the noisy crash reverberated through the dense vegetation with such authority that it seemed like all of the animals in the dark jungle responded in audible shock.

Like dangling links of a chain, Phillip firmly grasped his brother's left hand, while at the same time, William's right hand was entangled in the life sustaining Amazonian vine. The two men purposefully swung back and forth until Phillip finally found a sturdy enough limb on which to land. After about a half an hour of silently descending to the jungle floor the two brothers joyfully sat down on solid ground.

"Thank you," Phillip whispered as he turned to his only brother with tear laden eyes. "You saved my life."

"Nothing you wouldn't have done for me, given the right opportunity," William shot back at him and put his arm around the grateful sibling.

"What are we going to do now?"

"Well, we planned on getting settled in for the next two months before we started grad school . . . . I guess we're going to hike through the Amazonian Basin instead," William replied and turned toward Phillip with a smile.

"We need to let the Council know what happened as soon as possible."

"I'm sure we'll take care of that eventually."

"Phillip," William said as the pair began to stand up, "people in Arkonos said coming to the Old World was going to be an adventure, but I couldn't have imagined this is what they meant."

"Who knows what we'll discover."

"Well, we've got a long road ahead of us." The two men gathered what was left of their supplies and disappeared into the dark, mysterious jungle.

* * *

Part I – Awakening

-Present Day-

‖ *1* ‖

Roger had *some* idea why he'd been called into Specialist Rodriguez's office. Cosgrove Strategies Inc. preferred that their agents walk a discrete line between the civilian and the top secret world. Having numerous contacts with civilian scientists should be rather advantageous for Roger; however, in the case that they are *un*secured contacts, well that's another matter entirely.

"What the hell were you *thinking*, Vanden?" Rodriguez's words slapped across Roger's face.

"Sir, if you'd just hear me out . . . . I can explain," he continued nervously replying. "It's just that I thought, you know, this one had to be a glitch or something." Rogers's next sentence was cut off as Specialist Rodriguez slammed both of his fists on his dark walnut desk, the force seemingly propelling him to his feet in preparation for a loud lambasting of the obviously anxious man.

From one word to the next his voice emulated a pressure cooker about to explode, "that's the *damn* problem *Roger*; you *thought*!" Rodriguez, whose skin went from olive colored to red, was visibly attempting to control his anger in an effort to shield the office from thinking that they were next on his list.

"Yes sir, I guess I shouldn't have voiced my opinion. I just thought," Roger tried to complete his sentence again but to no avail.

"What did I *just* tell you about thinking?!?" Rodriguez crashed back and into his brown leather office chair, slumping a bit in frustration. He rubbed the dark rings around his eyes, which without words told a tale of hard work and unfulfilled dreams. "Roger we have rules here not only to protect you, but to protect our entire *operation*. The National Security Service (NSS) doesn't pay us to cause panic. Do you know how detrimental bad press and rumors are to winning contracts? You should have *never* tried to consult with your people in DC on this one. *Never*." Rodriguez's fingers rubbed his temples while much needed silence flushed into the room for a just few moments.

"Sir, I know if you just give me a little more time I can fix this thing," he said confidently, knowing that he had bested more cumbersome challenges in his middle aged life.

"Ehh . . . . . eh, eh," he said, shaking his head from left to right, "no more talking for you Roger. This thing is too far above your pay grade for *you* to fix. It falls in my arena now. What I need *you* to do is to go back to your desk, sit down, and keep working on this thing. Capiche?"

"Yes sir. I'm going now." Roger turned around and shuffled toward the exit happily knowing the conversation was over.

"And Vanden," Rodriguez called out as Roger turned back toward his boss with an attentive eyebrow raised, "you were right, this could be *huge*." After pursing his lips and slightly nodding his head in fearful realization of what he actually discovered, Roger turned and exited the spacious office, closing the door behind him.

As he walked back to his own office, he started to contemplate the ramifications of what he had done. *I'm sure the company will probably put a mark on my record,* he thought. He knew that in the end it did not really matter. Sometimes he considered a reprimand to be a necessary part of effectively getting the job done.

Roger was glad to not work for the red tape laden enterprise known as the government; nevertheless he still had to work *with* them. Cumbersome bureaucracy and split second decision making are like oil and water, and this is exactly why companies like Cosgrove Strategies exist. Roger knew that over half of the spy agencies' budget goes directly to independent contractors.[1] Publicly, the agencies themselves state that this is the case because of the enormous cost of "outside services". This is non-sense misinformation. Outside services don't cost that much! Intelligence services not bound by any semblance of constitutional law on the other hand; well, that costs quite a lot.

Having worked at Cosgrove Strategies, Inc. for almost two decades Roger has certainly seen his share of strange world events. During the late eighties and nineties they had a contract to monitor Russia and the former Soviet states for all sorts of things. Nuclear proliferation was certainly at the top of the agenda, but Roger learned that all manner of devious and insidious people are born out of imperial collapse. One man in particular surfaced to his mind.

---

[1] Shorrock, Tim, *Spies for Hire: The Secret World of Intelligence Outsourcing,* (New York: Simon and Schuster, 2008). *ALSO: from the Office of the Director of National Intelligence 2006.

Before the fall of the Soviet Empire Sergei Ingistov was a mid-level nuclear researcher, who during the last days Gorbachev's rule, was dangerously outspoken not just against his own government but even the United States. This was a rarity among Russian scientists at the time because many of them wished to apply to live and work in the US, where their Russian wages would have probably quadrupled.

As Roger began tracking Sergei, normally with electronic surveillance, but sometimes even on field assignments, he noticed something very odd about the man's behavior. After supposedly visiting with a number of professors in the United States and around the world, Sergei suddenly stopped publicly complaining about the various governments and corporations of the world. He just *stopped*. No more letters to world leaders and officials, no more attempting to shock news reporters with his statements, and he even discontinued writing his own small newspaper, "United as Individuals". At that point the alarm bells really went off, because for someone *that* outspoken to all of the sudden have a change of heart was *extremely* unlikely in Roger's business. More *likely* the case is that he started to keep a low profile so to not draw public attention to his actions. Whatever the case was, or could have been, it's irrelevant now.

About six months after Sergei stopped appearing publicly, some agents were routinely tracking him while he was at a nearby market in Moscow. It seemed like business as usual until the agents saw some kind of commotion and all of the sudden Sergei disappeared. Gone. He never came home, nor did he pack a bag or take any of his personal possessions. No one knows if he left on his on accord or was taken against his will. That was well over decade ago.

Roger physically shook his head and returned his attention to the present day. He peered at his sleek, flat screen monitor, shook the mouse to break the computer out of its slumber and then entered his sixteen digit passcode. The report which had gotten him a personal meeting with Agent Rodriguez flashed to life in front of him.

He leaned back in his chair and put his hand through his salt and pepper colored hair in contemplation. Roger had been tracking disappearing scientists, professors and other prominent people for almost a decade in an effort to find some sort of connection. After each incident the cell phone, land-line and internet records were always examined and that was the oddest thing about the majority of these cases – there was no communication. In Roger's world this is called 'operating off the grid' and it meant that normal methods of conversation weren't being utilized.

A few years ago he postulated that it would have been impossible to accomplish these types of abductions without some sort of independent, complex communication's system between the coordinating parties. Knowing that cutting edge technology was not exactly within his sphere of understanding, the next step was to contact an old friend – Herschel Bohr.

Herschel and Roger had gone to graduate school together at Princeton and were inseparable during those days. While Roger had mainly studied politics and government, Herschel on the other hand focused his attention on physics. Roger thought it was interesting that back then, they had always wished that the other would really "get" their field of study so they could share that part of their lives as well. Physics, specifically of the quantum variety, was not exactly graspable for Roger and neither was politics for Herschel. So they simply enjoyed each others company and realized that the absence of the same subject matter led them to relax more with one another – something they both desperately needed during grueling masters' programs.

Immediately after graduation Herschel started working for a research company called Vanguard Quantum Technologies, where he has advanced quite rapidly ever since. At Cosgrove, Roger had done much the same, earning numerous promotions through the years. The two have kept in touch sporadically after their studies, randomly meeting up at conventions and the occasional class reunion.

Roger remembered a conversation from a few years ago that had piqued his interest during one of the conventions at which they met. After a long day of excruciatingly boring seminars and rubbing elbows with some of the company high-ups, the two old friends did what they had always done best – drank. On the third round of scotch in a relatively posh up-town hotel bar, Herschel was relaxed enough to boast about his classified work a bit.

From what Roger could gather from the conversation (Herschel was nice enough to use what he called *plain language)* they were on the brink of a scientific breakthrough not achieved since the wheel was invented. As Herschel put it, "Alright, alright, think about it this way. Let's say I take two atoms and put them next to each other, right. By using a small bit of light I can program these two atoms to show 'on' or 'off' or 'both'. Got me? Now here comes the weird part . . . . then I could take one atom and drive it to say Winnipeg, Canada and then leave the other one, *right* here, at *this* very bar in New York City, and guess what? When I turn the one here from 'on' to 'off', the other atom in Winnipeg changes as well. They mimic each other perfectly. Now here's the even weirder part; they do it almost instantaneously, at least 10,000 times faster than even the speed of light." [2]

Roger remembered that he had actually said, "that's crazy," something he reserved for only the absolute oddest things he's heard.

"It may seem to be crazy," his old friend replied, "only because our present paradigm of how the universe works is in fact the crazy theory."

"Careful Einstein," Roger said as he hoisted his scotch in for a cheers, "you're starting to loose me."

"Wouldn't think of it," their glassed met one another a bit too clashingly which in turned caused the wait staff to take notice of the two.

"So, while this is all well and good in the crazy quantum physics world Herschel; what does it all mean to us . . . . in the here and now?"

"We believe that we can develop communications systems utilizing this technology to deliver 1's and 0's - which is the basis for all computers - in real time. Without having to wait for some archaic radio wave to bounce back and forth, science can advance much more rapidly. I mean hell; it takes about thirty minutes to get a signal back and forth to Mars. But even besides space exploration the communications and computer systems that could be utilized here on earth would make our present system look like the damned Pony Express."

* * *

---

[2] D. Salart, A. Baas, C. Branciard, N. Gisin, and H. Zbinden, "Testing spooky action at a distance," Group of Applied Physics, University of Geneva, 20, Rue de l'Ecole de M_edecine, CH-1211 Geneva 4, Switzerland.
For more information search: *Quantum Entanglement*.

‖ 2 ‖

Jakob took a silent seat on the couch. His father, Roger, was sitting next to him on a luxurious brown leather arm chair. The TV blared the evening news in the background; both father and son were fixated on the broadcast in an attempt to placate the awkwardness between them. The on-site reporter who was dressed in a crisp, olive colored suit tightened his posture and spoke:

"In tonight's special report I'll be examining a new designer drug, a drug which is *designed* to addict primary and secondary school children. Law enforcement and secondary school kids call it *Stakz*, while the primary schools kids call it 'Pinkz'. Whatever name you give it, it's at epidemic proportions. It looks like candy and the pieces "stack" up, hence the name. They are actually sweet to the taste, but unlike candy within minutes the drug creates an extreme type of euphoria and after about five minutes the entire experience is over. The child is then completely normal and there are no signs that they'd *just* been intoxicated. In fact, even in the middle of their euphoria it's very difficult to tell if they've taken the drug. Even stranger is that they have little or no effect at all on adults. First hitting the streets about three months ago, the drug has now spread from California to all the way across the country in that short time." The reporter heaved a breath in like a bagpipe player before continuing.

"While Stakz itself is stirring controversy, the other issue is how law enforcement officials have chosen to fight this scourge . . . . through the use of random school searches. Actually Diane this Echelon Township

School behind me," he moved a step to the right, revealing the police squad cars leaving the scene, "was just searched only a few hours before. It's now true that law enforcement officials have begun a nationwide operation.

"They are entering schools, both primary and secondary, and searching entire facilities. This includes all student lockers and private book bags, as well as faculty areas.

"One outspoken critic of these searches is Senator Langesé, who claims it's yet another violation of the citizens' constitutional rights," the young reporter raised a suspicious eyebrow and paused before speaking again.

"The Senator, along with several other lawmakers, has managed to get court injunctions to temporarily ban the searches in their states.

"Law enforcement officials tell Channel Seven that the epidemic is worsening in those areas not conducting the random searches. This issue is controversial and will remain so as long as our children are in danger. Diane, back to you."

"Thanks Bradley, in other news the Mayor has decided," the newscaster kept rambling on as father and son continued to sit together focused on the TV in an attempt to *not* focus on each other. Jakob finally spoke first.

"Crazy about that drug and those school searches, huh? It's tough to be a kid these days."

"It's tough and about to be a lot tougher when a lot of those parents wake up to a lot of dead children, which may be necessary, albeit unfortunate," Roger said pursing his lips tightly in confirmation as he sipped his scotch. Jakob turned his head and looked straight into his father's eyes in response to the odd comment.

"What do you mean 'dead children'?" Jakob asked before being interrupted by a call coming from the kitchen.

"Dinner's ready, c'mon time to eat!" Jakob's Mom's voice echoed throughout the house alleviating the awkward momentum between the two men, who both quickly got up and made their way toward the kitchen.

After a few moments of silently consuming the lavish meal Roger broke the silence this time. "So Jakob," Roger asked him after thoroughly chewing a bite of marbled, rare rib eye, "how do you like your classes this semester?" Gathered around the family dinner table were Jakob's mother and father as well as his six year old brother Kyle.

"They're pretty good, I guess, I mean there's one class I've really gotten into lately," he replied.

"Oh yeah, what's that?"

"It's an economics class, but well," he struggled to find the right words in order to transmit the meaning to his often disappointed father, "it's kind of like he, Professor Briarton, I mean, sorta shows you how it applies to politics."

"Oh, well then it's kind of an *intra*disciplinary class then, huh? I guess your third year is when you should start seeing how a lot of these subjects relate to one another and that's a good thing as long as you don't lose focus on your primary subject." Jakob's father spoke flatly about education regarding his son. As a child Roger had always excelled in his studies while his first born son, Jakob, on the other hand, had not. This was an immense let down for the father of two boys because he, like most fathers, expected their sons to be *better* than him, not worse. Right or wrong, Roger subconsciously felt that because he was the teacher of his offspring, this made *him* the failure. And above all Roger despised failure which he knows to be a sign of weakness.

"Yeah, I like it. There's a lot of class discussion, really gets the brain going, you know," Jakob took another oversized bite of his steak, and silence filled the air while his jaw muscles pulsed, rippling his cleanly shaven, youthful skin.

This was typically the part of the conversation when his Father would ask him if he'd given any thought about what he was going to do after college, and that 'all the best students were already lining up jobs'. He'd ask these knee jerk questions even though they *both* knew that with his 2.5 GPA, it was *highly unlikely* that Jakob was going to land a great job. His father would then point out the vaulted ceilings in his upper middle class home and try to motivate Jakob's academics with the threat of perceived poverty if he did not "try" harder - as he put it. The thought of the impending conversation made Jakob nauseous. Sensing the approaching pointlessness his Mother changed the subject.

"Roger, has Kyle taken his medicine?"

"I'm not sure. I didn't give it to him if that's what you mean," Roger said, noting the obvious change of topic in his mind.

"Mommy, hehe, where's the medicine," Kyle said demandingly yet oblivious to what was going on around him. He reached for his soft drink and thirstily took five gulps, easily finishing the beverage.

"What's wrong with Kyle? What do you mean 'medicine'?" Jakob inquired.

"Well we took him to the doctor the other day and he said that Kyle has some kind of brain disorder that keeps him from paying attention, so the doctor recommended he be put on this medication," his Mother replied softly as one would speak at a funeral.

"He's got *what?!?*" Jakob said, his face showing dissatisfied surprise knowing the ubiquitous nature of the study drug at his own university.

"Yeah honey, I know, I was shocked too. But the truth is when the doctor started to name all the symptoms - Kyle was a text book case. And I don't know if you've noticed or not, but his behavior has improved immensely since he started taking it," Jakob's Mom said matter-a-factly while giving a little pat on Kyle's light colored head in satisfaction.

"He's six years old and you've got him medicated. Mom. Seriously? I bet you took him to the same doctor who's got you all doped up too, huh?" Jakob sputtered frustratedly.

"*Don't you DARE* talk to your mother like that, *boy!*" Roger angrily slammed a fist on the table momentarily forcing the silverware to involuntarily dance about the surface. An awkward silence wafted like unwanted cigar smoke after the outburst.

Jakob's mom had started to take an anti-depressant about a year and a half ago and Jakob noticed the difference almost immediately. Sure, Jakob admitted that she definitely wasn't as depressed like she was before. No longer did she have those bouts of sadness which could last for days or even weeks, and sure, she found it easier to do her daily chores. But there was something else that happened as well . . . . . she did not love as compassionately. She did not smile as wide, and she wasn't really herself, whoever that was supposed to be. It was as if his mother was replaced by some middle of the road compassionless, fake, phony woman, and he despised this new person. Jakob had confronted her in the past and she had confessed that she 'finally *liked* herself *all the time* now,' he remembered her saying. She said that she felt more balanced than before. All this did not matter to Jakob if this new person wasn't his mom. To Jakob it was a chemical lobotomy. It was a quick fix. Without really looking into the actual causes of her gloom, some pharmaceutical pill pusher had slapped a shoddy bandage over her gangrenous wounds. And the worst part of it was that the same mindset had been forced onto his little brother. At least his mother had chosen to take drugs to change her personality – his brother had no choice. Jakob knew that Kyle would never be the same, and the revolving pharmaceutical door would probably keep spinning for the rest of his life.

"Maybe it's all the damn sugar he eats all the time. Don't you think *that* could make him hyper?!? Did you even *try* to change his diet before you drugged him!!?!" Jakob got in his comment but he knew it would be short lived, as his father never let a real debate occur.

"Are you a *doctor* Jakob? Huh, are you a medical doctor? Answer *ME!*" The tone of his father's voice had now moved past agitation and on to contempt.

"Look, I just . . . . . "

"*Answer ME!*"

"No, I'm not a doctor, Dad, but what I'm saying . . . . . " Jakob tried to convey his thought but was quickly cut off by his Father's much louder, starker voice.

"No, you're *not* a doctor. What you *are*," he intimidatingly postured his frame and pointed his index finger at him, "is a C student at a mediocre state university. And I'm pretty *damn* sure that the doctor that your mother and brother go to . . . well . . . let's just say he's a hell of a lot smarter than you. That's for *damn* sure." As Roger finished, Jakob leaned back in his chair in contemptuous disgust.

He *knew* it was stupid to even try to have a real discussion with his father, and for some ridiculous, unknown reason, he continued to attempt this impossible feat. It was one of his many masochistic tendencies and Jakob knew for the sake of his own psyche that he had to stop and now was as good as time as any. Why should he even continue to try? His mother has already had the equivalent of a lobotomy and his brother was too young to understand. Jakob knew that with Kyle's own pharmaceutical bliss he would remain unreachable for as long as he's stuck in the revolving door. His father was the only one who wasn't pharmaceutically polluted but it really did not matter anyway. Roger's mind was imprisoned by the most fierce gate keeper of all – himself.

He had been working for some sort of top secret agency for the better part of his life. Decades of service, as he called it, had led him to build up brick after brick of a 'God, country, family' philosophy that was too tall to even touch. From this high perch he looked down at everyone as Zeus on Mt Olympus must have, only he categorized every dissenting thought as belonging to hippies, commies and heathens.

Jakob was aware that the older his father became the less emotion he showed. His job was partially to blame for this – constantly operating in the shadows while rationalizing his immoral behavior for the greater good can make a man unemotional. Naturally, any form of depression or sorrow by those around him was immediately seen as a sign of weakness. Therefore Jakob's mother's chemical lobotomy was perfect for Roger. It's the way his father always wanted her to behave. She's finally the perfect woman for him.

"I've got to go. I've got some studying to do," Jakob said emotionlessly standing up and pushing himself from the table as well as the pointless conversation.

"That's the first good idea you've had all day. You *better* study hard or you'll never make anything of yourself. Frankly your attitude stinks," Roger called out while Jakob was heading expediently toward the door.

He grabbed the front door handle, twisted it violently and said to himself, "I'm so done with this." He secretly vowed to not return again.

* * *

‖ 3 ‖

Chairman Gorshial's grayish, wispy finger minutely stroked his forehead. A slight amount of the weight from his bulbous head was now resting on his digits as he scowled at the report in front of him.

"Incomprehensible!!!!" his fist struck the table and with it a wave of adrenaline induced pain crashed through his body. "It's not time yet," he pleaded, "we haven't fortified our sphere of influence enough to achieve our 'Goal of Continuity'." His finger continued to move across his forehead slowly, perhaps two millimeters at a time taking in every ridge and peak of the bone structure.

Chairman Gorshial, peered from behind his svelte, 10' long by 3' wide, gleaming pure metal desk, and finally calmed down enough to again meet eyes with the focus of his rage.

Kralsich's face was stoic as stared back at the Chairman and then spoke with distinction, "*you* know what our next action, however precipitous, must be," his eyes statically locked with Chairman Gorshial's. "After all I penned the currently decisive 'Alternative Solutions in the Event of a Constrained Time Frame: Goal of Continuity', which I presume we shall select for immediate enactment." Kralsich's tone was evenly matter of fact and why would it not be? He had in fact written the Alternative Solutions Transcript and in essence predicted the future, although through his intellect Kralsich did not see it that way. In his complexly cognitive way, the Transcript, with which Gorshial had so much contempt, was merely a possibility in a realm in which anything is possible. One is, however, able to trace factors, which would lead to the probability of one possibility over another. In Kralsich's mind those probabilities had coalesced into the 'Alternative Solutions in the Event of a Constrained Time Frame: Goal of Continuity', and he was therefore sitting in front of Chairmen Gorshial's desk, his posture appearing *quite* confident.

"It's seems as though your proposal, accepted by the Council of the Many, was indeed quite prophetic," uttered the Chairman with hint of irrelevance. "Your contribution has become essential to our goals. This is magnanimous. My colleagues will update you on the logistical details."

Kralsich and Gorshial both stood up and correspondingly dipped their heads a few centimeters down and back up again. The Chairman, again seated behind his simplistic metallic desk, watched as the younger, taller Kralsich exited the moderately lit office.

After the massively elongated door swung closed, the Chairman tapped a cold, copper colored button on his desk. A holographic face appeared and was quick with the appropriate salutation. "Yes Chairman?"

"See to it that Kralsich is given the appropriate documentation in order to continue his research. And Hickel," he said dryly, his face expressionless.

"Yes Chairman?"

"I want all of his accessing fully tracked and reported only to me, *understood*?"

"Yes Chairman; fully tracked."

* * *

‖ 4 ‖

Leather creaked as Jakob's hand gripped the wheel, fighting off the centripetal force of his hurried turn into the campus parking lot. "Typical," he spoke aloud and then thought, *no place to park.* The battle of equilibrium was momentarily lost by the clutch – his '68 Bronco lurched forward led on by the formidable two barrels of the carburetor bursting into action. His vehicle bounced straight over two speed bumps, at the same time his head turned to the left to observe a few young ladies exiting their jeep, blanketed in sunshine. They appeared to be smiling at *something.* Jakob assumed it was at him and was quick to look rather uninterested. *They loved to be chased,* his brain repeated, *especially those two.* The thought had unconsciously played in his head, conversely the act of *ignoring* everything his body told him to do . . . . . well, that takes conscious, disciplined control.

The engine shut off as his vehicle finally squeezed in a spot. He snatched his book bag off the back seat, slung it over his shoulder and began to make his way to class. With his feet shuffling beneath, he yanked his phone from his pocket and checked the time. *Shit!* Five minutes to make a fifteen minute walk. He still could not even *see* where his class was from this distance.

The truth is, at first he was rather uninterested in this particular class, but after a few great discussions/lectures he was sold. The tantalizing questions Professor Briarton asked made it easy to see that he did not care about the status quo or about questioning somebody's belief system. This unwavering style sometimes proved controversial as some students openly resisted following his line of reasoning for fear of where it would take them.

Jakob enjoyed this type of thought because it typically leads him to the most important question – 'why'. He's *always* had an intrinsic captivation with understanding the 'why' in everything. Without it, he's unable to truly encode new facts into his memory. Perhaps this is a primeval function of the brain – to protect itself from extraneous information.

He finally approached Padua Hall; his eyes scanning both left and right. *Nobody around outside – that means I'm REALLY late.* Pushing through the entrance way to the building he took a deep breath, cleared his head, and ever so gently opened the door through which he proceeded to enter.

"The mid-terms may be an insurmountable failure for approximately half the class," Professor Briarton, his body posturing with frustration, continued to bellow at the class, "to be quite honest with you all, as a Professor it's quite disheartening year after year to see students becoming progressively more *un*-intelligent. It's fair to say this is actually the antithesis to what we university types attempt to accomplish. Nevertheless, even the ones of you who were sapient enough to deal with my essay questions typically have one of two things horrendously wrong with you: (1) You regurgitate melodramatic propaganda in place of an actual thought process or, (2) You're like Jakob over here and believe that my classroom is like a cinema – *the first fifteen minutes are previews,*" He said, his expression calm but his voice level rising to a crescendo.

Jakob's opaque facial capillaries engorged themselves with blood, as he was half a second from being completely seated on the far left row. *Almost made it.* He said nothing, simply throwing a succinct, salute like wave to the Professor - less *is more in this case* – and finally sat down.

"In place of today's lecture we're going to pursue a different venture," he paused momentarily pushing back a more impatient facet of his personality, "today we're getting back to basics, to fundamentals. This is so because to *this* Professor it has become undeniable that, as evidenced by the ones among you who tend to only be able to repeat what you hear, you don't have an iota of understanding in relation to how the world works. Let's start with the most contentious question of the three on the essay test which was . . . . . ," he paused as he rustled through the test to find the precisely worded question, "ahhh, 'In the context of individual liberty and the constitutional amendment to ban alcohol, has the United States of America created and executed the 'War on Drugs' appropriately?" He knew it was a loaded question, which was purposefully constructed to illicit a negative response toward an ingrained policy. His intention was test if his students were simply towing the official government line. Intuition in this case proved true.

Professor Briarton's medium sized frame began to look the class over as he paced back and forth giving his students fifteen seconds to ponder a response before he randomly called on someone. It was a technique that he often used to ensure that everyone was kept on their toes. The fifteen second pause was used in the second half of the semester. In the first half he employed a ten second pause which kept the class moving even slightly faster. At this point in the semester his students had become so accustomed to only having ten seconds to prepare an answer that the extra five seconds puzzled them, but in the end artificially sharpened their learning senses. It was this moment that Briarton seized upon. *Fourteen, fifteen,* and he spoke, "Ryan Herring what is your response?"

"Ummm, I said that if I can drink and smoke cigarettes and they are bad for me," he continued on rather nervously, "then why can't I do other things that aren't good for me." Professor Briarton again began to pace and his hand slithered from his forehead down to his chin, his eyes widening with impatience.

"Alright," the Professor elongated the word, "but the question says 'in the context of individual liberty and the constitutional amendment to ban alcohol', right?"

"Well yeaaah," Ryan replied, "hey that's just like, what I thought, you know."

"Alright, alright, let's just see here," his eyes darted around the room, "Kimberly . . . . ." he craned his neck back to inspect the roll sheet, ". . . .Marlton, what was your answer?"

"Well, I thought, you know, that drugs are really bad for our children, and you know, alcohol isn't *as* bad so that's why drugs are illegal and why we have the war on drugs," her answered lingered like cigarette smoke wafting in the room without any circulation. Professor Briarton waited for about ten seconds to see if someone would interject. *Anyone,* he shouted internally.

The Professor stood in the center of the lecture hall for just a moment longer. His hands pulled down the sides of his slightly baggy suit causing it to curve across his shoulders. He straightened his posture.

"Professor?" Hayden called out.

"Yes Hayden," the Professor returned.

"I agree with Kimberly." Professor Briarton could not stop the quiver of his brow from showing his inexplicable distaste for these responses, which clearly ignored the first premise of the question.

"'*In the context* of *individual liberty* and the constitutional *amendment* to ban alcohol," Professor Briarton said much more articulately than was necessary. After four seconds there was still no response to the reiteration, and he, disbelieving that this was *really* what the students thought, decided to take a rather unprecedented survey.

"Everyone please close their eyes," he pronounced rather harshly. The eighty-plus students shifted rather nervously in their seats, wrought with uncomfortability. "Everyone *please* close their eyes," he repeated, only this time his voice resounded with far more bass. While some heads still twisted back and forth, most everyone complied. "How many of you have ever done an illegal drug?" he asked.

"You mean *any* illegal drug?" someone shouted in anonymity. Professor Briarton widened his eyes in disbelief yet again.

"Yes, I mean *any* illegal drug at all," he uttered. Ever so slowly a little more than fifty-percent of the class very cautiously, half-way raised their hands and much more expediently lowered them. "Thank you," he directed to the ones who still had raised hands, "you can lower your hands now." Understandably during the process eyes suspiciously darted back and forth paradoxically checking on the honesty of their peers.

"Well, there we have it," the Professor said sardonically, "around 90% of you agreed with the government's 'war on drugs' on the test, while at the same time around 60% of you have tried at least one illicit substance. Would anyone like to account for the disparity?"

An obligatory amount of awkward silence ensued until one brave soul was able to muster the courage to speak.

"It's like," Patty answered while her bleached locks highlighted her conversely burnt skin, "just because we try it doesn't mean that we want it readily available to everyone and *especially* not to our future children . . . . . who are the future of the world."

Time for another survey, he thought. "Would most of you agree with this?" he inquired and paced through the lecture hall. "Alright, so . . . . . let me see if I get this straight," he paused for effect, "you all would rather have a law that makes something completely illegal, with rather stringent consequences in place, to protect the 'masses'," he made a 'quotes sign' with both hands. "But because you're much more intelligent than them, go and try the substance anyway in the shadow of illegality? Am I getting this correctly?"

"Kind of," Brian Sanderson loudly stated from the back row of the stadium seating. "The truth is that most working class people wouldn't go to their jobs and feed their kids if they had easy access to that kinda stuff. It would be detrimental to society as a whole." Brian felt quite smitten with his answer. Having decided what would be better for the masses, inherently his facial expression gleamed with arrogance.

"I see," the Professor peered down at the ground and began to pace back and forth, his presence dwarfed by the twelve meter tall ceilings in the lecture hall. "So, you all here," his finger swung in a circular motion enveloping the whole of the class, "*you here*, are able to make decisions for the betterment of society – keep the 'workin' folk' in line as it were?" His eyebrows were raised as high as the noon sun.

"*Well*," Megan responded, her high society nature subsuming the first word, "we *are* the best and the brightest." Her wide smile suddenly outshone her overly correct posture and glisteningly tan legs.

"Does anyone have anything to say to the contrary?" the Professor said matter-a-factly while concurrently cutting his mouth off from the disdain swirling in his mind.

"Well," Jakob began, "who are we to do something and then tell other people they can't do it?" he questioned.

"Best and the brightest. Duh!" Megan slyly uttered so that only her inner circle of sorority minions could hear.

"What I mean to say," Jakob continued, "is, we, the self ordained bourgeois, think we can control not only our own lower classes but also other lower countries." The majority of the class had a puzzled look, while the rest were uninterested in his comments. "I just . . . . . don't think that's morally right."

"Why don't you think it's right?" the Professor, having just deeply enjoyed Jakob's comment like a breathe of fresh air in an oxygen depraved room, asked with a smile.

"Well if you look at our own Declaration of Independence and our Constitution you can see that the founding fathers thought everyone (which meant only white men at that time) was created equal. Do the rules not apply to the upper classes," he replied. "It feels like we're King George III telling our little 'colonies', be it lower classes or countries, how they should act - that's all. It's like we've reverted to the very thing that we fought to break away from."

If not for these momentary reprieves of emerging intelligence Professor Briarton would probably have given up teaching a very long time ago. To consistently find these moments of clarity in a single student was indeed something very precious, nevertheless the Professor was careful not to expose his attitudes too openly to the other students. For he understood that the climate in academia today is very much establishment based and reprisals consisted of professorial glass ceilings as well as invisible trap doors leading to a type of Socratic exclusion.

"An interesting thesis," Professor Briarton said dryly, "I mean clearly it requires a bit of polish but . . . . please, Jakob, could you tell me how this fits in with our current topic?"

"Well, I guess I mean that 'groups' are being controlled or simply manipulated by a more dominant group. *Look* at the amount of arrests in the drug 'war'.

It's unbelievable that about 40% of the 3 million Americans in prison are there for simple possession of a drug. And you KNOW most of them are poor, and the 'war' is escalating with no end in sight."

"Yes, you do have a point there. The drug 'war' does disproportionately hurt the poor, but it's important to realize that this isn't some kind of top down function where people are actually *targeting* the poor. It's just that poor people are *more* likely to get pulled over and searched because they are *more* likely not to have the money or time to keep the government off their backs about inspection, registration, insurance, license, etc. They also have less economic opportunity than the upper classes and are therefore *more* likely to resort to the black market to make money," Professor Briarton said in response, fearful that he may have expounded too much on Jakob's idea.

Megan, subconsciously realizing that the battle of ideas was shifting further from her level of comfort, jumped in, "Poor, rich, white, or black the law is the law," she said with her eyebrows up and her head bobbing. "It's like, you know, if they're poor . . . so what – these are the rules and they are there because drugs are a menace to society."

She smiled while her eyes darted from sorority sister to sorority sister seeking the gratifying looks of approval she so craved. One by one Megan's eyes meet her 'sisters' and one by one their facial expressions heaped onto Megan her drug of choice – social approval. Her heart, still thumping and pumping wildly from when she made her statement, began to steady with gratification. She hungered for more.

"I *hope* you're not implying that it's ok to do drugs . . . . . or that poor people should not be arrested for doing drugs," she added becoming ironically more illogical *and* confident.

"Oh, no, that's not at all what we're saying, Megan," Professor Briarton very calming said. He knew not to upset the situation any further. Upper class individuals like Megan *know* people. They know people who can cause Professors to loose tenure or something nuanced like getting passed up for a promotion. He knew he had gone a bit far with his analytical response to Jakob. *One day*, he thought, *I'll break Megan down, but that day is not today.*

"What we're saying is," he continued, "that, well, first - does the law fit in with our values of liberty and freedom? And second – is the law evenly applied? That's really what we're trying to get at here."

People like Megan don't have their own thoughts, his mind wondered. *They constantly repeat what has been told to them. They don't reason things out – they recall them. This is why the application of media 'buzzwords' is so influential. When used in a story they create an associative brain reaction which makes it difficult to reason outside of the preconceived memory.*

"Well, ok," she finally muttered, "I was just reminding you of how bad drugs are; they're a scourge on society, that's all." Her attitude laden demeanor poured onto the class room for all see.

Professor Briarton, who had been standing in the middle of the room, took a few steps toward Megan and politely delivered his conversation closer, "and we thank you for pointing that out." His wide smile was reciprocated by Megan and he turned toward his Power Point lessons knowing that the Megan time bomb had been meticulously defused – at least for know.

"Let's get to these slides," he said commandingly. With a whoosh of air the projector lit the pale screen and Professor Briarton began going over the standard book learning material for his course. He liked to open up the first ten to fifteen minutes of class with tantalizing discussion; however, this University did not give him free rein by any means. Sticking to the course guidelines, mandated by the University's administration was, of course, obligatory.

Being well aware that certain things were beginning to be put into motion, Professor Briarton was doing just fine keeping a low profile . . . . . . *just fine*, he thought.

* * *

‖ 5 ‖

A few years after Roger had discussed quantum technology with Herschel during the convention, Roger contacted him about developing a detection device to see if someone was already using this technology. Hershel scoffed at the ridiculousness of the request and even took it as a personal insult. 'Don't you think that, *I*, being the foremost top researcher in the world would have heard about something like that,' Roger remembered him saying. *It was funny seeing him all worked up like that over this stuff,* Roger thought. Once Herschel had calmed down, Roger convinced him to design a small satellite based device that could spin around the globe and detect the signatures of someone using a Quantum Communications Device (as Herschel called it).

It took Herschel about six months to write a scientific analysis of what to actually try to detect. Specifically, Herschel said it would spot the electromagnetic signature from the activation of a Quantum Communicator. He finally produced a paper and began to consult with the Cosgrove scientific staff in order to develop a detection device that would suit their needs. It amazed Roger that the entire device which in total took a year and a half to design and build, was about the size of shoe box.

Then came the difficult part – he had to convince the Defense Administration to allow the device to be launched into orbit using one of their spy satellites. Roger and Herschel's cause was helped tremendously by its miniscule size. Finally after an enormous amount of bureaucratic red tape, they agreed to include his unit on a satellite which contained an additional twenty classified experiments on board.

The monitor in front of him displayed only some of the startling results from the first few months in orbit. When Roger initially viewed the data, he thought that it had clearly experienced some sort of malfunction.

After only a few months, the satellite detected the surprisingly frequent, electro-magnetic signatures of quantum communications (or Quantum Bursts as Herschel says) in hundreds of major cities around the globe. Even after eliminating sources like quantum research facilities and a few physics departments in universities, there were still thousands of Quantum Bursts dotted throughout the world.

This was particularly vexing to the in-house intelligence agents, because to their knowledge no known society had been able to cultivate quantum physics for use in communications. So that means that whoever these people are, they not only have mastered a form of technology that we have not, but they also have a global network of agents lying in wait. This all sounded fairly ridiculous to Roger which led him down a path of questions that eventually got him reprimanded.

Because it was *so implausible* that a vast spy network with radically advanced technology was operating undiscovered around the globe, Roger decided that there must be some other *plausible* explanation for the Quantum Burst phenomenon. Therefore, he forwarded the map data onto a scientist with which Cosgrove Strategies had used as a technology sub-contractor in the past. And so the story goes that this sub-contractor was equally perplexed and alarmed as Roger was, so *he* showed it to some of *his* people, and finally the information eventually made its way back to Roger's boss - Agent Rodriguez - via a high level intelligence friend *he* has.

Needless to say this was an uncomfortable situation for Roger as it made him appear rather incompetent. The only reason he did not get in more trouble is because the sheer amount of Quantum Bursts looked so preposterously improbable that most people who saw it dismissed it as either a hoax or a malfunction. If not for that, most likely Roger would have been packing his things while a pair of armed security guards kept an eye on his every move.

Nevertheless, the mystery remained; what *the hell are these?* He squinted at the screen. Because the satellite could only detect Quantum Bursts within a mile or so, Roger could make out the city in which they occurred, yet he could not pinpoint the *exact* location.

That's when he noticed it. Leaning in further toward his monitor he found his own city on the map, with its very own Quantum Burst.

* * *

‖ 6 ‖

Thump, thump, thump, Jakob's knuckles rapped on the dense door with the words 'Professor Phillip Briarton' written on it. "Come in," a voice from within called. The Professor's office was sparsely decorated. Other than an imposing solid oak desk, there were only a few artifacts strewn about along with what looked like some old money framed and mounted on the wall.

"How's it going?" Jakob obligatorily asked.

"I can't complain," Professor Briarton replied trying to be as 'cool' as possible – leaning back in his chair at the same time.

"I just came by to chit-chat for a while," he plopped his two hundred pound six foot frame in the sleek brown leather guest chair.

"Well, I always encourage that sort of thing. Would you reach behind you and get that door?" The Professor was always mindful of his surroundings.

"Sure," Jakob agreed. His sturdy arm pushed the door closed.

"So what did you want to 'chit chat' about?" Professor Briarton inquired.

"I guess . . . . . I've just been a little confused about some stuff in class lately. And not the stuff in the book, I get that."

"Exactly. That's what the material is in there for, to make you feel confident and soothed. We'll get to that later, please, continue."

"It's some of the stuff in the lectures - it's confusing. I mean I get what you're saying, but the . . . . . well . . . . . I just."

"Jakob, slow down for just a second. This isn't just about the drug lecture today, is it?"

"No, that one is easy - I'll give you that. I mean who couldn't compare the prohibition of alcohol to the drug war. Yeah. I mean, you had Al Capone and the gangsters in the 20's and 30's. And today? What do we have? We've got everything from international narco-kingpins to gun toting dealers in the hood."

"Not bad Jakob. Let's see if you can take it a step further by asking the most important of all: '*Why*?'"

"'*Why?*' It always leads you to ask more questions and dig deeper doesn't it. Well, I'd say the reason you have all these gangsters is because . . . simply . . the dealers need protection."

"Why do they need protection?" The Professor inquired.

"Because the cops don't provide any. If something goes wrong at a drug deal. What happens?"

"Put that in economic terms, just like we practiced in class. By the way, very good how you went straight to the 'micro' example to figure out the 'macro' problem. Please, go on."

"Let me try this again," Jakob tightened his posture before continuing. "In the legal world when a business deal happens and one of the parties is unsatisfied with the deal that's taken place – a contract dispute or something – they can go before a judge in order to settle what basically is a property dispute between citizens."

"Ahh huh," the Professor nudged Jakob forward and looked to the side.

"The judge makes a ruling and all parties involved usually accept the outcome. In the drug world when a deal goes sour none of this occurs. First off there is no contract to go by, so right off the bat you have miscommunications and bad memories coming into play. You've got obvious outside pressures from the drug war including all the goodies like wire taps and moles. And if all of that wasn't bad enough, you've got no third party mediator to guide you through if there's some sort of problem!" Jakob audibly laughed at himself.

He continued, "And in the business world there are degrees of punishments available: felonies, misdemeanors, etc. But in the black market world there is only typically one type of punishment: death."

"Alright, Jakob. You clearly know your way around these arguments. Let's dig a little deeper, shall we," Professor Briarton asked as he leaned back in his chair and let all eight fingers and two thumbs press together ever so exactly in front of his face. "We've talked a lot about the outright lies which existed about alcohol during prohibition and we've also touched on that same phenomenon in the war on drugs. Wherever propaganda exists you have one group of people who are trying to control the thoughts of another group. This automatically implies purpose and pre-meditation. So, why were drugs outlawed in the first place? A couple of hints: 1. who gains? 2. who loses? Hint: It's never just one reason or group."

Jakob looked around the room satirically, "is this an assignment?"

"Funny, Jakob. No, it's not an assignment. Just consider it extra credit. You don't even have to write it down. Just think it over and stop by my office any time."

"Alright, no problem. Oh, by the way . . . . what's with all that money on the wall?"

"Oh, that," Professor Briarton glanced to his left at his collectable bills framed on the wall, "those are currencies which have collapsed."

"Right, you touched on paper money a few times during the lectures."

"To be honest with you Jakob that's what I wrote my dissertation on – monetary policy."

"Really . . . . . continue."

"Now you're telling me to continue, huh? The tables have turned," the Professor chuckled. "Really though, money is an interesting topic. I know you've heard some of my brain teasers. You up for one?"

"Sure," Jakob said flatly.

"Let's say we're floating in space in a fantasy universe and there's only $100 and a barrel of oil. Now because there are only those two things in this little mini-universe then a barrel of oil must cost $100 because the paper money *represents* the value of *things*. You cool so far?"

"Wouldn't have it any other way."

"Alright. Now let's say – all of the sudden – another $100 appears and now we've got $200 and still only one barrel of oil. How much is a barrel of oil cost now, Jakob?"

"I'd say $200."

"And you'd be exactly right. What we've described here is monetary inflation. It can be particularly immoral because the people who shuffle financial paper around are the most aware of it. What this means is that a farmer or factory worker who has spent his entire life working in order to one day retire could see their savings vanish, while the paper pusher who only lives on managing the money of a productive society could avoid this slight of hand catastrophe.

But I'm getting a little ahead of myself aren't I?" The Professor forcefully twisted his wrist so that he could flip his golden, loose watch into sight. "Tell you what Jakob; I've got a meeting in about ten minutes. How about we pick this up the next time you find time to drop by my office."

"Yeah, sure . . . . I'll be around," he responded while getting up and sturdily shaking hands. Professor Briarton's and Jakob's eyes met in a moment of mutual connection – green mirroring blue, respectively.

Jakob turned and had the massive door halfway open when Professor Briarton remarked, "Ohh, and Jakob."

"Yes, Professor."

"Try not to be late next time," he said.

"I'm not promising . . . . but I'll definitely try. See ya!"

Jakob, his back pack in tow, turned for one last time, exited, and even remembered to close the door behind him.

Now standing, the Professor took a few steps, and calculatingly twisted the dead bolt in order to silently lock the door. He sat back down in his brown leather high-back office chair and leaned his head back for a few moments, staring at the ceiling. Thoughts of the day blitzed around his mind crashing and caulking with the past. Snapping out of his daze, he grabbed his key chain and unlocked the bottom draw of this well built desk. He pulled out a small black device which resembled a cell phone. Before flipping open the device, his thumb slowly combed the sleek black surface for imperfections. There were none. A small display background lit up in cold blue letters, "MORE DETAILS TO COME. YOU HAVE 5 DAYS TILL THE DEADLINE. THE PLAN HAS BEEN ENACTED." His mind raced, *I don't have much time. Holy shit I don't have much time.*

* * *

‖ 7 ‖

Chairman Gorshial stared at the holographic images in front of him. Tediously going over this amount of data was a job suited a bit more for an analyst than a Chairman; however, Gorshial was aware of the sensitive nature of this assignment. Fear of public ostrification had prevented him from calling a Starter Employee to pour over this quagmire. Although collecting a plethora of information, as Gorshial's assistant Hickel had been instructed to do, was by no means illegal; it would surely be looked down upon by his peers. It may even lead to all sorts of stones beings turned over in Gorshial's life just to see what else they could possibly uncover.

The information collected on Kralsich was horrendously extensive. Beginning at the age of two personality data had been recorded to the tune of hundreds of individual assessment per year. Gorshial was standing in the Holographic Access Pad, better known simply as HAP, and began sifting through the records with great displeasure. HAP did not look like much. Just two 9' by 9' by 1' smooth black pads, one to step onto, and one suspended about 10' above.

When a need arose to review multiple documents it worked a bit like a file room. Only in this case it was possible to see any file room, and actually pick up and hold the pictures, files, or whatever else may have one time been in a 'scrap book'. 'Scrap book', the word itself threw Gorshial into revulsion. *How dare they adopt such silly, mind wasting initiatives*, he thought. *We have SO much to accomplish without being sidetracked by poisonous cultural inundations. We are BETTER than this!* While his insides were raging and erupting, his face remained frozen, motionless. Not so much as a stray muscular twitch was evident. Nothing.

From where he was standing, directly in the middle of the platform, file and tablet cabinets completely encircled him. Gorshial thought that the only way to take a little wind out of the sails of the young and up and coming Kralsich was to explore the depths of his short life. *Perhaps something would explain his overactive ambition*, he thought. *Perhaps something far more insidious could come out of this. Something incriminating even . . . .* he opened a random drawer and forcefully yanked out the holographic computer tablet.

Upon finding a recorded, formal Life Assessment from age eight, Gorshial's curiosity was piqued. Staring at the video on the sleek tablet, one of the Assessors began to read a prepared introduction which detailed how a young Kralsich had chosen to study a myriad subjects and refused to officially designate a 'major subject of interest'. This apparently caused the Assessors concern because by age eight most children had already shown preference for one subject over another - but even still - were by no means limited within those academic bounds.

The child defended his life choices vigorously not with the fiery passion of the rest of the children, but rather with eloquently chosen words. On several occasions the Assessors could be seen conferring with one another openly; not something which would be considered normal at all. Their faces appeared puzzled as the child spoke. The young Kralsich had articulated that because equilibrium in nature was surely a necessity shouldn't we assume that an in depth study of ALL subjects would manifest balance in the individual? The Assessors reasoned with the boy by asking him to choose a subject at least temporarily, with the expectation that it could be revisited later at his prerogative and that there were no boundaries to what he could study. The boy replied that it seemed as though the assessors were not comprehending what he really meant, which is that he objects to the imposition of choosing. He finished by saying that he would never allow his mind to be cordoned and compartmentalized by those with obvious ulterior motives. Audible gasps could be heard in the video and the recording abruptly turned to black.

Gorshial set the holographic tablet down. His fingers danced across the most prominent ridges on his grayish forehead as thoughts poured through his mind. He stepped off the HAP platform and commandingly said, "System Off."

All of the tablets and filing cabinets pixilated for just a moment before vanishing, leaving only the two smooth platforms in their wake. *Is he simply a contrarian? Or something far more sinister?* He thought to himself. To display blatant, yet starkly cognizant defiance at such a young age is surely odd at the least.

By this time Chairman Gorshial had shuffled back over to his elongated desk and sat down comfortably, still contemplating, still wondering what sort of man Kralsich really was. *I cannot have some young, openly defiant know-it-all ruining my legacy.* His fist slammed against the solid metal desk as a shockwave of sound pelted the enormous office walls. *How is he making these predictions?*

* * *

‖ 8 ‖

"Gimme whatever's on special," Jakob said positioning himself atop his regular bar stool. "Draft if possible," he added. Doug nodded, turned, and filled a 20 oz imperial pint full of bubbling, cold beer. He placed it in front of Jakob with a wobble, causing a glob of the foam to hoist off the side.

"I think you're going to like this one Jakob. A local distributor accidentally over-ordered about 50 kegs of this stuff. It's a nice, really hoppy, *sharp*, Pilsner," he commented, wiping up the excess beer off the traditional oaken English bar.

Jakob spoke over the ambient buzz of humming conversations as he waited for the foam to settle, "Why are you always taking me on these 'around the world beer tastings'?"

"Ya see Jakob," Doug started to say as a smile slowly stretched across his face, "you're pretty smart talking to professors and what not . . . . but at the same time; you lack the ability to distinguish and categorize."

"I'm sure you've got a point to all this. So, I'm listening, go on, continue."

"Yes, as I was saying. People who appreciate good beer, that is to say, they appreciate the production, rote consumption, and most importantly the sampling of new creations, do so because they enjoy the art of distinguishing and categorizing. You can see this in more traditional sampling pursuits like wine, cheese, or even caviar tasting. And this same behavior is evident with a ton of different activities. The real question is: Why is man driven in this way? Think about it. I mean to constantly desire to distinguish and categorize even the absolute slightest of differences in the senses, is obsessive at best and psychotic at worst."

"And *you're* trying to get me into *this?*" Jakob blurted out with a smile.

"Absolutely! You more or less study economics, I mean - this semester at least!"

"Thanks Doug."

"Well economics is just the ecosystem of mankind. We've moved out of the naturally existing food chain and created our own. It's not completely different by any means; in fact, a lot of the same rules under the old system still apply to the new one, like a higher likelihood of disease if you have too many of just one species.

"Really though, that's all economics is. If you could go into nature and look at blue jays and say . . . . . the blue jays built 153,493 nests this year. That's an 8% drop over last year. Analysts believe this may have something to do with a Maple tree disease which caused a twig shortage in the Northeast this winter, or something. See. It's the ecosystem of man.

"Unfortunately *modern* economics has become a hopeless quest of trying to quantify the unquantifiable. . . . . . . namely mankind. We're far more complicated than those blue jays. We constantly change our minds for a vast number of reasons. How can you predict *human action?*"

"I don't think you can," Jakob shot back.

"Exactly. And yet the entire academic discipline has been turned into nothing but a bunch of math nerds, while those who understand the theory behind the complex interactions known as economics have been cast out of most of the universities. Hopefully your beer tasting will help you categorize all of that!"

Jakob stared at Doug *the philosophic bartender* for a few tepid moments before slowly bringing his now almost headless beer to his lips.

"Damn, that *is* good." Jakob called out with widened eyes and a crooked smile on his face.

"I knew you'd like it."

"It's a lot hoppier than that last one you had me try. It really gets ya right here on the back of the tongue toward the sides."

"That's where your tongue is able to taste bitter substances. You know Jakob," he started speaking softly and wiped away a fake tear, "you've really come a long way." Jakob grabbed the bar towel out of Doug's hand and jovially threw it at his face.

"No seriously, when I first met you, all you ordered was rice beer and were absolutely convinced that everything else was just a rip-off. And now look at cha!"

"It's been a fun ride so far!" Jakob said as he tipped his drink toward the bar keep.

"Learning how to quickly distinguish and categorize things is going to be your greatest asset. You've got to understand the animal you're studying. If you were a cattle rancher you'd have to know everything there is to know about cows, right?

"Yeah, I guess so."

"Well if mankind is obsessed with distinguishing and categorizing stuff you better damn well figure out why."

"Thanks Doug. Whenever I become famous I'll make sure and give you all the credit," Jakob nodded.

"Wouldn't expect anything less of ya!" He craned his neck toward the other side of the bar and noticed several groups of people walking up. "Let me go grab these guys real quick, ok."

"Cool," Jakob said simply, taking another long, soothing drink of his beer as Doug took care of the newly arrived patrons. He set the glass back down on a napkin atop the bar and stared off at the people openly quaffing.

Economics is like studying the ecosystem. Hell, 'eco' is even in the name. Jakob couldn't help thinking how Doug had always managed to discover these interesting little things. He thought that it's probably related to the copious amount of 'people watching' that he did. Bartenders are supposed to serve drinks, keep people calm, and clean up. There's probably a lot of time in between his official duties to observe how various people interact.

Jakob noticed that the medium size bar had begun to fill up a bit. The crowd at Harold's Pub was mostly college age due to the proximity of the university, but this place was different than other college bars. Having obviously been built by a sampler of London's pubs, the interior was filled with enough solid oak to build a fortress. Add polished brass to that and the London pub façade was complete. So it wasn't a surprise with this level of class, to see a few visiting parents enjoying their child's company while reminiscing about their own college years.

Doug made his way back over to Jakob, smiled and said, "See anything interesting out there?"

"Just thought I'd ma . . . . . " he was mid-sentence when he spotted her coming through the front entrance. Megan. There she was, standing at the hostess stand flanked on either side by her token sorority sisters.

"Wow. Now there's somebody to people watch," Doug commented his arms folded across his chest. Even though the bartender was in his mid-forties he still never felt it was inappropriate to hand out advice about young women.

"Alright Jakob, I'm assuming she's a friend of yours, seeing how you haven't so much as twitched since she's walked through the door. Let me give you a bit of advice. Forget about her. Those sorority types are nothing but troub . . . . . ," his sentence trailed off as Megan turned and approached the bar, just then coming within earshot.

"Well look who it is," Jakob said as he swung around to face her, "the *fuzz*. Have you come to take down all the college kids around here?" He let out a chuckle as he noticed that his first beer and the sight of attractive women had unexpectedly loosened his tongue.

She laughed and said, "You don't know the first thing about me do you?" She leaned in a little and was now only inches from his face as her voice got raspier and more seductive, "But I'd bet you'd like to." Jakob sat motionless until her charade was finished.

"Riiiighhhht. Does that shit actually work on people? So what am I supposed to do now Megan, huh? Kind of look flabbergasted and beg you to have me? What is this - some kind of movie?" Jakob whimsically turned his head from side to side acting as if cameras were in the room. Megan took a step back and quickly gathered herself enough to formulate a response.

"In your dreams," she muttered and spun around, minions in tow, before she walked off back toward the hostess stand.

"C'mon, that's all you got," Jakob laughingly called out again. He spun around to face the bar again only to catch Doug shaking his head.

"Well that could've been worse; at least she didn't slap you." He let out one more laugh as he turned and began serving some rather unquenched students seated nearby.

Jakob had known Megan since they were teenagers. She grew up fairly wealthy with her Dad amassing a small fortune as some kind of overseas engineer. Jakob got to know her when their family returned to 'settle down' for a while after traveling with her Dad abroad. The entire family had not lived stateside for almost a decade up to that point. She went exclusively to the best American schools overseas. People say that she can speak two or three languages but nobody's ever heard her.

Before Megan became the most recognized face in their high school, Jakob and she were good friends. When Megan got back from being oversees she felt lost and did not really get along with everybody at first. Jakob befriended her, and even though he did not have answers to all of her very international questions, he always listened.

A lot of those questions helped eventually foster a disposition of understanding and compassion in Jakob. They spent hours discussing some of the extreme poverty in places like India that she saw. All the while Megan and her family always lived in lavish mansions with many house hands at her beckon. Megan realized they were people like her and sometimes felt guilty about their hardships.

Her father saw it a much different way. Megan was informed that those servants were not like her, nor like him. He told her that their family was more successful because they were *better* than those other people. Over a six month period Megan's mind fought a battle with Jakob on one shoulder and her father on the other. Eventually they began to see each other less and less as Megan became progressively more involved in society clubs, galas and cheerleading, while Jakob, who didn't enjoy the same level of affluence, began working more and more.

Jakob saw a very slow change in Megan during the last few years of high school. She stopped going out of her way to help people like she had done. It wasn't long before she was spreading insidious rumors and publicly humiliating people all in a selfish effort to climb the high school social ladder. She began to view others around her as chess pieces to be moved and sacrificed at will. All of that actually fits in line with her father's thinking. Because if you view people as less than yourself, then in your mind you'd actually be doing society a *service* to use them as a stepping stone to get ahead. Megan has been honing that very skill since high school and she was now *brilliant* in its application.

* * *

Later that night after Jakob closed out his lower than expect bar tab, he carefully drove back to the apartment, while his mind began to wonder back to some past conversations which he'd shared with Professor Briarton a few weeks ago. It was after class and Jakob had knocked and then subsequently entered the Professor's office. The conversation had meandered a bit like a creek through a swamp, when about ten minutes into an hour long discussion; they had chosen a topic which stuck – money. Even then Jakob had noticed that you could always get the Professor talking about money!
The debate, which conversations normally morph into with Professor Briarton, centered on 'hard vs. soft money'. Hard money, the Professor explained, makes a lot of sense to the common individual. The paper note, a dollar in our case, represents a fixed amount of exchangeable material. This basically kept whoever the money printers were, the government back in those days, honest. *Right,* Jakob thought. Think about the void with one barrel of oil and the $100. If you can print the money then you'd be able to have as much oil as you'd want in the beginning before everyone realized there were more dollars in circulation. The Professor made it clear that this type of power is basically the Midas touch. It allows individuals and organization to turn paper into gold. *What a concept,* Jakob thought, as his mind instinctively wondered how one would acquire such a skill.
Jakob learned that today the world operated with paper currency that's more or less created by governments (or their very friendly 'independent' central

banks), and not backed by any thing. Starting after World War Two, the Professor continued, only nations (NOT individuals) could exchange paper money for gold, and if countries wanted to exchange the paper they could only exchange it with the United States. This so called 'gold window' was eventually shut about thirty years later because the United States had printed up a massive amount of money to pay for the Vietnam War and expanding social services (Guns and Butter as it were). With more dollars in circulation and the same amount of gold, many nations began to exchange their dollars for gold, however, this situation quickly depleted the United States' gold supplies. At the height of the panic a French warship actually demanded their gold while in New York's harbor. Eventually Nixon was forced to close the 'gold window' and thus ended redeemable currency. So basically since the early seventies the world has been trying the grand experiment of a world fiat currency system – paper with nothing behind it but the 'credit worthiness' of the country that issues it.

  The Professor then reiterated something he talks about in class often – how does the government raise money? Borrowing it, printing it and taxing it (the last two are really the same thing).[3]

  Whenever a nation wishes to spend money on a 'need' of some kind they have to use one of the above mentioned ways to raise the money in order to proceed with the project. Politicians find that because they can

---

[3] Bernanke, Benjamin. "I couldn't agree with you more that inflation is a tax". July 16, 2008. Congressional Testimony. United States House of Representatives.
See Also:
http://www.pbs.org/newshour/news_summaries/2008/07/summary_16.html
Video: http://www.youtube.com/watch?v=D4yBrxmEOkY

borrow it or print it, why would they ever want to raise taxes? Raising taxes may allow the project to be funded, but what does it really matter if the politician doesn't get reelected anyway?

Jakob thought back to his conversation with Doug about 'eco' nomics. Imagine if . . . . birds had to ability to print money. And let's say there was a slight shortage of food, worms in this appetizing case. The birds would most likely 'print some money' in order to 'purchase' some worms so that none of their brethren would starve to death. Of course some of the birds that usually do other productive things, like building nests in this case, would have to go out and gather the worms to bring to the other birds. This could cause deficiencies in other areas. Furthermore the birds could have misjudged the severity of their worm shortage and actually *overproduce* worms leading to an over abundance of food and a shortage of nests.

It's tough to get everything just right, Jakob remembered the Professor saying. Professor Briarton always brings up the Post Office when people in class recommend that the government should take on a new enterprise. *Have you BEEN to the Post Office lately,* he would ask. Then he'd always go on and talk about how Einstein said that doing the same thing over and over again and expecting a different result is the definition of insanity.

Jakob realized, *why would I trust the same people who run the post office to manage the money supply without real transparency? All of this assumes the people who operate the system are not only competent but also altruistic . . . . what happens if the wrong guy gets into power or if government power is transferred to another entity!?!?*

Remembering back to a particular day in class when a student asked rather rudely, *does any of this actually mean anything to me?* The Professor, in a rare moment of candor, walked purposefully in front of the seated student, looking down at him and said, *do you think that your grandmother would rather make toys or bombs? Because you see, if the government so chooses it can divert money that used to be spent making and buying toys to manufacturing bombs. That's what the power to tax and print means – CONTROL.* Afterwards he turned around, acted as if he had not yelled at the student, and resumed teaching.

With Jakob nearing Hidden Hills, the ridiculous name of this cheaply constructed pre-fab apartment complex, he put on his right blinker to signal the turn. Remembering that he did not have anything for breakfast, Jakob quickly clicked his blinker off opting instead to drive up the road to the convenience store, and that's when Jakob really became suspicious.

Taking the long way home through various neighborhoods after a night at Harold's Pub was nothing new for Jakob. He knew a number of his friends who always avoided major roads after midnight, which made the black car behind him taking the exact route nothing unusual in his mind. When Jakob switched on his blinker the car followed suit, but the unusual thing was that the sleek black vehicle also followed suit when Jakob turned *off* his blinker.

Well, maybe he needs something for breakfast as well, he thought. Jakob made a left into the convenience store without signaling this time, while carefully watching his rear view mirror. As he pulled into a parking space he noticed that the suspicious car kept going straight without incident. "Paranoia," he said aloud while shaking his head and walking into the small building.

After picking up enough food to stave off his morning hunger, Jakob drove back to Hidden Hills and parked his Bronco in front of his single bedroom apartment. While walking up the outdoor stairs to his front door, he spotted something strange. Craning his neck to side and looking about fifteen parking spaces down, he saw it – the suspicious, sleek black car parked in his own parking lot.

He felt the hairs on the back of his neck stand up as he fumbled with his keys, desperately trying to unlock his front door. Upon entering the apartment he dashed over to the dining room window, and with the lights still off, he ever so slowly peaked out of the blinds at the mysterious black car. Suddenly the side door opened and from within the sedan appeared a man dressed in a black suit. Jakob could barely catch a glimpse of the suspicious looking figure from the tiny sliver of window, but from what he could make out the man was walking toward the rear side of his apartment. As Jakob lost sight of him through the narrow view, he hurried to the back balcony so that he could continue to track the steadily moving figure.

Slowly and ever so quietly he unlocked and then slid the back glass open. Once on the balcony he fearfully waited until he heard any suspicious sounds. Deafening silence seemed to go on for minutes. Finally, a branch creaked under someone's foot and the sound almost caused Jakob to stir in panic. *He must be right below me,* Jakob thought as his white knuckles gripped the balcony's railing.

The man was moving toward the thick tree line which sat only about fifteen feet away from the back of his apartment building. Jakob *very* carefully peaked his head over the edge of the balcony and now caught sight of the figure's shadowy silhouette.

Just then, Jakob noticed the man was holding something in his hand . . . . it was some kind of weapon. Before he even had time to run inside and call the police, an incredibly high pitched sound, followed by the sudden crackle of electricity discharging, became audible. Jakob was frozen in angst still watching the scene unfold as the man entered the woods and proceeded to apprehend the person who he had just electrified, or whatever that device was. Strangely the second man, who had been sitting in the woods doing who knows what for who knows how long, now seemed to be completely compliant with the black suited man who had zapped him!

The pair filed away from the back of the apartment and consequently Jakob moved back to the window in the kitchen to observe them walking. It seemed that the apprehended man was slightly drunk! He clumsily moved in whatever direction the dark suited man pushed him.

It was at that moment Jakob noticed the strangest thing about the entire incident. As the apprehended man was being led into the passenger seat of the mysterious black car, he finally faced Jakob. There were no irises, nor color of any kind; the only thing Jakob saw was the haunting reflection of the white's of his eyes. He pulled back from the window, the hairs on his arms now standing at attention. *What the hell was that?* He said to himself. One last time he peered out of the window and saw the black car, now with two passengers, slowly leaving his apartment complex, and tried to convince himself that none of it was real.

* * *

‖ 9 ‖

"Let's talk about this," Professor Briarton turned his head toward the projector screen. An overhead image of suburban America saturated the lecture hall - easily seen by everyone. "And this", another image of a planned suburban housing development flashed on the screen. "And this, and this, and this," he continued flipping the images very rapidly until the class had seen overhead images of thousands of houses, all of them strikingly similar. "Why do we live like this? Why does the average American drive forty-five minutes back and forth to work everyday? How did this all come into existence?" The Professor again clicked the image changer in his hand in order to show a lone oversized barrel of oil. "Without this," gesturing toward the image, "none of this", now gesturing to a picture of suburbia, "would be possible. And most importantly of all, without these," he now gestured to an image of five formidable navy battle ships, "none of this," now an image of suburbia again, "would have come into existence."

Clearly a few of the more jingoistic students in the back of the lecture hall had misinterpreted his comments because a loud, "hell yeah," was audible from everywhere in the room.

"A few of you may be wondering where exactly I'm going with this, but I assure you it will become abundantly clear in a few minutes. So, why exactly would the suburbs develop because of oil and how is that statically linked to the military? Many of you have probably heard a few potential presidents promise 'energy independence.' Honestly I've heard the last eight or so presidents all guarantee the same thing - but guess what? None of them, *none* of them have delivered on this promise. Only a small fraction of the oil we consume actually originates from this country, but half of the oil consumed in the world is used right here in the US of A. In order to reconcile this, the US has had to traipse around the world and find enough of the black stuff to satisfy our cravings. And traipse we have," he said with emphasis as the next image filled the projector screen.

"Here is a map of the world. Notice the countries which are darkened in different shades of blue. The darkest shade represents the countries with the most oil. So you can see that Saudi Arabia, Iraq, and Russia etc all have substantial oil reserves. Now, the next image is also of the world, but this world map shows the locations of all the United States military bases in foreign countries." He clicked to show the next slide.

A few audible "wows" were heard throughout the class. "Impressive isn't it," the Professor said. "Seven hundred bases in a one hundred and thirty countries. Let's see what the last two images look like when we fade them both out and combine them," he clicked to the combined image. A few gasps and "oh my gods" were echoed throughout the lecture hall. "Yes, I know. It's clear that the US likes to put military bases atop its "strategic resources" to use their own nomenclature. In total, the United States has military bases on sixty-seven percent of the world's oil. As a side note, it was at seventy percent until Venezuela kicked us out.

"So what does this mean? Well, for starters we could surely assume that despite any of the official policy lines of why we're in a lot of these countries, the real answer is probably oil. I mean this could be a coincidence but seriously, welcome to the real world. We're the largest consumer of a product and we want to make sure that we can continue to purchase it as safely and inexpensively as possible.

"The two main reasons that these bases exist is because we don't want governments who currently sell us oil to be overthrown and replaced with governments that won't sell – at a good price of course. The other reason is that our navy provides security for our oil tankers which physically transport the oil. So class . . . . *what* does this mean in economic terms?"

"It's a subsidy," Jakob commandingly called out from the back of the class.

"Correct. It is a subsidy. Plain and simple. That's all there is to it. Oil is a form of energy and it competes with other forms of energy on the market, but gets an unfair advantage because the military is paid for out of your income tax, not at the pump. This is one reason that renewable energies haven't even had a shot at competing with oil."

"But they subsidize 'green' energies now too," Megan called out from the front of the class with a smile.

"Exactly. So, is that a good thing? Is it good that the government in all of its postal wisdom tries to decide which energies we should use? They effectively are making the price of all energies a bit cheaper. Wouldn't it be better to do away with all the subsidies than to subsidize everything? When governments subsidize things doesn't that mean that they indirectly decide what you should purchase, thus taking away some of your freedom of choice? What does that mean to us? It means this!!" He clicked to show one of the random images of the American suburbs.

"How many of you grew up in a neighborhood which roughly resemblances this picture . . . . a show of hands please," the Professor called out, craning his head to see all the way to the higher rows of the lecture hall's stadium seating. "So about seventy-five percent of you, huh? And do you think that if gas had cost about eight dollars a gallon that your parents, or even *grandparents* for that matter, would have moved so far away from their places of work? Probably not. Most likely if the seven dollars a gallon scenario were to have been true, living in the areas outside of a city would have been confined to farmers, the super rich, and weird creepy hermits," the lecture hall filled with mixed giggles at the rare joke.

"You wouldn't have seen a massive move to the suburbs, as there simply would have been no way that average Americans could afford the travel expenses.

"So, what is the most used method of deduction in economics? Class?" the Professor signaled the Pavlovian response with raised eyebrows and a hand to his ear.

"Follow the money," the entire class called out in a communistically uniformed drone.

"Right. If you follow the money in this case it becomes obvious that the US has subsidized the building of the suburbs.

"What's wrong with that?" Megan trumpeted. "I mean, it's given those people a bigger house, a yard, and a higher standard of living. I'm not seeing the problem." Her coven of sorority sisters considered this to be an obvious slap in the Professor's face, and delighted in the victory of *their* side.

"Good job Megan. Those are all of the *benefits* of the subsidy and coincidently the same arguments on which politicians use to campaign. They, like you, also don't name any of the negatives associated with this form of central economic planning. Luckily you, as opposed to the politicians, have *me* to guide you through any downside the subsidy has. For starters," he changed the image of the American suburbs to one of a map of Asia.

"Half the world's population lives on this continent and very few of them enjoy the luxuries that we do. But all that's beginning to change very rapidly. China and India are *very* much different than they were twenty years ago.

"Remember, we consume half the world's oil and we're only five percent of the population. So what happens if the rest of the world decides they all want to drive cars and live in the suburbs just like America does? Everyone cannot live like us . . . . it's just not sustainable in the long run or for that matter . . . . . it's not even sustainable in the medium run."

Jakob called out, simultaneously signaling with a raised hand, "We'll invent something. Something . . . . . that'll let our cars run cheaply . . . . a new energy source of some kind." Confident in his response he ceased talking and waited for a response, staring into the eyes of the standing professor.

"You're right. That's a possibility. We could in fact discover some new wondrous energy source. Nuclear fusion has a lot of promise I'm hearing – it's the energy that comes from combining atoms rather than spitting them. It works just like the sun does. However, what I'm hearing from scientists is that even a fifty year window for this technology to become useful would be amazing," he looked down and shook his head, "and we definitely don't have fifty years. "As far as renewable energy goes, it just doesn't produce the power. One nuclear power facility can produce the approximate energy that *twenty thousand* wind turbines create. So, right, we could invent some thing, sure. But it's a bit like going to fight a lion without any weapons, and assuming you'll invent a sword on the way there. Possible . . . . . sure, but highly unlikely. What else?"

A collective sigh was released, the pulsating sound of the bell blared out for all to hear. "We'll pick up here next time," the Professor called out, projecting his voice more forcefully than even the background noise.

With the expedient students congesting the exits as if a fire were at their backs, professor Briarton signaled to Jakob as he waited. Jakob turned and paced toward the Professor, backpack in tow.

"You called?" he said jokingly.

"Yes," Professor Briarton replied, "do you have any extra time this afternoon to stop by my office? I have something I wanted to talk with you about."

"Yeah, sure . . . . . say in about an hour?"

"That'll work," a smile stretched across the older man's unshaven face in approval. Jakob turned and filed out the door with the other students, while the Professor began carefully packing up his lecture materials, one at a time.

His mind raced with anxiety. *I really don't want to have to rush this thing.* He visibly shook his head in disgust. *I can't believe I'm going to have to do this today. There's no way he's even close to being ready.* He slipped his laptop into the carrying case moving aside a thick manila folder marked with the words: Jakob Vanden.

* * *

‖ 10 ‖

Sitting at a desk for long periods of time was something to which a professional Prognosticator like Kralsich was readily accustomed. This particular one was especially useful to him. Its size was that of a typical office desk, but made of what appeared to be solid black granite. Above it another piece of black granite the same size as the desk but only a foot thick, was hanging from the ceiling. This left Kralsich about four feet of height in which to work.

The Holographic Access Desk, better known as a HAD, was stacked with files. Kralsich moved his left hand over to the next file in the stack. His grayish thumb and index finger began to clasp it. Only there was nothing *actually* there. His thumb and finger were really touching one another and did not *feel* a file. Nevertheless the holo-file moved as commanded by Kralsich to the destination directly in front of him.

He flipped it open and began analyzing the data therein. His eyes scanned the document in blocks of five to eight words at a time. His mind was able to perceive the meanings of words simply by gazing at the chunks of sentences, broken down in a patterned way. Within minutes he was finished with the entire fifty pages of the rather dry report.

As he closed the folder and literally tossed it back onto the stack from which it came, it had become clear that the situation before him had grown increasingly complex, making his duties all the more difficult. Looking off into the distance his mind erupted volcanically, violently combining the new data he had just read with the old which was still presiding rather confidently despite contrarian thoughts.

His mind, now overloaded by processing the newly acquired information, flashed back to a vacation he had taken a few years ago. Spelunking was one of Kralsich's most sought after diversions. The images of the adventure flashed before him, the beauty of the jutting, massive crystal structures had enchanted his mind in a way that no art ever could. His flashlight shone steadily into the transparent structures. The light fractionalized through both the crystal stalagmites and stalactites lining the enormous five mile long hall known as the Great Cavern. It seemed as though an infinite number of colors could be seen as minute movements in his hand were amplified into colossal spectrum shifts miles down the hall. At the time, Kralsich felt as though that just by *witnessing* the complexity of the illumination, that doors of consciousness were being opened in his mind which had previously been bound shut. After five days alone in the enchanted place mediating throughout, Kralsich stood up, knowing that he had accomplished what he had come to do, and left to make his four day journey home. *Amazing*, he thought to himself.

At that moment his mind revisited reality driving his eyes to again gaze upon the files in front of him. By enacting his 'Alternative Solutions in the Event of a Constrained Time Frame: Goal of Continuity' this particular file had become rather unpredictable. He realized it was indeed essential to rush the subject's development. Still residing in the back of his mind was *if by chance*, it did not play out as expected. *If by chance* the subject did not except reality and chose instead to cling on to those obviously unreal things in front of him. *That is highly unlikely,* Kralsich thought. If the improbable did become reality the Prognosticator knew what would have to happen at that point.

He leaned purposefully back in his chair, his wispy hand finding its way to his forehead. The hand slid slightly across his bony cranial structures pausing periodically in contemplation. Once more grasping the file in question, he angrily threw it down onto his Holographic Access Desk, the other files swooshing around from the 'wind'. A picture slid out onto the cold black desk - a picture of . . . Jakob Vanden.

* * *

‖ 11 ‖

Jakob tapped lightly on Professor Briarton's office door. "Come in," he heard a voice from inside reverberate through the solid wood.

"Hey Professor," Jakob said as the door parted with the frame, revealing the Professor sitting in his office.

"Jakob, nice to see you, please have a seat," he took off his reading glasses and turned his attention toward the younger man. "I'm glad you stopped by."

"Well, I wanted to turn in my 'extra credit' assignment about the drug war that we discussed last week."

"Oh, you didn't have to do that, I just expected you to drop by and kind of chit chat about it. You know, nothing formal."

"Yeah, I know that's what you said, but umm . . . sometimes I organize my thoughts a bit better if I get them down on paper, you know what I mean?" Jakob said as he pulled the single sheet of paper from his book bag and handed it to the Professor.

"Yes, I do know what you mean," his hand grasped the paper and subsequently pulled open a desk draw in order to store it.

"But I also came because I had a few thoughts that I wanted to talk to you about. Remember that discussion we had about inflation and all that?"

"Ummm, yes I believe that was the one about the barrel of oil floating in space," the Professor smiled because of the absurdity of the image in his head.

"Well, I've been wondering, you see, I've always heard we had a free market system, but it doesn't seem like that to me sometimes."

"Go on," the Professor leaned back in his chair secretly pleased that Jakob was beginning to ask the right questions without any coaxing.

"Well, in class a few weeks ago you called the interest rate, which is set by the Central Bank, the 'fulcrum of the economy'. This interest rate is the overnight lending rate that banks borrow money from the Central Bank, but it really leads banks to set all of their interest rates by it. So in practice the Central Bank sets all the interest rates in the country? Maybe I'm missing something but it seems like that's a centrally controlled economy. I mean the banks lend money out to people based on this set rate. How is that a free market exactly?"

Jakob's face wrinkled with questions as he realized that the story he'd been told his entire life did not match what was before him. His mind instinctively tried to defend the old paradigm, but Jakob consciously quieted the knee jerk reflex and continued to intently listen to the new ideas shifting his notions of reality.

"You definitely have a point there Jakob, there's certainly some control going on. The Central Bank doesn't directly set prices and tell people how much to grow/manufacture but they definitely turn the spigot of money on and off, thereby *indirectly* having an influence on them.

"The truth is that when the bank makes a 'loan' it's not really a loan at all. They 'print' most of the money. They don't really loan it. And then they only have to keep a very small percentage of the cash at the actual bank. Ever hear of a bank run? If they don't have the required reserves then they can borrow it from other banks or the Central Bank itself. If the interest rate is set really low, say at 0% or 1% then it acts as an incentive to lend out money to people or to buy government bonds. This environment is extremely profitable for the banks, and is also a de-incentive to saving.

"In this, the Central Bank is encouraging lending (money printing), which leads to price inflation and typically very bad loan selection on the part of the banks. The end effect is that wild speculation is rewarded and prudent saving is discouraged.

"That was the boom. During the bust all the banks have to do is keep the difference between what the bond pays and interest rate is set at. *Easy money*.

"Don't forget though, with every dollar printed that means the pre-existing money becomes less valuable. It's kind of like slicing a pizza pie – you can slice it into 57 tiny slivers, or you can cut it into 4 huge slices – it's still the same amount of pizza." The Professor tilted his head to the side to express the simplicity of the argument and continued talking. "You remember the barrel of oil floating in space, right? It's the same concept really – you've got more fake, paper money chasing the same amount of real, scarce materials.

"The interesting thing is if you apply money printing to the animal world it would have much the same effect that we see in the human world. If dogs were suddenly allowed to consume all the food they wanted with no natural resistance, they would become fat and bloated. This is also the case during the boom years of the boom-bust cycle which is mainly caused by money printing. Regular people gorge themselves on consumer goods while 'hungry' speculators drive up the prices of everything. Both groups get the capital they need with freshly printed, ubiquitously available cash. After the boom ends and the bust cycle begins, the masses point fingers at all the greed, gluttony and corruption of the private sector. They say that 'we need more regulations' and 'we need more government to watch the markets and stop the greedy speculation'. No! No! We need to stop printing money! Because Jakob . . . . you can try to make sure a dog doesn't over eat by watching him the entire time, but wouldn't it be better to simply not overfeed him?

"The government, who typically encourages the Central Banks to lower interest rates too far thus *causing* the problem of too much money in the system, now grabs more and more power to regulate the markets. Why don't they just treat the cause of the problem (money printing) instead of treating the *symptoms* (greedy speculation, fraud, corruption)? In the past people have advocated for the type of system which we have today so that 'money would be the servant of man rather than vice versa'; in practice money has become the servant of a *few men*. The moral implications alone are difficult to ponder.[4]

"Another thing . . . . . if you trace all the freshly printed money around, you'll find it doing strange things sometimes. The most notorious example is a bubble. This isn't to say that bubbles are necessarily *caused* simply by money printing. No, no . . . . . they're caused by a number of things, but what money printing does is *exacerbate* them."

"When you say a bubble, you mean like Tulip Mania, right?" Jakob inquisitively replied.

"Exactly, this happened in the Netherlands in the 1600's. Due to the introduction of few new varieties, in combination with some very skilled selective breeding, the Dutch were able to sell a product that had high demand associated with it. Everybody *had* to have these beautiful flowers just like the latest gidget gadget or phone or whatever you'd see today. This bubble started in November of '36 and was mostly done by the following

---

[4] Hülsmann, Jörg Guido, *The Ethics of Money Production*, (Auburn Alabama: Ludwig von Mises Institute, 2008).

May . . . . only six months, or one growing season. That was back when communication was slower too!

"Think about how long the bubbles last today. Some trail on for the better part of a decade. This happens because governments won't let the bubbles deflate. They realize that the whole system is teetering on a shaky fractional reserve pyramid. Remember, when the banks give out a loan they only have to have a fraction of the actual cash – the rest is money printing magic. Letting the prices fall would crash the whole system."

"Ahh . . . ," Jakob nodded back in understanding, "so compared to back then that's why bubbles last so long today . . . . they're printing the money up and then just shoveling more in to keep the bubble furnace going. When that doesn't work they move to bailouts and tax reduction incentives.

"Hmmm . . . so," Jakob smiled and tilted his head, "what's the next bubble I should be investing in!"

"You joke, but a lot of people dedicate their entire lives to that very endeavor and some of them become *filthy* rich. But you know as well as I do Jakob that it's not about the money anyway . . . . it's what you do with it that matters.

"Anyway, like I was saying, if you look into the real causes of Tulip Mania you'll find out that the Dutch government intervened into the normal way that people do business. They sort of changed the rules in the middle of the game. Back then the Dutch government manipulated the rules of contracts while today we manipulate the interest rates - among other things. In the Netherlands' case the result was one season of future's contract madness.[5] In our era, generational sized bubbles are inflated and popped.

"And don't forget that there's no containment system to keep the damage from spreading."

"What do you mean by that," Jakob's face crinkled curiously.

"The Central Banks of the world try to lower interest rates to increase growth and raise interest rates to decrease growth. Simple formula really when you think about it. The problem lies in them actually knowing when to turn these spigots of economic activity on or off. What should they do when only *one* sector is moving too fast? What about certain states that maybe underperforming economically? Should they turn off the spigots to the entire nation?

"The Central Bankers, who are not actually part of the government, are undoubtedly under political pressure – as they should be! Their decisions can make or break billions of people who have a right to know what their elected and appointed officials are doing. I'm off on a little tangent here, but bare with me, ok?"

"Oh, please . . . . . I thought you were just getting going!" Jakob quipped aloud brushing his hand through his sandy colored hair.

"Well like I was saying . . . . . containment. The speculative bubble that surrounded Tulip mania was contained mostly to that sector because money wasn't really printed like today to fuel it, nor did the government bailout the speculators afterwards. In today's world, on the other hand, all that money printing is not 'contained' and it undoubtedly inflates the prices in a multitude of sectors, industries and regions. Whenever that happens, the Central Bankers are

---

[5] Thompson, Earl (2007), "The tulipmania: Fact or artifact?" (PDF), *Public Choice* **130** (1–2): 99–114, doi:10.1007/s11127-006-9074-4

supposed to act by raising the interest rates, (to 'pop' the bubble) but because of the political pressure to continue the boom they will most likely wait too long. They then will continue to be behind the curve in market predictability generally making matters worse along the way. One wonders if the entire system was created in order to manufacture *instability*.

"There is one thing we know that this system has beyond a shadow of a doubt accomplished since being established."

"What's that?" Jakob asked with his index finger and thumb supporting the weight of his concerned, muscular face.

"Central Banks have always provided the funding for governments to go to war. *Every time*," the Professor's face momentarily became somber before continuing. "Typically in collusion with the central banks, many of the largest private banks end up financing *both* sides of a war."

"*Interesting*."

"I also believe this type of system leads to another nasty thing."

"What's that?" Jakob's interest was always piqued when the Professor was willing to open the intellectual door a bit wider.

"Have you noticed how quickly things break?"

"Ummm, not really any more than usual."

"Of course not. You were brought up in this world so you've been socialized to believe that it couldn't exist in any other way. It's kind of like if you grew up with pink elephants roaming the streets. You wouldn't think it was abnormal at all to see a brightly colored, trunked animal eating the trees on campus would you?"

"No, I guess I wouldn't."

"Right, but *someone* else from *somewhere* else would look insane to you if he objected to these pink creatures wouldn't they?"

"Yeah, I see what you're saying," Jakob looked off to the side and pondered the extensive implications of the allegory.

"Well, when I was younger things lasted longer than they do today. I mean seriously we can't design a car that can go over a hundred and fifty thousand miles before it leaves us stranded on the side of the road? Even to play devil's advocate a bit, *they say* it's better for innovation to keep churning forward, constantly designing new things – we advance quicker they tell us. What about a toaster? Why do I need to buy a new toaster every few years? That's absurd! Does it toast my bread better with new technology? C'mon. No, no, the constant wearing out of everything is in large part due to money not holding its value. Think about it.

"You're a manufacturer that earns money by selling your goods. You're therefore aware that the money you receive today will be worth about three to four percent less in a year based solely on inflation. Sure you can play the financial game and make some money on risky investments, but the truth is you're a manufacturer not a financial wizard and you'd sleep much better knowing that you had consistent cash flow. So there's a *huge* incentive to design a product that will wear out quickly, thus forcing the consumer to purchase another one in five years or so. You do this because you know that in five years the consumer will pay fifteen to twenty percent more for the same product versus if you had simply held onto the original money."

"Yeah," Jakob shifted his weight and responded, "but isn't that in what you called nominal money instead of real money. I remember you said that 'real money' is defined as what your money actually *gets,* verses 'nominal money' which is just the number. And the number only means something when compared with the other things in the market."

"Wow. Even though you're late to class you never fail to keep up. Impressive."

"Thanks Professor, I try my best," waves of endorphins rushed through his head, a clear reaction to a compliment from someone Jakob admired.

"So, the manufacturer is driven to always get his hands on fresh cash and this consequently makes him modify his business plan to produce a good that will ensure that goal. If he were to make a product that lasted for a really long time, he would be holding in his hand the cash that simply disappears into thin air. While his competitors, who would be manufacturing inferior products but thus ensuring constant cash flow, would have a clear competitive advantage.

"Even if the manufacturer does happen to find a 'good' financial broker to manage his assets, in the end it won't matter anyway. The boom and bust cycle which is created/exacerbated by the manipulation of interest rates will always lead to a 'bust' whenever all the bad investments have been realized.[6] So even if the manufacturer does invest his money 'properly' he will still be subjected to the eventual downturn."

"Hmm, I never thought of it like that."

"Well, you're not supposed to. That's the whole point. The powers that be want you to buy into this world and to continue your unquestioning devotion to the purchase of mal-designed products.

"Really, a lot of people think that the worst side effect of fiat money is the exacerbated boom/bust cycle, when in reality the subtle changes in *human behavior*, as evidenced by the manufacturer's decisions, are the most pernicious. The truth is, the public doesn't even recognize that this system has changed their decision making process. It's like living with someone who starts

---

[6] von Hayek, Friedrich, *Monetary Theory and the Trade Cycle,* (London: Jonathan Cape 1929).

putting on five pounds a month. A year later you probably wouldn't even notice it unless you picked up an old photo."

Jakob's head nodded up and down in both agreement and contemplation. He stiffened his posture. "Do you think that the move toward hyper-consumerism is related to that?"

"I think that people's motivations change when they're exposed to the artificial pleasures of a boom cycle, yes . . . . definitely.

"Another devilish part is the pure unsustainability of this system," Professor Briarton pointed a finger in the air and pursed his lips.

"What do you mean by that Professor?" Jakob asked with obvious inquisitiveness as he scrunched his brow.

"Ok, well, what's the first thing you learned years ago in economics 101?"

"Umm," Jakob looked off to the left as if the answer was posted on the wall, "ohh, yeah, scarcity. There is only a finite amount of resources on the planet and the mad grab for these resources leads to supply and demand characteristics playing out."

"Exactly. And I thought most freshmen black out their first year at university with copious amounts of alcohol consumption. You're always going against the grain!" Professor Briarton cheerfully grinned and in reciprocation Jakob returned a partially subdued smile. "Yes, you're right Jakob. There is only so much metal, oil, etc in the world, although on a side note, the most difficult economic force isn't scarcity, but rather what to do with the surpluses – however that's a conversation for another time. What's certain is that we're using a hell of a lot of non-renewable resources right now.

"And because of this pyramided fractional reserve banking system, governments will not allow negative growth for fear of crashing the entire wobbly

Ponzi scheme. They therefore drive people to use resources ever more rapidly, thus causing our population to *double* in the last fifty years alone. Ok . . . so we have *projected* infinite growth in a world with finite resources. What happens when they run out?"

"We'll invent something new."

"Right. I always hear that argument. We'll just figure it out. Create some magical invention and puff, everything will sort itself out. Sure. That's *possible*. I'll give you that. But remember my metaphor I used in class about the lions and inventing a sword on the way to a fight? Personally I'm the kind of guy who would build defenses *before* the skirmish."

"Yeah, you gotta a point there. So why aren't we preparing or at least recognizing the problem?" Jakob asked, stroking his chin.

"That's a *really* good question Jakob. Some would say corporate and individual greed. Some would say original sin of mankind. I personally believe something far more nefarious than that." Professor Briarton shook his head slightly and pursed his lips.

"And what's that?" Jakob asked, as he leaned toward his mentor in anticipation.

"Well, we don't have quite enough time to explore that today," he flashed a look at his wrist watch. "But let me just put it this way. Those people at the top of the pyramid, they don't *accidentally* do things. You yourself have seen the small slivers of a control economy and it only goes deeper from there – I can assure you of that.

"Sure, those on the bottom don't feel that way because they've got the freedom to start their own businesses and that's the definition of a 'free market' in their minds. I'm sure cows in a field feel quite 'free' to eat all the grass they want until they start testing their barriers. The only difference between us and them is that most of us never see the fence that's keeping us in. For those who try to test the barriers . . . . well . . . . if a cow escapes then the farmer is going to be comin' with the truck to get 'em back in line – that's for *sure*."

The Professor nodded his head quickly up and down as Jakob continued to stare directly into his eyes. Neither one of them said anything for at least the next ten seconds as the information was digested into the young man's consciousness. Professor Briarton knew he had taken a bit of a leap, but was also aware that only days remained to prepare Jakob for what was about to happen. *He will accept reality*, the Professor said to himself.

His thought was interrupted by the ringing of the bell, prompting Jakob to jump up from his chair and turn toward the door of the small office.

"I'm late again," Jakob said flatly as the information he just received weighed his mind down with wild thoughts and implications.

"Well, it's clearly my fault this time, sorry about that," the Professor said. The dual meaning of his sentence was understood by both men. It wasn't Professor Briarton's goal to make heavy thoughts weigh on Jakob's soul but it was, however, a necessary step in the process.

"Ahhh, don't worry about it. I'll get over it," the pupil replied. Additionally the duality of *Jakob's* sentence was not lost on the Professor, and he internally celebrated the victory.

Jakob smiled and started to exit the room as Professor Briarton's words abruptly halted his gait.

"Oh, I wanted to ask you. . . . well, I know this is rather sudden, but these kinds of opportunities don't come along often. Do you have any plans this weekend?"

"Ahh, no I don't. Why? What's going on?" Jakob replied.

"As you already know, sometimes I advise the government on economic issues. And as it happens, I've been summoned by a Senator to discuss a few upcoming issues with him. It's no big deal really, but if you're not doing anything you could tag along as an assistant. You know, see how the whole process works."

Jakob's eyes widened in shock at the invitation, but not wanting to appear giddy, he quickly regained his composure and simply replied, "Yeah, definitely. So who's the Senator?"

"His name is William Langesé."

* * *

‖ 12 ‖

Jakob toyed with his food in the massive Union Center Cafeteria. The facility was expansive. Hundreds of rows of elongated tables filled the hall. From where he was standing, he could still easily see the pulsing neon signs of all the major fast food companies. Students snaked out into huge lines ravenously hungry for the overly processed chum. Jakob skipped those chemical laden feasts for a lesser known university run food counter called Mom's Cookin'. They prepared a university version of home cooked meals and Jakob ordered a grilled chicken breast with two sides of vegetables.

He looked around for somewhere to sit when he saw his friend Brandon, or Bran as he liked to be called, and delivered the obligatory, "what's up," as he sat in a vacant seat across from him.

"Not much," Bran replied. In recognition of Jakob, Bran's square, flat face swiveled toward him. He then neatly emptied the contents of his brown bag lunch onto the table in front of him.

"Watcha got there?" Jakob asked while craning his neck to see a plethora of neatly chopped, raw vegetables along with a large chunk of turkey.

"Oh little of this and that from the fridge. . . . how 'bout you?"

"Well, you're the food scientist. . . .*you* tell me!"

"May I," Bran asked, gesturing toward the food.

"Wow. A taste test from the professional, please, by all means," Jakob quipped with a smile.

Robert methodically took a bite out of the chicken and the two vegetable side dishes. After chewing for a few minutes and then taking an unnecessary moment to look off to side in contemplation, he opened his mouth.

"Judging by the taste, the chicken was definitely processed and frozen at some point before it was cooked. It looks like this piece of meat wasn't actually a *real* chicken breast at all, but rather little pieces of chicken that were ground up, probably bleached and then poured into a mold which only emulates the original version in shape.

"The vegetables clearly came out of can. This isn't to say that they didn't have any flavor. I guess that's why butter overpowered my senses with every bite. Because they were canned vegetables, it's guaranteed that the magical process of pasteurization had been utilized which is just a fancy word for 'boiling the hell out of them'. Unfortunately that means that a lot of the vitamins which naturally exist have been broken down and rendered inert. That's why most things that are pasteurized must have vitamins added to them *after* the fact. You know, like ascorbic acid in orange juice."

"Well that was fairly thorough. And this was the most nutritious thing I could find! I've been trying to eat naturally occurring foods like you told me about, but a lot of times it's hard to get it right."

"Now you see why I pack my lunch," Bran shot back with a smile.

"You know to be honest with you, the economist side of his brain is thinking of the insane amount of energy waste that goes into the creation of these canned food stuffs which virtually everyone in this country consumes. Couldn't the cafeteria buy local food from farmers cheaper, rather than serving us all of this tasteless, vitaminless rubbage?

"I mean think about some farmer in a far away place growing tons of food to be canned. The cans, made of tin, must be extracted from the earth and processed which is of course a fairly energy intensive undertaking. The food must be cooked (pasteurized), thereby wasting more energy. Finally, it's shipped a far distance by freight to get to its destination – more energy loss – and then cooked *again!*"

At that moment he realized that the over reliance on cheap energy has clearly shaped the way people eat. The growth of the suburbs wasn't the only effect of cheap oil. *Imbalance always reverberates through a system,* he thought.

"Maybe this sort of thing makes sense if your community is in place with an inhospitable climate, but this goes on in places where fertile land lies fowl as farmers receive government subsidies to *not* grow certain crops," Jakob finished and again worked on what was left on his plate.

"And what about the fact that we all eat "dead" food?" Bran interjected after swallowing a large bite of romaine lettuce. "The vast majority of what people eat consists of items that are pasteurized or cooked to the extreme. How many people do you know that eat a *lot* of *raw* fruits and vegetables? I don't know many to be honest with you. Another huge change is the switch from a grass based diet to a seed based diet."[7]

"What do you mean by that?" Jakob inquired.

"W*ay* in past, our diets consisted of fresh fruits and vegetables along with grass fed animals, ok?" Jakob nodded in response as he continued chewing his cafeteria meal. "Then came agriculture and with it, the advent of storing surplus grain. First off, the grain has to be refined/processed which is a fancy term for stripping out most of the vitamins. This was great back then because food could easily be stored in times when it was

---

[7] Pollan, Michael, *In Defense of Food*. (New York: Penguin Books, 2009).

scarce, and thus famine could be avoided with careful planning.

"Because sitting food stuffs gave the government tremendous power (specifically the power to prevent starvations) they naturally subsidized/ordered the planting of a multitude of grains. This of course leads to over production and rather than simply being a protection against famine, the grains turned into the main source of calories for the people. Naturally, animal production is increased as the surplus grain is feed to them instead of grass. Just to exemplify how unnatural this is, cows have to be given antibiotics in order to prevent an infection when they're feed too much grain. And of course rather than getting nutrients from the grass which the cow used to eat, we now too get another serving of grain instead.

"This same grain/government story has happened again and again in varying forms throughout human history. The difference between this cycle and the others is that industrial food science has propelled it vastly farther than before. The diet of mankind has never been so irrevocably changed in all of human history," he pointed finger cuttingly into the air, emphasizing the importance of his words.

"Bran, you never beat around the bush do you? So do you think that some of this can be connected to the horrible physical and mental afflictions which seem to infect almost everyone? I mean if it's any indication, I think about half of Americans are on prescription drugs."

"Of course these things are connected. I mean how could nutrition and health not be connected!" Bran laughed haughtily at his own comment. "The odd thing," he said, as he continued to shovel his food into his mouth, "is that nobody even thinks to ask these questions, and if you do ask," his eyes widened in disbelief, "everyone looks at you like you're some nutty hippy."

Jakob's mind flashed back to the conversation he just had with the Professor. *If you were raised with pink elephants roaming the streets would you think anything of it? If you went around trying to tell everyone how odd it was they'd think you were probably mad.*

Lightning dazzled and crackled in his mind as he realized the massive implications of that allegory. It seemed that every time he questioned established thought, he got put down before people ever even qualify the facts. *They don't even SEE the pink elephants,* he thought, *and that's why they're so quick to say they don't exist.*

Jakob remembered back to his childhood when he was convinced that he absolutely despised watermelon. The odd thing about his disposition was that he had never tried *actual* watermelon, but rather only its artificial counterpart which was produced in a lab. He wondered how many children thought they did not like various *real* fruits because of their lab produced substitutes in candy. Perhaps waiting too long to discover the difference would simply lock the mind down into never appreciating the real thing.

"Yeah it's all pretty crazy when you think about the modern diet," Bran continued as he motioned with an outstretched finger at Jakob's tray. "Another unintended consequence of processed food is that most of it is highly addictive. As you know I've spent some time in South America with my family and seen that various native Indian tribes use the Coca plant, from which cocaine is manufactured, in ways that I hadn't seen before. They made teas with it and some people simply chewed the leaves as one would with tobacco. The narcotic effect on people was about like that of a few cups of coffee and would certainly not be associated with its processed cousin – cocaine.

"I started to think about it, and I realized that processed coca and processed foods of all kinds might have something in common – addiction. Survey after survey confirms that the vast majority of the people admit that they have a self control issue with respect to food. What was making people suddenly lose dietary control where they had not in the past? Then I thought of a better question. . . . . Why don't people typically loose control with tea or coca leaves? The answer is because it's the refinement of a product that makes it more addictive."

This wasn't the first time that Jakob had been exposed to one of Bran's rants and he was fairly certain it wouldn't be the last. Jakob liked the way he explained things and enjoyed it when he took the liberty to talk about food science, which by no coincidence is also his major.

"So you're saying that refined foods are like all vices whether it's gambling, tattoos, drugs, and some people are naturally more susceptible to its calling than others."

"Yeah, I think you got it. I mean, think back to when people found or purposely grew beets, corn or sugar cane long ago. They weren't causing any health issues because people enjoyed their treats in moderate quantities. This was so because the increased volume of eating naturally occurring fruits and vegetables fills people up much more than processed food. Nowadays, on the other hand, modern food scientists basically break down food into their chemical components, you know, like high-fructose corn syrup, refined sugar (mostly just sucrose), caffeine, and an unbelievable variety of oils. . . .and then," his eyes widened for effect, "they recombine them with taste and color enhancers along with plenty of semi-toxic preservatives and. . . . . walla! You've got yourself a processed food. Unfortunately the refining strips the fruits and vegetables of most of their vitamins so now guess what food scientists do? They add processed vitamins back into the food! Of course the absorption rate of these reconstituted vitamins is much lower than their naturally occurring sources. Thus even though people eat large quantities of processed foods, their bodies are still not receiving the correct amount of vitamins. Some people think this is one factor in overeating. A vitaminless diet never satiates their hunger.

"On the other side of the obesity argument, there are those that believe industrialization has led to a general decline in food prices and thus, people over eat now simply because they can," Bran paused for a second and laughed at the idea before continuing. "This cannot be correct because the obesity spike should have been more pronounced *when* the actual price decline in food *happened*. The obesity spike does, however, correlate with the introduction of a *substantial* amount of refined foods into the diets of consumers. *This correlation is no mystery*.

"Wow, I hadn't thought about it like that before," Jakob commented.

"And I'm quite certain that there are scores of people who would like it to stay that way," Bran's face was momentarily petrified in stone-like seriousness.

"Well. . . . anyway. You know I play Lacrosse, right?" Bran inquired, which seemingly changed the subject.

"How could I forget?" he said with a sarcastic smile.

"Isn't it ironic that my coach would continually hound us about not eating any "junk food" (really just another term for refined or artificial foods), while none of my Professors do the same. *It's like they believe the brain is not an organ in the body*," he said, while simultaneously an index finger, like a woodpecker, rhythmically tapped on his dark complected forehead.

He unwaveringly continued, "When the body is poisoned to the point where it can no longer regulate its own functions and this becomes evident in blood pressure, vitamin, cholesterol, and glucose imbalances, then I assure you that every organ is being adversely effected which *naturally* includes the brain."

The two men sat in silence while finishing their entrees. Within minutes Bran abruptly leaned back in his plastic molded, cafeteria chair and uttered, "gotta go. I think I'm going to sit this one out, if you don't mind."

"Huh?" Jakob surprisingly said. Bran's eyes motioned toward the right, and he signaled with a raised brow as he stood up. Jakob's head twisted to the side and saw that Megan was walking toward him.

"Am I interrupting something?" Megan looked down at Jakob as she spoke.

"Nope just leaving," Bran said grabbing his trash and walking off.

Jakob finally faced Megan and said, "have a seat." His leg kicked out the chair across from him, and he indicted with his facial expression for her to sit down. For a moment Megan acted indecisively but with false reluctance finally sat. Before being settled she toyed with her rather short skirt and adjusted her blouse in an obvious attempt to catch Jakob's eyes scanning her body.

"So ahh, couldn't find anybody else to sit with?" he said sarcastically.

"Does that give your little self-esteem a boost?"

"It doesn't hurt," he replied as a smile stretched across his face. The truth was Jakob could see right through her, and she knew it. He did not mind playing along with her perfectly symmetrical face and flowing blond hair – at least the scenery was nice.

"Look, I'm really not here to socialize."

"Oh, really?"

"I've noticed that you and Professor Briarton seem to be on pretty good terms."

"I guess you could say that," he thought about his upcoming trip this weekend to meet Senator Langesé, but instinctively held his tongue for the moment, "ahh. . . .go on."

"That's the only class I *don't* have an A in, and I want one. Do you know what's going to be on the test in a few weeks?" Jakob dropped his fork on the tray in front of him, knowing he had to play hard to get in order to leverage the request into something *he* wanted.

"I'll tell you what Megan, I'd be happy to go over what's on the test with you – on one condition of course."

"What?" Megan's eyes rolled so far back in her head that passerby's could have mistaken it for a seizure.

"We go out and have a few beers together. . . ."

"Uh, what?"

"And you explain to me what the hell happened to you in high school that made you like *this*. I'm not going to try to change you, don't think that. I just want to know what did this to you. So what do ya say?"

"Fine," she replied as she took a rather angry gulp of her diet soft drink.

"See, that wasn't so difficult. How about you say - we meet up this Monday around seven at Harold's Pub?" Although part of him wanted to brag, in the end he did not tell her about his trip with Professor Briarton to meet Senator Langesé. *That's just the sort of thing that's better left unsaid – people could get the wrong idea,* he thought.

"Fine," she repeated. Megan immediately got up and grabbed her tray and drink.

"You're leaving? You haven't even touched your food."

"I did not come here to eat," she said emotionlessly as she turned and began to walk off.

"And Megan," Jakob called out, "no sorority sisters, ok."

"Arghhhh." She did not have to use any actual words, but Jakob would take that sound as an acknowledgment that she heard him.

* * *

‖ 13 ‖

"So, you must be Jakob, very pleased to meet you," Senator William Langesé extended a hand out to the younger man and he shook it firmly. For just a moment, Jakob imagined cameras capturing the event; however, there were none present. While looking each other in the eyes, Jakob was immediately taken with the warmth that the Senator exuded, and could somehow instinctively feel that he was an empathic man.

Then, along with Professor Briarton, they took their seats naturally following the lead of their senatorial host.

It had taken the better part of Friday afternoon for Professor Briarton and Jakob to make the trip to Washington, DC. Upon arriving fairly late in the evening the two men had retired to their rooms for the night and awoke early in the morning so that they could use the Senator's only available time slot.

"It's been too long William," Professor Briarton remarked rather candidly to the Senator.

"I know Phillip, we'll have to make better use of our free time in the future," Senator Langesé commented. While Jakob wasn't *exactly* sure what Professor Briarton did for the Senator, he still felt that they were both being a bit informal.

Senator Langesé's office was the most spacious one Jakob had ever seen. He looked around at the eloquence of the room, and noticed that it was most likely built in the 20's. Perfectly preserved art deco shapes and carvings of varying levels of complexity lined the walls and even the furniture was clearly from that era.

After remaining silent because of an intimidated respect for the situation, Jakob leaned forward from the sturdy, brown leather arm chair and spoke.

"Senator Langesé I wanted to start off by thanking you for taking some time out of your *extremely* busy schedule to have me here."

"It's not a problem at all Jakob. In fact, after Professor Briarton told me how gifted of a student you are, well, the time issue took care of itself," the square jawed Senator complimented. Jakob grinned ear to ear at the praise from not only his mentor but also a serving Senator.

"Jakob," the Professor calmly turned toward his pupil, "I don't think you realize how rare an opened minded individual is. The biggest road block in the teaching process is when students hold false, preconceived notions as absolute fact. The majority of my time as an educator is spent trying to undo the misconceptions that the students believe are true. Then, the *actual* learning process can begin. . . . but first you must to have a clean slate.

"With you on the other hand, it seems like your misconceptions haven't solidified around a false façade of religion, nationalism, and whatever else, as with the other students. Falsehoods were simply pushed aside without an emotional uprising. You've been to my class before. . . . . it might as well be an exorcism going on in there, just this one has to purge the students of all of falsities rather than demons."

"Is there a difference?" the Senator murmured while adjusting his posture and raising his brow.

"The real question is," Jakob now felt confident enough to intrinsically respond, "why do they believe things that are false in the first place. To some degree adolescence is really a slow pace, brain washing process. Think about it. . . . parents transfer their world view to their children before they're consciously aware enough to make decisions, and then they tell the kids 'don't question me'. If this weren't enough on its own, the process is reinforced by peers, the media and teachers. Most people who can break out of it probably spend the majority of their 20's undoing all the damaging propaganda of their youth. Luckily for me I've got Professor Briarton," he said, looking at his mentor in smiling admiration as he balanced his compliment.

"That's very insightful Jakob," Senator Langesé gestured with his hands as he spoke, "I think what you described is related to a subconscious fear of almost all parents; namely that children will turn their backs on their own upbringing. Out of this fear, the majority of parents *do not* teach their children critical thinking skills, but instead teach them to simply obey. It's interesting that we actually teach what is already an inherent component of the human race – follow the crowd.

"Speaking of . . . here, what do you make of these" he reached over to a table beside his chair and threw five magazines on the table. "I was trying to find a political magazine about the Senate at a grocery store, and these were the only ones at the checkout. Just for convenience they tell you how to dress, converse and please a man!"

Jakob and Professor Briarton looked over the glossy fashion, celebrity, sports, and gossip magazines and realized there were no political, science or economic publications of which to speak.

"Hey look, don't get me wrong I love sports, but it's strange that the demand is so low for real life stuff, don't you think?"

"Yes, but at the same time, most of that stuff at the checkout counter – your candy bars, gum, entertainment magazines – are just there to catch impulse buyers as they wait captive in the line," Professor Briarton commented. "Still. . . . . I see where you're going with that. Maybe it's a reflection of those missing magazines, but. . . . I mean if you talk politics or economics in a café you'll find that the topic of conversation is very quickly changed to. . . . . . surprise, surprise, the subjects of a checkout aisle magazines. And there's nothing inherently wrong with that per se. . . . but it begs the question: Why does such a large segment of the population not care about the real world? If you happen to find someone who is willing to talk about those 'taboo subjects' then the conversation typically devolves into 'right vs. left' ridiculousness."

"I know exactly what you mean Professor Briarton," the Senator cradled his chin before continuing, "I think that right vs. left phenomenon is rooted in a misunderstanding about the role of government. You see Jakob," he turned to the young man and stared him intently in the eyes, "my political philosophy differs from those on the right and left. I usually put it this way: Conservatives generally believe that society should stay the same or be rolled backwards, while Progressives believe that society should advance forwards. The thing that unites the two philosophies is that they *both* think the government should be used for their aims.

"I, on the other hand, believe that society should progress, or conserve or do whatever it would like to do without interference. That means – keep the government out of social engineering and *let people be.*" He clenched his fist adamantly, while Jakob was clearly taken with the intensity with which he spoke.

"I've noticed that too. Both of these sides seem to use the government as a battling ground for their social agenda and they trample over every law in the book to do it," Jakob, now leaning back in his chair, quickly noted.

"They don't just trample on the regular ol' laws Jakob. . . . . most politicians, along with soldiers, *swear an oath* to uphold and protect the constitution as well," Senator Langesé pointed out. "Have they even bothered to read it? That actually reminds me. . . . by the way Phillip, I've got a great way to end a frivolous right vs. left debate – just ask the people 'when is the last time they read the constitution?' Then say 'well how can you judge a politician if you don't even know which policies will cause them to break their constitutional oath'!" The Senator let out a belly laugh allowing his true jovial nature to shine through.

"Yeah, Professor, like you were saying about conversations," Jakob, looking off to the side in contemplation, interjected, "I do know what you mean about certain topics being off limits. It's like, whenever you break one of these unspoken rules, you can actually *feel* it in the room," he nodded at Senator Langesé. "Most people don't realize this because like cows in a fence they never stray too far," Jakob looked over at Professor Briarton in appreciation of the allegory. "If you go on about celebrity gossip, sports, rumors around town, or a number of other subjects, everything is fine and normal. But if you veer off the beaten path and venture down a road of critically thinking about what governments and big business are doing together, then you better be ready for an abrupt subject change, because I can guarantee you that somebody in the group is feeling *very* uncomfortable talking about those things. 'Hey, just keep it light' they always say. I respond with 'As far as I know, I've only got one life to live and I'm not going to waste it exclusively on superfluous banter'."

Just then, the phone beside Senator Langesé lit up and a female voice chimed in, "Sorry to bother you Senator, but the protestors are here again. How do you want me to handle them this time?"

"Just a second. *Unbelievable*," the frustrated politician tapped the mute button and buried his face in both hands, "you try to help people and they despise you for it."

"William, what's this all about anyway?" The Professor responded.

"You're familiar with the Stakz epidemic right?"

"Yes, that's the new designer drug that's all over the schools. I've been following it very closely."

"These school searches that they're doing are out of control," the Senator's eyes got wider as he spoke. "They're practically strip-searching the kids now! But there are also some *very* well funded anti-drug groups that believe *I'm* endangering their children by getting a court injunction to temporarily ban the searches. I truly wonder if any of those parents have ever checked their *own* child's locker for drugs. Why couldn't *they* stop by on their lunch break or something? For so many people the very idea of that is ridiculous, and yet they wouldn't blink an eye if some jack-booted official did it for them. They do this because these people are scared to be parents so they slowly cede all of their natural duties to a central authority with the hope that the 'collective power' of government can get it done. Admittedly, it's also not helping that many people must work really long hours, and so they just don't have the time to be parents. . . . . but that's an economics issue, which is of course is Professor Briarton's domain.

"Right now we are only beginning to see the consequences of a majority rule system," the Senator continued speaking while running his hand through his full head of dark, thick hair, "which the founding fathers actually feared more than a monarchy. [8]

"The truth is, we're supposed to be a republic which *utilizes* democracy. . . .*not* the other way around! It's mob rule. . . . . which means there are no rules. You see Jakob, a republic," Senator Langesé stopped for just a moment and let a deep breath in and then out again

---

[8] Paine, Thomas. *Common Sense,* (Philadelphia: printed and sold by W. and T. Bradford [1776]; Bartleby.com, 1999).

before going on, "well, you know the Pledge Allegiance, right? You pledge an allegiance to the flag and the *republic* for which it stands'. This *republic* has core rules ensuring that no one tramples on the people's basic rights. Property rights, the right to free speech, and the right to not be searched without probable cause are just some, to name a few. Unfortunately after systematically twisting, contorting, or simply ignoring our own laws for so long now, they have become. . . well. . . flexible to say the least. Or you could say our laws – *almost all of them* – seem to be changeable with a simply majority (over 50%). In the past the constitution needed a 2/3's majority to be changed, but the thing is today Jakob," Senator Langesé leaned toward the younger man and spoke softly, "we don't bother with the 2/3's majority - we pass everything with a simply majority. And *poof*! You didn't even need a 2/3's majority, see! Both parties have set this precedent and neither one of them wants to give the enormous privilege up. Sure they may complain a little when the other party uses it, but never enough to change the system.

"With all of our 'guaranteed' liberties now subject to a simple 50/50 vote, there are no boundaries. Think about it. . . . what's to stop a government official from coming into your home and inspecting it for energy efficiency? Just a simple majority, and it's done!

"And so it goes, the republic dies. Horrible events – terrorism, economic, weather - are seized upon as opportunities and pre-written bills thousands of pages long are passed in the middle of the night by a Congress who couldn't possibly have read them in that timeframe. With extreme circumstances presenting such an opportunity for those wishing to further this agenda, it's hard not to imagine the worst. Here we are today," the Senator tightened his chin and pursed his lips, "the Stakz epidemic. . . . . just another problem that people are overreacting to. . . and lo and behold, the government has the solution. Which, as usual, means that you need to give up more of your 'guaranteed' liberties. The repetition is haunting," he finished exasperated and returned his face to his hands. Although the Senator's core personality was optimistic by nature it was clear that years of cold hard, political reality had taken its toll on the man.

He decidedly broke his moment of sorrow and slapped the mute button on the phone, "Vicky," he called out.

"Yes Senator?" She responded.

"Do nothing," he said resoundingly.

"Nothing sir."

"Nothing at all. Thank you."

"No problem sir." He disconnected the line and smiled at his two guests.

"No mater what happens, I know I'm right. Protestors or not," the Senator said, his face tensed with seriousness.

"William, you *have* heard those rumors about Stakz, right?

"Of course I have, so?" He scoffed at Professor Briarton.

"Well, what happens if they turn out to be true?" By this point Jakob was quite confused but nevertheless could feel the tension between the two men. His head turned following each speaker intently.

"I *highly* doubt they're true," William responded with his brow furrowed.

"Humor me. . . . . just assume they're true. What happens then?"

"Then," Senator William Langesé leaned closer to Professor Briarton and said, "my br. . . . ., my friend, they've set the perfect trap for me."

Jakob was still intrigued by the odd conversation between the two men, and not to be left out, commented, "what do you mean 'set the perfect trap'?"

Senator Langesé realized that he and the Professor had probably been a little candid when speaking in front of Jakob. He quickly regained his conversational composure, "well Jakob, let's not spread these rumors any further than we have to."

"You mean about Stakz, right?" Jakob asked rhetorically. "My dad was saying something about that not too long ago. Yeah, he said something about a 'lot of dead kids', or something like that. Is that what you guys heard too?"

Professor Briarton's and Senator Langesé's heads jerked toward one another and their eyes immediately locked in stunned confirmation that the rumor was probably true.

"Your father said that, huh Jakob?" The mentor asked his pupil.

"Yeah, and he was real weird about it too. He just made the comment and kinda clammed up."

"It doesn't matter anyway," the Senator exclaimed, "I'm going to stick to my principles and go from there!" He clenched his fist, now full of renewed, principled vigor.

"Alright, just be careful, ok?" Professor Briarton responded.

"Professor what have you heard? What's the rumor?" Jakob, still left out of the conversation, inquired.

"Let's just hope it's something that will never happen." He said plainly.

"I still sincerely doubt," Senator Langesé said somberly, "that people could be so *cruel*, as to do have actually *done* something like that."

* * *

‖ 14 ‖

Jakob looked down into his glass of beer, the bubbles moving and coalescing like bacteria in a Petri dish. "You know that beer's alive, it's unpasteurized," Doug said looking down at him seated at a table alone. "It's strange that you're looking kinda lonely over here at a table – why aren't you sittin' at the bar tonight?"

"I'm meeting somebody to study with," Jakob, remaining purposely aloof for effect, looked down at his phone to check the time, "and she should've been here already."

"*She* should have been here already, huh? Are you sure this has anything to do with studying?" Doug finished the sentence with a bit of a smirk.

"Well, I guess you'll find out in a few. . . . . " Jakob's sentence was cut short as Megan approached the table causing both men's heads to involuntarily turn in response to her presence. Doug shook his head in jealous approval and threw out a quick, "I'll see you around," before turning and attending to his bar patrons.

Jakob, always the gentleman, stood up as she approached and said, "good evening."

"This isn't a date or anything. It's an obligation. Nothing more, nothing less, you got that?"

"I wouldn't have it any other way. Have a seat." Megan nodded and maneuvered into her chair, concurrently adjusting her hair and clothing to their appropriate seated configuration.

"This is kind of funny, really," Jakob said, "here you are the perfect 'A student' asking me, the 'C student' for help in a class. Why do you suppose that is?"

"Because Professor Briarton's class is for the unintellectual. He's not clear about what's going to be on the test and his lectures are usually *way* off subject. Really, it is perfect place for *un*focused individuals like yourself." Megan's head tilted to the right and her eyebrows rose at the end of her response. Jakob thought it to be quite brazen that she would attempt to insult his intelligence when *she* was the one asking for help. Megan was a genius when it came to justifying her own inadequacies as she had clearly just done.

"Well I've got a different theory why you're having trouble," Jakob began.

"*Ohhhh,* tell oh young genius, who's better in one out of *five* classes," she laughed at her own insulting joke and batted her almond eyes in fake anticipation.

"I'm about to."

"Well go ahead"

"I will."

"Go!"

"Oh that's what I'm about to do," Jakob continued with confidence. "You can't handle this class because the majority of the material forces you to use reason and logic to re-examine everything that you've been taught to believe your entire life. And because you can't tolerate to have your beliefs questioned you clam up and fight Professor Briarton so much that you're missing the entire point."

"Yeah, and what exactly *is* the point."

"Don't you listen? I just said it," Jakob face looked puzzled at her response, ". . . . .use reason and apply it to your decision making process."

"Well I do that in plenty of my classes. I've always gotten A's in all of my philosophy classes," her voice changed as she quoted, "*The philosopher is in love with truth, that is, not with the changing world of sensation, which is the object of opinion, but with the unchanging reality which is the object of knowledge.* Plato."

"Do you even know what that quote means, Megan?"

"*Yes,* I know what it means."

"No you don't. You know how to memorize it and repeat it. You can memorize anything; I've watched you since high school when they used to make us recite poems and the Preamble and stuff like that. You don't *know* them. Sure you've gone a *little* further than we used to back then. Now you actually memorize what someone *else* has told you they mean, and then you choose one of the little bubbles on the test. . . .giving yourself an instant feeling of intelligence. I could train a monkey to do that. Think about how you study for tests. I've *seen you!* You just group everything into nice and neat little headings and subheadings with little numbers in between. And all of that is *perfect* for filling in little bubbles as quickly as possible. That's all. That is *not* intelligence."

"I'm sure I'm going to listen to a *C* student lecture me about what intelligence is. Jakob, look at yourself. You've always struggled in school ever since I've known you. If we're *really* going to be honest with each other, I was thoroughly surprised that you even decided to *go* to college; what with *your* aptitude. . . .I just did *not* think you had it in you. And it looks like, except for this *one class*, I was right."

"Why are you so unable to really *perceive* anything I'm saying? You think that because I find reasoning, understanding, and truly thinking, preferable to memorizing a bunch of disparate facts without ever knowing why I'm doing it - that makes me unintelligent? That's absurd."

"You know Jakob," Megan began to speak softer with a plastic tone of compassion, "I remember when my family was overseas. At that time my Father was working on various engineering projects and every once in a while he'd run into an engineer that was questioning the sort of projects that the company was assigning to them. You know what he always found out about those people Jakob? You know what he found? They typically lacked the aptitude to complete them. That's why they started to question the long term viability of them. Their minds had to *reason* away their obvious incompetence. Don't you *see?* That's *you*. You don't have the mind for higher learning and because of that you're looking around and saying to yourself – 'there must be something wrong with the system'. When really Jakob, it's you. There's something wrong with you."

"Wake up Megan. Look around you," he gestured both arms in a circular motion as the infuriation began to build inside of him, "look at our world. First we go to elementary school, then high school, and during both of these places our teachers are constantly doing what? What do they *really* expect of us?"

"I don't know Jakob – wild guess here – they expect us to learn," she shook her in response to what she thought was a stupid question.

"That's part of it. But what are we learning – facts figures, and propaganda. We sure as hell are never taught to think for ourselves. When students ask 'why do we need to know this', which is about the best question any rational human being could ever ask, what is the answer normally? 'Because otherwise you'll fail', or 'because I said so'. Critical thinking is punished. The students who can memorize and then repeat unquestionably get the best grades in these early schools, and the sad truth is our schools are designed to weed out the real thinkers.[9] Because if your primary and secondary school teachers don't think that you're good at

---

[9] Gatto, John Taylor, *Dumbing Us Down*, (Canada: New Society Publishers, 2005).

rote memorization, then you're obviously *not* college material. Then, if we're actually in an undergraduate program at college, your first three years of it is mostly the same thing that you did in your primary and secondary school years. More multiple choice and bubble filling, more learning without questioning – it's not until your senior year that you actually get *some* smaller class sizes and maybe even a few essay questions. And sure this may not be the case at a lot of Ivy League schools, but the truth is that your 'grades', in reality a measure of how docile you are, have to be so high to get in, that there's almost no way a free thinking individual can even attend those schools.

"So where do we go after that? Some go to grad school where they start to force some of the mindless zombies to do *some* actual thinking but very little at this point. And you can be *damn* sure that these people will think grad school is very difficult because they've never had to actually *use* their critical thinking skills before. But by this point it doesn't matter anyway because most graduate schools are so focused on one discipline that there's no time to think outside of the box even if they wanted to. Besides all that, if you start publicly going against what your professor is saying you can be *damn* sure that you're not going to finish top of your class. This fear usually leads to the worst kind of censorship – self-censorship. And then what?

"After this massive distillation process those people who are the 'best of the best' move up into the high-level government and corporate jobs they've always dreamed of. What do you think they're going to do then? Change the system? Fix things? Make waves? No, they'll do exactly what they've been trained to do their entire lives - to *not* critically think and they certainly will *not* go against the grain. This thing has been playing out for a long, *long* time. And it's exactly why our entire society seems to be getting worse and worse every year – because it is."

"Jakob your lack of success has made you bitter and delusional," she placed both hands on the table and used the force to propel herself out of her chair. "I don't need your tutoring. I'm really not sure how you're doing so well in that *one* class, but it doesn't matter either way. I've already reported Professor Briarton to the Board."

"For what?!?"

"For advocating students to try drugs," Megan said haughtily.

"That's ridiculous! You're joking." Jakob's face wrinkled with surprised disdain.

"Well I'm not joking. I reported him on official channels already but now, Jakob," she leaned toward him, "I'm going to make a 'few phone calls' to some people I know so that I can get the process expedited. I hope he won't even be around by the end of the semester."

"Why are you *doing this*? Destroying a man for your own vanity is even lower than you."

"It's not about my vanity Jakob. After hearing you ramble on about all this non-sense, which I'm guessing is mostly coming from Professor Briarton; I can only *imagine* the damage he's doing to other students. I'm doing this to protect the people, not for my own vanity." Megan picked up her purse, adjusted her hair, and took two steps away from the table pausing before her exit. "Good luck on the test," she muttered sardonically with a polyester grin.

"Megan, don't do this!" Jakob called out over the noise of the bar, but he said it to no avail while she scuttled out of Harold's Pub.

To Jakob, Professor Briarton wasn't just *a* professor, he was *the Professor*. He was the only professor that ignited a spark inside him and made him feel like he wasn't a failure. He had a way of turning the tables on the world by implying that it's the world that has the problem 'not you, Jakob'. For him to be ousted from the university meant that Jakob's spirit would die just a little, and more importantly it meant that what Jakob considered evil would triumph over good. Maybe if he warned the Professor they could avert the situation together. Even though it was almost eight o'clock Jakob had often seen the Professor working late in his campus office.

"I've got to see if he's there," Jakob said aloud.

"Got to see if who's there," Doug asked as he walked over to the table with the intention of refilling Jakob's beer.

"Ahhh, nobody Doug. Sorry man, I gotta take care of something," Jakob starting getting up from the table and fished a five dollar bill out of his wallet, slapping it down on the table in haste. He quickly dashed toward the exit of the pub with Doug calling out to him.

"Strike two with Megan, huh? It's alright, that ballgame's not over yet!" Doug shook his head and began clearing the table for the next patrons.

* * *

‖ 15 ‖

In addition to the shoe boxed sized device which had hitched a ride on a satellite in search of Quantum Bursts around the world, Herschel had also developed a quantum briefcase detection device. Although it was slightly larger than the satellite model it did have the added bonus of being able to pinpoint a Quantum Burst to within a few meters of the source. The only problem was that you had to be within one mile of the Quantum Burst to *even* begin to detect *anything*.

So Roger, naturally curious about the Quantum Burst detected in his very own city, was currently driving around in his SUV with one eye on the road and the other eye looking toward the open 'briefcase' which was safely seat belted in like a passenger. Herschel had told him that the device would start to chirp loudly if it detected even the faintest of Quantum Burst. Roger never listened to technicians or programmers about what a device was *supposed* to do; even a good friend like Herschel when talking about untested equipment tended to speak with a hundred percent certainty when a fifty/fifty chance of a successful operation was more realistic.

After seven hours of driving around the city with nothing to show for it, dusk was now setting in, and Roger was just about to call it quits. He had just spoken with Herschel, well, he had just argued with Herschel about the operational effectiveness of the device and Herschel did not exactly have any good news. He had told Roger that a quantum communicator (he was abundantly clear that he was just theorizing because a few months ago he did not believe such a device *even existed*) wouldn't leave a signature unless it was in use.

This is why the satellite placed detector was so effective. That device has been spinning around the earth for months, detecting each Quantum Burst like time lapse photography would have.

Roger decided to allot about another hour to the seemingly vain search before he would call it quits. He had already driven around the entire city three or four times without a chirp, beep, or peep from that stupid device.

I'll just cut through campus on the way home and call it quits for the day, he thought to himself. Just when he made a left onto Palmetto Street, the interior of the SUV, silent throughout the day, echoed with a beeping noise that stirred the ghosts of long dead professors drifting around campus.

"What the fuck, Herschel!" Roger said aloud to himself. "Where the hell's the volume switch?" He quickly pulled over to the side of the road and examined the device with renewed purpose. *First things first,* he thought as he turned the knob down to an audibly acceptable level. *Alright, let's see here.* The bulk of the 'guts' of the device was located in the lower section of the plain black suitcase, but on the upper part is where the instrumentation lies. On the right side of the screen a series of numbers and odd symbols which meant absolutely nothing to Roger, were changing and flickering quite rapidly. In the middle of the display, a sonar like device showed from where the signal was emanating, and to the left a number was displayed directly below a label saying 'meters to source'. *173 meters to the source, damn, that's coming from on campus!*

Excitedly Roger looked back up at the road while concurrently putting the bulky SUV back into drive when he had to abruptly slam on the brakes to avoid hitting a campus police car which pulled directly in front of him. *Ahhh, what the hell is this!*

Looking down at the officer in the vehicle from his much taller SUV, Roger could see that he was rather unhappy about the two inches of space in between the two cars. Roger quickly exited the SUV to talk with him. Likewise the officer exited his vehicle to speak with Roger.

"Stay right there, *don't MOVE,*" the officer called out, internally suspecting the absolute worst about the suspicious SUV parked in a no parking zone, without a university decal, *and* driving erratically. "Keep your hands where I can see them." By this time the officer had his hand on his tazer (or cattle prod) and judging by his facial expression Roger knew better then to 'give him a reason'. *No need to do something stupid and get cattle prodded by this buffoon.*

"Officer," Roger said smiling in an attempt to defuse the situation, "I'm a contractor with the NSS. I can show you my credentials but it's a bit difficult to do so with my hands raised up."

"Alright. Turn around and put one hand on the vehicle and hand me your wallet with the other," the officer called back in compromise.

"Sure, sure, no problem," Roger said as he complied, handing him the wallet as requested. As the officer began examining his Cosgrove ID with a NSS seal clearly visible, Roger realized how powerlessly controlled he felt at that moment. Deep down he knew this was just a modern 'fight or flight' response and was aware how absolutely necessary these police procedures were, but at the same time he understood why the innocent sometimes run in the face of such dominating authority.

"Alright Mr. Vanden," he said looking down at the ID, "I'm going to have to run you through the system real quick, ok. It's just a formality. I'm sure everything'll check out fine." The officer would have felt tremendously more comfortable if Roger had been wearing some sort of uniform which would have identified him.

Plain clothes contractors did not give him the fraternal endorphin rush brought on by a sense of tribal togetherness as uniforms do. Because he was not consciously aware of this primal-tribal phenomenon, he simply felt uneasy. After a few minutes the officer stepped out of his vehicle and again approached Roger.

"Sorry about the confusion Agent Vanden. If I may ask, what exactly are you investigating on campus today?" He inquired as Roger pulled the wallet from the officer's clasp.

"Unfortunately that's classified, but I'm sure it's nothing to worry about," Roger replied. He had already been chewed out by Specialist Rodriguez for his CIA leak and he was damn sure not going to let this information get out to some low-level campus police imbecile.

"Well I can appreciate that, sorry to take up any of your time. You have a good night," the officer turned, got back into his patrol cruiser and sped off.

"*Idiot*," Roger said aloud after the officer was out of earshot. Like in any fraternal society, the higher ranked members always looked down on the lower ranked ones, despite how they treat each other publicly and when amongst common enemies.

Roger climbed back into his SUV only to find that the signal was no longer flashing. "Damn it!" He slammed his fist on the dash board in anger. *There's got to be some sort of save feature on this thing.*

He searched the device but could not find anything. *I'll have to take it back to Cosgrove and give Herschel a call to figure this out.* He slammed the gear selector down to drive and jumped on the accelerator causing the vehicle to shed some unwanted rubber. Roger sped off to Cosgrove Strategies dialing Herschel for instructions on the way.

* * *

‖ 16 ‖

Jakob yanked the double doors ajar at Padua Hall and dashed down the hall toward Professor Briarton's office. *I've got to warn him.* He recklessly careened around three corners before happening upon the door of his office. He frantically knocked, and just as quickly called out to him in case the Professor did not want to answer his door so late. "Professor Briarton, it's me, I've got something to tell you!"

"Come in," the Professor's muffled voice called out from within the office. He pushed opened the door to the rectangular room and breathing heavily said, "something's happened Professor!"

"Jakob," Professor Briarton smiled while still looking slightly concerned, "what's the matter? Here, here. . . . . have a seat. Tell me what's wrong."

"It's Megan, she reported you to the Board and is trying to have you fired."

"Well, ok, what's her reasoning exactly?" The Professor asked, keeping a sheath of reason and calm in the face of Jakob's contrary emotional ramblings.

"She said you're advocating drug use to students, but really she was just upset about a conversation that we had at Harold's Pub," he struggled to catch his breath. The Professor smiled widely at Jakob not because he thought that the situation was irrelevant but on the contrary, he knew this would fit in perfectly in the limited time-frame with which he was dealing. He readied an appropriate response.

"You know, Jakob," he said, getting up from his behind his desk in order to put a hand on the young man's shoulder. "I've found that the best way to deal with situations like these is simply to let them blow over. I'll tell you what - I was supposed to take a trip next week to Argentina to advise their government on some economic matters, but I may just move it up a day or so. You know I may just leave tonight, as a matter of fact!" He said excitedly. "You want you tag along?"

"Really? Seriously?" Jakob's face stretched wide with surprised anticipation. "But," his demeanor turned to concerned, "what about class. I can't miss class."

"Well, let's just say it's nice to have a professor on your side," he replied with eyebrows raised and finished with a wink.

"Ummm, ok, let's do it," Jakob replied while nodding his head expediently up and down. "When do we leave?"

The Professor looked down at his watch. "Well, if we hurry we can catch the red eye that leaves in about three hours. Do you think you can be ready by then?"

"Yeah, I don't see why not! I'll just rush home to my apartment and pack a bag. How about I meet you at the airport in about two hours?"

"Alright Jakob, I'll see you there," the Professor said while the younger man jumped out of his seat and began to exit the office. "And Jakob, this is going to be life-changing kind of fun. . . .you know what I mean?"

"Oh yeah, it's going to be great. See you in a few hours," Jakob said leaving what seemed like a flash of color where he had just hurriedly vacated.

Professor Briarton closed the door and twisted the lock to ensure no one would enter unexpectedly. He knew this trip was definitely going to be a life changing event, however, simply not in the Argentinean way that Jakob imagined. Although the Professor did not particularly like deceiving people, he knew that a utilitarian, greater good style philosophy, in this case at least, ultimately benefited those who were doing good things. This isn't to say that he completely agreed with this philosophy in every situation, oh no. He was acutely aware that the vast majority of crimes against the human race have been justified by saying 'I must sacrifice the few in favor of the many'. Professor Briarton knew that was ultimately the path toward destruction for all around him. A limited, moderate use of this philosophy could in fact provide needed benefits to everyone. He was certain that it would in this case as well.

He situated himself back behind his solid wood desk and took a relieved seat in his high back leather chair, knowing that Jakob's perceived 'problem' had become the Professor's good fortune. Grasping his keys, he carefully unlocked his bottom desk drawer and pulled it out. Behind some files his hand clumsily fished out a small black device which resembled a cell phone but obviously was something much more complicated. He flipped open the svelte device and began typing allowing cool, crisp blue letters to illuminate the screen. IT'S DONE. MYSELF AND VANDEN WILL BE ARRIVING IN APPROXIATELY 21 HOURS. PREPARE THE RENDEZVOUS APPROPRIATELY. He waited for about ten seconds before a receiving this reply. AFFIRMATIVE WE WILL BE READY. WELL DONE BRIARTON.

He held the device in his hand for a few moments to ensure that was the last transition and just as he was beginning to close it, the screen switched from its normal cool, blue hue to angrily flashing bright red. OUTSIDE DETECTION DEVICE DETECTED. OUTSIDE DETECTION DEVICE DETECTED. *What the hell?!?!!?*

As fast as his phalanges could move he typed frantically knowing that time was clearly not on his side. MY DEVICE FOUND A DETECTION DEVICE; HOW IS THAT POSSIBLE? This time the interval in between typing and a receiving a response was only about three seconds. WE DON'T KNOW, IT SHOULD NOT BE POSSIBLE. DISCONTINUE USE OF THE DEVICE.

SELF-DESTRUCT AND FIND A BODY OF WATER FOR DISPOSAL. WE WILL MEET YOU AT THE SCHEDULED RENDEZVOUS. COMMAND OUT.

The Professor quickly entered the code for self-destruct knowing that the internal parts of the device would be chemically liquefied within seconds so that the technology wouldn't fall into the wrong hands. He also planned to take the long way back to his house so that he could toss the device out of his car window and into a lake along the way.

Who the hell is trying to detect Quantum Bursts? They don't even exist to these people! For my Quantum Handheld to be able to recognize a detection device they must have been fairly close whoever it was. That means I don't have much time.

He grabbed a few files as well as his Quantum Handheld and stuffed them into his briefcase. Turning toward the computer he quickly printed something out and tossed it haphazardly on the desk. Whipping his head back and forth to make sure he didn't miss anything, Professor Briarton approached the door and took one last look back into his office – knowing he'd probably never see this place again.

* * *

"Professor Briarton!" Jakob called out with an excitedly raised hand from across the airport lobby. His anticipation of what was probably the most thrilling trip of his life was more than evident to anyone within eye or earshot. "Over here!" The Professor's head snapped in Jakob's direction and they met at an equidistant point from each other.

"Ahhh, you made it," Professor Briarton said with a smile and a hand on Jakob's shoulder. "Let's go and get our tickets, shall we?" He asked as the two men moved toward the snaking line.

When the Professor noticed that Jakob only had one bag, he asked, "do you have anything to check on?"

"Nope, just carry-on, I figured it would be a lot easier this way – keep it simple - you know."

"You're a smart young man, Jakob. Have I ever mentioned that to you before?"

"On occasion Professor, on occasion," Jakob replied with a nod. After getting their boarding passes the pair wondered about looking for their Terminal.

"Well, alright," the Professor said while scanning the travelers streaming all around him. They nimbly navigated through the throngs of fellow travelers eventually reaching the entrance to the Terminal. After entering the standard airport line maze, they, much like slithering snakes, began to slowly follow the people in front of them as others grouped behind them.

Jakob had not been on a flight since he was a child. In fact he had only left the country once when he was twelve to visit Niagara Falls in Canada on a family vacation. Naturally he was curious about the impending security measures to which he would be subjected. His neck craned and bobbed past the travelers in front of him in order to observe the spectacle. He noticed several people who were pulled to the side and being physically patted down by the security agents. Professor Briarton, after noticing Jakob's nervous curiosity, discretely leaned over and spoke softly to calm his fears.

"Just be cool about these guys. They just act tough to try and make people nervous. They really don't do much except prevent the same thing from happening twice."

Jakob looked at the instructions to his right and realized the Professor was right. The security measures read like a list of 'how we screwed up in the past'. He started to match each measure with the terrorist incident: 1. No explosives. Something about Pan-am flight something or another popped into his head, but he must have been too young at the time to really recall the incident. 2. No sharp objects. The box cutters said to be used on 9/11 came to mind. 3. Please remove your shoes. That was from the shoe bomber, right. 4. No liquids over three oz. - that was from the UK when people used liquid explosives (although he thought that really should have been covered under the 'no explosives rule' actually).

As the two men neared their turn to enter the security apparatus Jakob looked over all of his things and again checked his pockets out of irrational concern. The list of rules and regulations were so daunting that Jakob began to have angst as to whether he had inadvertently broken some of them. He frantically reached into his pocket, jingled around some change and felt a paper clip. *Is this a sharp object?*

"Boarding pass and identification, please."

"We already showed it to the Agent when we entered the line," Jakob replied as the Professor, not wanting to bring any attention to himself, motioned to Jakob not to say anything else.

"Here you are officer, Jakob. . . . . do you have your boarding pass?" The Professor nodded his head down and winked at his younger pupil so that the agent wouldn't see and Jakob, notoriously unorganized, shuffled through his papers to find the documents.

"Thank you. Next please," the man said coldly. The two men, suitcases precariously in tow, shuffled up to the next checkpoint. Jakob eyed some of the agents who were before him and remarked to himself that they looked a bit dodgy. He thought about how they recruit these people and noticed from their long, drawn down faces that most of them *clearly* had lived rather difficult lives. Perhaps the goal was, in fact, to fill these positions with people who were capable of reciprocating the cruelty they had experienced in their own lives back onto the passengers.

"Please remove your shoes and empty all of your belongings into the trays!" An agent, who was seated behind an x-ray screen, called out loud enough to have his voice echoed throughout the entirety of Terminal C. Jakob looked to the left and right for a bench so that he could remove his shoes without hopping up and down on one foot, unfortunately there wasn't one. He noticed a few elderly passengers who were clearly having difficulties but gathered not so much as a sympathetic look from the officials. With his shoes removed and pockets emptied into the bin in front of him, Jakob sought out the next obstacle in the virtual rat maze.

"Next," an agent standing in front of the x-ray machine called to whoever would listen. Jakob turned around to ensure that he wasn't cutting in a line and as he looked back toward the x-ray machine he heard another, "*NEXT*".

He moved forward into the machine as he gathered a chest full of air into his lungs. "*Beep, Beep, Beep,*" the machine angrily belched with a red light flashing above the apparatus.

"Please step to the side, sir," the agent commanded. Jakob did as he was told, but with anxiety building inside of him. "Have you accepted any gifts or other item from anyone?"

"No."

"Is this your carry-on?"

"Yes, that's mine."

"Would you please spread your arms and legs?"

"What for, I haven't. . . . . "

"Would you *please* spread your arms and legs, sir?" The agent called out this time with added authority. Jakob complied with the request while simultaneously coming to the conclusion that, in addition to empathy and reason, questions need not be applied to this situation. *Why don't they treat the passengers like human beings; why don't they just answer our questions? My tax money pays for this, and these are the services I receive?*

The Agent thoroughly patted Jakob down, a bit *too* thoroughly in Jakob's opinion. *Where was the line,* he thought. He felt humiliated and violated as the officer patted his crouch to ensure no weapons of mass destruction were in his underpants. *Could I complain? Is this normal? WHO would I complain to? The very agents who were conducting the search? They'd probably sit me in a room all day. Not worth it.* Fear gripped him as the agent finished the search. He didn't want to be a burden on the Professor.

"Please remove your belt."

"Excuse me?"

"*PLEASE* remove your belt," the Agent purposefully clenched, sending his jaw muscle into obvious spasms. Their eyes stayed locked in contempt while Jakob's hands slowly removed the leather strap holding his pants up.

"Place it in that the bin and step through the metal detector, please." Jakob slowly walked through, again unconsciously holding his breath in anticipation of an alarming noise. After passing through the machine without incident he began to breathe again and the agent again accosted him so that he could go no further.

"Is *this* your suitcase?" The uniformed man held up Jakob's small carry-on.

"Yeah, that's mine," he replied, following the agent off to the side away from the metal detector.

He rifled through Jakob's belongings and then the man's face contorted into a horrible expression as if he'd found a stick of dynamite. When his hand emerged victoriously from the now wrinkled clothes, a tube of toothpaste was securely in his grasp.

"Is *this* yours?" He rhetorically asked.

"Yes."

"This is a forbidden liquid and is not allowed in your carry-on," he said unemotionally.

"Actually it's a gel," Jakob said with a smile in an unsuccessful attempt to lighten the mood even though the man's rude nature did not warrant it.

"We'll have to confiscate it." The Agent threw the villainous tube of paste into a huge container which looked like a mass grave for gels, cleansers, lotions, nail filers, water bottles, and even an extra-large bottle of baby formula. Interestingly enough, for what could *all* be potentially explosive devices in the eyes of the confiscating agents, the holding container was oddly placed in close proximity to the security personnel. Even stranger is that on several occasions Jakob witnessed agents throwing the "hazardous materials" into the bin without even tagging the items. If one of them did turn out to be a bomb of some type, they wouldn't even know to whom it had belonged!! A potential terrorist could try over and over again with no recourse. Although keeping in line with the way this entire operation is run, more than likely a bomb would have to actually explode in their container before they took any steps to change the current situation. They were just reactive . . . . never proactive.

After the search of Jakob's carry-on was complete the agent haphazardly stuffed all of his belongings back into his bag and said, "Have a nice flight." Jakob did not reply, nor did he look the man in the eye, he simply gathered his things, returned cover to his shoeless feet and walked into Terminal C.

After shuffling about fifty feet in a humiliated daze, staring at the exact items for purchase which had just filled the Agent's holding container to the top, he realized he had completely forgotten about Professor Briarton. Turning his head a hundred and eighty degrees Jakob was relieved when he saw a familiar face and waited a few seconds for him to catch up.

"Sorry you had to go through that," the Professor apologized. "It's all so ridiculous isn't it? I mean if you look a bit deeper into this whole terrorism thing you'll start to ask yourself: if these people are indeed everywhere (sleeper cells and all that), if they are *really* trying to do *anything* to kill us. . . .*where* are they? I haven't seen a mall, a sporting event nor a school attacked. These would obviously be easier targets than planes, right? Where are all these supposedly 'evil' people anyway?"

"I know," Jakob replied, "when you actually examine all this security you can see they're not really doing anything anyway! There's always something else that could be attacked."

"Oh, but they are doing something Jakob. They're keeping people afraid. And it's *very* effective because scared people give away their rights in order to feel safe. The truth is that there is no possible way to 'secure' a society and have it remain 'free'. Could you image airport style security in every mall, school and church in this country? A man once said that those who are willing to sacrifice liberty for security will get neither."

"Wow, I never thought about it like that," Jakob said, his scrunched eyebrows showing concern as they continued to head toward their departing plane.

"The more pertinent question is: *why* would people want to attack us? I think we all know how Americans would feel if Saudi Arabia had military bases in *our* country and *our* politicians could only get elected with tacit approval from their leadership. And I assure you Jakob, if the 'terrorists' had technology they would never resort to these cowardly acts, they would simply bomb our cities from the sky as we do theirs," the Professor knew that he had to continue Jakob's education quickly in order to prepare him for what he was about to see.

"Yeah. . . .that's an interesting way to look at it."

"I mean seriously, I cannot believe that any intelligent individual would take all the evidence of our glaring imperial abuses, set them aside, and think that they attack us because we're 'free'. It's absurd. There are plenty of *other* free countries to attack. . . .but only one imperial power . . . oh excuse me. . . . I mean 'super' power to use the term de jour"

"Gate 37," Jakob looked down to double check his ticket, "there's our gate Professor."

Despite the deep conversation Jakob remained surprisingly upbeat about their journey. Every time the Professor told him something that should be shocking or astounding it no longer was. In fact Jakob had realized that he had previously thought about little bits and pieces of these things for some time. However, for whatever reason, he had never put them all together in a succinct picture like the Professor was able to do. For instance, Jakob was always suspect about a 'War on Terror' when he came to the simple conclusion that it could never end. What president would be daring enough to declare an enemy defeated which you could not count, wore no uniform, and could therefore still strike at any moment? Even a President that saw the folly in such a "war" could never end it because that would simply invite another attack, and consequently tarnish his career.

How did I simply push these thoughts to the back of my mind without REALLY examining them? What made me think like this? Jakob knew he would have to contemplate this in depth later so that it wouldn't happen again. He never wanted to repeat being 'asleep at the wheel'. More importantly he was well aware that the Professor knew a lot more than him, and Jakob was still eager to peal off more layers of the onion despite the occasional stinging in his eyes.

"Now boarding flight 3-4-5-8 to Buenos Aires. All passengers in section A (first class) may now begin boarding," the slender flight attendant called out from behind the podium into the microphone. Jakob looked down again at his ticket to see what section letter he had, and to his surprise they were in fact first class tickets.

"I can't believe the university splurges on us like this – not that I'm complaining," Jakob said, quick to show his appreciation.

"Well, to be honest with you, the university pays for coach and I covered the rest with my own money," the Professor admitted.

"Professor Briarton I can't accept this, I just. . ."

"Ehhh, eh, eh. Jakob this doesn't come without strings attached," the Professor continued as they moved with the first class line to board, "all I ask is that you do the same thing for someone else; whenever you find yourself in a similar role, ok?" Jakob's body was warm with endorphins from the indirect compliment.

"Without a doubt. Thanks Professor."

"Don't mention it, c'mon let's go ahead and board." They walked up together to the flight attendant who was checking tickets and went down the boarding hall toward the plane. The Professor had a horrible feeling in his stomach because he hated deceiving Jakob. The truth was the university did not pay for any part of the tickets and that they had no idea either one of them was even *going* to Argentina. The *real* truth was that Argentina was definitely *not* their final destination and that Jakob would not be fully conscious for much of the journey - for his *own* safety, of course.

* * *

‖ 17 ‖

"Alright, I've got that plugged into my computer from the Detector – now what?" Roger called out toward his speakerphone.

"Now, do you see that blue switch on the left side of the briefcase?" Herschel's voice blared through the speaker.

"No. I don't see it!" Roger called out in frustration, "I'm this close to calling our technician in. You *said* this would be *easy*!" Roger was becoming more and more impatient as he knew time was of the essence now that he had detected a Quantum Burst on campus.

"It's there, trust me. Check the right side of the briefcase, would ya?"

"Yeah, yeah. . . . . I see it. Ok, done."

"Alright now give it just a minute. Your laptop should automatically download the software from the network and then show you the *exact* GPS coordinates of the Quantum Burst you detected."

"Yeah, I see it," Roger said. "It's installing the software now."

"So you really detected a Quantum Burst?"

"That's what your machine said. . . .*if* it works."

"Oh it works, I assure you it works. Who the hell are these people, Roger?"

"I dunno," he said physically shaking his head, "but we're just about to find out. Ok, it's done. Now what?"

"It should be displaying the location on your screen and if your office has a blueprint database the exact room number of the university office should be loading now."

"It's pulling it up. *Got it* – Room 236!" Roger slapped the keyboard a few times and found the university's website. He entered the room number in their directory and within seconds a name appeared: Professor Phillip Briarton. "Professor Briarton. . . . . that name sounds familiar. . . .*holy shit*, that's Jakob's professor!"

"You know this guy?" Herschel inquired through the phone.

"I know *of* him. He's my son's professor. Jakob talks about him all the time. What the hell is going on here?"

"I don't know Roger. But if it were my son mixed up in this thing – *whatever* the hell it is – I wouldn't be talking to me right now. . . .I'd be taking action."

"Yeah. . . . . ok Herschel. I gotta go." Roger did not even let the normal good-bye pleasantries ensue before he slammed his fist on the phone to disconnect the line.

He hurriedly yanked open the bottom drawer of his desk and felt around some files toward the back. Emerging in his grasp was a semi-automatic pistol. He chambered a round, grabbed his laptop and made a dash for the door. *I don't always agree with Jakob on everything, but whoever this son of bitch is, he's about to answer some my questions.*

After recklessly driving through the city with his dashboard blue lights on, Roger finally arrived at the university's Padua Hall around two o'clock a.m. and pulled his SUV onto the curb directly beside the door.

He bolted out of the vehicle and withdrew his firearm, kicking in the front door to gain entry. Walking methodically down the hall he checked each corner, and quickly came upon his destination – Room 236.

After checking his right and left flank, he stared at the solid door in front of him. Letting a breath slowly in and out, he grasped his weapon with both hands, and in one smooth motion crashed his foot through Professor Briarton's door. His gun scanned the small office for something to shoot but the tiny room was empty.

Roger holstered the weapon and began to have a look around. Atop the Professor's desk he spotted a printed airline itinerary for Professor Briarton and his only son – Jakob.

"Son of a bitch!" Roger said aloud. He scanned the document for a destination, quick to pull out his cell phone at the same time. It showed they were heading to Kraków, Poland. He immediately called his office and a female voice answered, "Cosgrove Strategies Inc, this is Kristen how may I direct your call?"

"Kristen, this is Agent Vanden. I need a Code 7 Foreign Extradition for two American citizens immediately," Roger barked into the phone.

"Yes sir Agent Vanden. What is the destination?"

"Kraków, Poland. It's flight 3-5-2-5 and it should be landing within a few hours."

"And what are their names, please?"

"Phillip Briarton and," Roger hesitated to say his son's name knowing the scrutiny it would soon bring him, "Jakob Vanden."

"Excuse me sir. . . . . did you say Jakob Vanden?"

"Yes, you heard me. I don't have time for this; we have to assemble a Polish team A-SAP! Just put in the *fucking order!*"

"Yes sir. I'm calling now."

* * *

Roger had been staring at the six different monitors for well over an hour now, his eyes darting frantically from one to the other in an attempt to catch a glimpse of his son. He was seated inside Unit 3 of the technological superior Cosgrove's Operations Center.

These closet sized units allow Cosgrove's Agents to monitor and/or direct operatives in the field.

Presently, Roger was linked up via an audio and video feed directly to a group of contracted Polish operatives which Cosgrove keeps on retainer for situations exactly like this one.

"The flight landed thirty minutes ago but there's still no sign of either one of them. Over," Agent Bravo said with a slight Eastern European accent.

This doesn't make any sense, he thought, *they should be there.* Roger continued to watch the screen in front of him as passenger after passenger came through Concourse B, however not Jakob nor Professor Briarton was among the crowd.

Roger's phone buzzed with activity.

"Agent Vanden," he called out into his phone, never taking his eyes off the monitors in front of him.

"Sir," Kristen said to Roger, "I believe I've found something that you may want to see."

"Yeah, what's that?" He replied uninterestedly.

"Well I just finished the standard tracking checks on everyone involved in your active case and I found something odd with Professor Phillip Briarton. It appears that he was supposed to fly on ten *different* flights today."

"*Really?!?* So where is his destination after he lands in Kraków?" He continued to speak with eyes glued to the screen.

"Umm, no sir I don't think you're following me. He booked flights for Frankfurt, Shanghai, New Delhi, Johannesburg, Moscow, Mexico City, Buenos Aires, Sydney, Barcelona *and* Kraków all leaving at about the *same* time."

"WHAT?"

"Yes sir, that does appear to be the case. All the flights were booked at the last minute and all of them were first class – that must have cost him *a pretty penny."* Roger did not reply, but rather, just sat in silence. *He could be anywhere. I've wasted all my time on assembling this team in Poland for nothing. It's over. They're gone. I fell into his trap.*

"Agent Vanden. Are you still there?" Kristen asked.

"Yeah, I'm still here. Kristen. I need you to find out what flight that *son of bitch* was actually on. Can you do that for me?"

"Yes sir. I'll get right on that. It's going to take a little while of course, but you knew that already."

"Yeah. I know." He punched the red button to terminate the conversation and turned his attention back to the Polish Agents.

"Agents Alpha, Bravo, and Charlie. . . . . we've received some new information about the flight – the targets are not on the flight. I repeat the targets are *not* on the flight. Stand down."

"10-4," Agent Bravo replied. If Roger was absolutely sure about one thing it was that Professor Briarton left that paper on his desk so that he would find it and that meant two things. One: The Professor and his son sure as hell *were not* in Kraków. And two: Somehow he knew that Roger was coming.

He got up from the command center and made his way out to his SUV in the parking lot. The sun was beginning to come up and Roger, having wasted his entire night, was about to go home and catch some shut eye before continuing to track down Professor Briarton. However, first, he needed to see something for himself – his son's apartment.

* * *

On his way to inspect the apartment for clues, Roger's mind buzzed with speculative activity. *Was he kidnapped? Did he run away? Is he part of a sleeper cell? Has he been sent to spy on ME?* A plethora of wild thoughts flooded his mind. He shook his head to physically regain control and went through the facts trying desperately to stay focused.

A few things were certain in Roger's mind. To start with Professor Briarton must be part of some sort of highly sophisticated international organization. This is so because: 1) he was clearly the individual who was in possession of a Quantum Communicator which had supposedly not even been invented yet, 2) his sudden abscondence is suspicious to say the least.

This secret international organization is probably larger than anything ever discovered which is evident by their sophisticated technology. Further substantiating this hypothesis, Herschel's satellite discovered Quantum Bursts in every major city in the world. This is unprecedented.

Whatever the goals of this organization may be, they were intelligent enough to put their agents in place as professors. In this role an agent like Professor Briarton has full discretion to publicly push his agenda. He simply cloaks it under the banner of academic freedom and in such a role his complicated jargon substantially decreases the power of the sound bite happy media to attack him. Whether or not Professor Briarton was already pushing his agenda publicly didn't matter to Roger. The proof that this organization has some sort of subversive agenda was evidenced by the sudden change in his son's behavior.

Jakob questions everything, he thought. *That one conversation we had months ago about history. . . . . all he kept saying was USS Maine, Lusitania, Pearl Harbor, Gulf of Tonkin and on and on about the engineers and architects who want the truth. His mind has been totally contorted about this country. He doesn't listen to doctors or psychiatrists, he thinks the news is a farce, he thinks the markets are rigged, and he thinks voting is a waste of time. Oh my God! His entire world view has completely changed under my nose and I didn't even realize it. How did Jakob get involved in this?* He pondered.

Arriving at Hidden Hills apartment complex in the morning wasn't exactly the smartest move on Roger's part. Students were naturally mulling about half asleep like zombies but moving nonetheless. After finding a parking space Roger briskly made his way up the steps to the front door, found that his key slid comfortably into the lock, and entered.

His son's student apartment looked fairly normal. Roger slipped on some plastic gloves before continuing. After excluding the normal mess one would expect to find in a college students place, he did not detect any signs of foul play. The kitchen was actually *cleaner* than normal with all the dishes having already been washed. He knew that was fairly unusual for someone who was a bit messy like Jakob.

The trash had just been taken out and there wasn't even a replacement bag in the receptacle! This is exactly the sort of behavior that occurs before someone is going to take a *voluntary* trip.

He made his way into the bedroom and found that Jakob's carry-on suitcase, a gift from his father for Christmas, was missing. Upon rummaging through his bathroom, he noticed that a number of his son's toiletries were also absent.

Everything was beginning to point toward Jakob not having been abducted but rather leaving on his own accord. *If he had been under duress and forced to leave then the trash wouldn't have been taken out nor the dishes washed!* He thought.

Roger was keenly aware that his son's behavior had changed in the last few months. Jakob was quick to assert his opinion, even if it created conflict, and he seemed frustrated with everything and everybody around him. It *was* possible that he had been brainwashed somehow by Professor Briarton and went along with him under 'mental duress'. Whatever the case may be, Roger wasn't going to let his eldest son get into any trouble. That much was for certain.

He started going around the apartment and very deliberately and quietly making it appear that there had been some sort of struggle. Roger gently lowered the dresser to the ground, threw some clothes about, and emptied the contents of a few drawers. This way Jakob would have a fighting chance no matter what he may have inappropriately decided during a moment of senselessness. At a minimum the Stockholm Syndrome defense could get his son off the hook, but the truth was that it's much more believable if you can prove there was at least *some* sort of resistance.

When he was finished doctoring the scene, Roger turned, looked at the mess, and muttered, "What have you done Jakob. . . . . what have you done?"

He shook his head in confusion, exited the ransacked apartment, and then drove home to get some much needed sleep.

* * *

Part II – Contemplation

‖ 18 ‖

Jakob's eyelids parted open to reveal a rather fuzzy image of Professor Briarton looking down at him. Slowly his mentor's smile came into focus.

"Professor?" Jakob managed to sputter in a raspy voice.

"Shh, shh, just lie still for now, everything's ok," the Professor replied reassuringly.

"What happened?" Jakob eyebrows scrunched together in confusion, "am I in the hospital?"

"Well, a hospital. . . . . of sorts, but don't worry I'll explain all of that in a minute. What's the last thing you remember? We'll start there."

"Umm, I. . . . . ," he looked around like a prize fighter who had just taken one on the chin, "I. . . . . was on the plane and. . . . . I. . . . . I. . . . . had that drink you bought for me to help me relax and fall asleep and. . . . . well. . . . . I think that's about it. . . . . yeah I can't remember anything after that." The Professor looked over at man to his left, who Jakob falsely assumed was a doctor, and they both confirmingly nodded their heads at one other.

"Jakob, I know you've advanced quickly in the last couple of weeks. There's no doubt that at times it's been kind of hard to digest all the information that you've received. I'm guessing it's totally changed your view of not only your country, but more importantly, the entire world, hasn't it?"

"Yeah, I guess you could say that. It's been tough, but I'd rather know the truth than stay ignorant. Professor, I've opened up so many of Pandora's boxes that there's no point stopping now. What's this all about anyway?" While attempting to sit up he quickly became aware of how weak his body was and consequently laid back down on the blue cloth bed. At that point he realized after looking around that this was definitely not any kind of hospital he'd ever seen before. Admittedly, Jakob had never been to a South American facility, but he definitely hadn't imagined it being so svelte and new in appearance.

"Jakob, what if I told you that everything you knew about history was a bit like the Noah flood story in the Bible."

"What do you mean? I'm not quite following you Professor."

"What I mean is, that it is *based* on fact, but the details are kind of either exaggerated or made up to fill in the gaps."

"Umm. . . . . Ok, I'm listening," he said with slightly more vitality in his voice.

"Jakob, apply everything you discovered recently about what is *wrong* with the world. Think about the lies and utter deception which has come from the top and is accepted as *unquestionable truth.* I mean from the pharmaceutical world, to the poisons in our food and water we call nutrition, to the dumbing us down in schools, to a control economy, to the war on drugs and terror – I could obviously go on and on. Now mind you that all of this occurs in the information age, in an age where the truth is readily available but nevertheless comprehensively ignored. An Age of Apathy to say the least, one in which we have the *capability* to discover the truth but choose to ignore it.

"Now go way back to a time when the *vast majority* of people couldn't even read and write. Now tell me what sort of deception could have been perpetrated in a time like that by the rich and the powerful."

"I would say," Jakob was still struggling to clear the cob webs out of his lethargic brain, and he paused for a moment again gazing at his surroundings. He noticed that light was emanating from long, strip like panels which were recessed into the walls. It had a very warm glow to it, much like sunlight. He tried to regain his focus, "what I meant to say is that, well, look at what the Catholic Church told people. They out right lied all over Europe for a millennium about everything from indulgences to who knows what else."

"Exactly, now apply that same framework of what happened in the Catholic Church to not just Catholicism but to all man made religions throughout the world *and* the ages."

"Yeah, I can see that."

"Now apply the framework to all fields of study and subjects – politics, economics, medicine, sociology, and naturally, history to name a few. And then apply it throughout the eons of time. . . .*and* multiply it by a thousand compared to today. Because back then you couldn't surf the net and find out about something you did not know. You and your ancestors could have been lied to for so long that all it would have taken is for one person to believe the lies, and they would teach it as fact to their child, and then they would teach it as fact to their child, and so on and so forth. Are you following me?"

"Yeah, I gotcha. I've definitely seen some of that through a few of the conflicts with my Father over discovering these things – he just didn't *want* to. . . . . no he just *couldn't* hear it," Jakob said matter-of-factly eliciting an instant, simultaneous head turn by the other two men in the room.

"Right, like the conversation with your Father," he replied as the two older men finally broke their gaze. "What I'm saying is, the people who have been brave enough throughout the ages to *stand up* to these evil people at the top who despise empathy, reason, and love, have been persecuted since the beginning of time. If anyone of these brave people challenged the status quo they typically ended up dead: Gandhi, Jesus, and Martin Luther King Jr., to name a few. Sometimes they'd even have official trials like with Socrates and Galileo, but the results were oddly one sided. Hell, people today are so mentally shackled that even when they hear of Socrates' trial, philosophy and ultimately his death. . . . .they *still* don't get it."

"I'm following you Professor, but where are you going with this?" Jakob was now beginning to sit up because the conversation had hit such a crescendo that it was too hard to simply stay lying down.

"What I'm saying is. . . .imagine if there had been a place throughout the ages to escape from such mental oppression. A place where *only* the enlightened and unshackled could enter, a place where the virtues I mentioned earlier – empathy, reason and love – could flourish *completely* unhindered without fear of recourse. That place would be astounding, wouldn't it?"

"Of course it would, but that's just. . ." Jakob's eyebrows furrowed tightly above his head as he began to notice, absent his blurry vision, the clothes the other man was wearing, and the materials all around the room – all of them look different, but not 'South America different'. He turned his head several times back and forth, "that's just. . . . . ri . . . .dic. . . .u. . . . .lous."

"Jakob, do you feel strong enough to stand up just yet?" The Professor inquired.

"After what I think you're telling me, you couldn't keep me down even with leather straps! Give me a hand would ya?" Jakob reached his arm out and Professor Briarton quickly reciprocated. He sat up first for a minute to let the blood fill his head and then proceeded to get on his feet, albeit still a bit wobbly, but on his feet nonetheless. "As strange as all this is, at least you don't have me in one of those horrible hospital gowns. . . . . . who came up with those anyway?" All the men laughed together not so much at the joke but rather out of relief that Jakob was indeed accepting his strange, yet unknown surroundings.

"C'mon Jakob, there's something I want you to see," the Professor extended an arm to him in an effort to act as a safety net in case he was still not sure footed enough.

"I'm fine Professor, feeling much better actually." He reached down and touched his toes after yawning and stretching his limber arms above his head.

The three men walked out of the medical facility and down a tall corridor with smooth, gray rock walls. They turned left down a hallway marked with a sign - Observation Balcony. Below the English lettering was some sort of scribbling which looked similar to ancient cuneiform. With the Professor in the lead they climbed about thirty meters of steep, stone steps before reaching the top.

Jakob's eyelids sprang open, and despite the increased amount of light, his pupils widened the closer he walked to the edge of the huge balcony. The platform was easily forty stories up. Even though he was in some sort of gargantuan sized dome, sunlight bathed and illuminated everything in sight. He squinted to see the other side of the structure and noticed living quarters at least a hundred stories tall. There must have been millions upon millions of apartments which were carved out of a sheer wall of rock. *This is no dome,* he thought, *it's the interior of the largest mountain on Earth!*

His soul became overwhelmed by the enormity of this place, contrary to being just a gray, sordid rock face as one would have expected, there was green lushness as far as any eye could see. From atop his magnificent perch he peered at fountains, parks, and people spread about like ants.

He was very curious how, being that they were clearly *inside* a mountain, this place was illuminated *so very* brightly, Jakob tilted his head toward the top of the 'dome' and saw chutes of light coming through cylinder shaped cut-outs in the rock. He followed the path of the light until his eyes caught sight of something he had never seen before. The tunnels of illumination were directed toward a system of mirrors until they final struck some sort of light diffusion apparatus. Unlike what he would have imagined, it was not uncomfortably bright, quite the opposite in fact. Upon striking the diffusers it was *refracted* and showered a warm, subtle glow on everything around him.

"So, what do you think?" The Professor said, speaking quietly yet confidently. Expecting his own mouth to move in response to the question, yet discovering that it did not, Jakob had truly learned the feeling of speechlessness. "I know. . . . . it's extraordinary isn't it. This place. Here. Now. In a world with almost universal despair and hopelessness there is this island – this island, this sanctuary from everything that is unempathtic, unreasoned and hateful. And you are here now too." The Professor had been standing directly behind Jakob but now moved toward his left flank and put a hand reassuringly on the young man's shoulder.

"How many people are here? How *long* have they. . . . . where did they. . . . . " question after question arose expediently from Jakob's dazed mind.

"I know you have many questions and they will *all* be answered in due time. For now though, we have much to see and experience. I believe that you'll be at home here. Come, let's get you settled in."

"Wait, wait," Jakob shook his head in sudden realization, "so on the plane. . . . . you drugged me?"

"We didn't want too Jakob. I sincerely apologize for having to do that, but understand this. . . . . it was for your own protection."

"What do you mean *my* own protection?"

"Oh yes. . . . . for your protection. Remember, information is a precious commodity and with these commodities come responsibilities. Knowing the location of this place. . . . . well, that's a responsibility that you do not need to be saddled with anytime soon."

"I understand why you wanted to conceal this," he looked up and down again at the vastness before him, "but, Professor, you lied to me." His face crinkled with concern at the breach of trust.

"I'm sorry Jakob. I am. Many of us here have sincere difficultly with deceiving people in order to achieve a greater good. This is something that our society, which is guided by strict ethical and moral rules, has had much difficulty reconciling. If we were to simply stay hidden from the world and not reach out as we now do, then we could easily maintain our moral code. However, if we did that, slither away in isolation to protect our ethics, the light of the world would not shine, but on the contrary, it would suddenly be hidden under a rock. The real struggle is maintaining our morality in the face of compromises such as you being deceived. Am I the same person after I've committed this transgression against you? All I can say is, Jakob," he looked his pupil squarely in the eyes, "I'm sorry."

"So how did you do it? How did you get me from Argentina to here?"

"Well," Professor Briarton heaved a deep breathe and reluctantly told the story, "after we landed your sedative wore off enough for you to walk out of the plane on your own accord. You appeared slightly confused but most of your grogginess looked like drunkenness so no one was suspicious.

"From there we boarded another privately charted plane to fly to the Falkland Islands which is a few hundred miles off the Argentinean coast. Again, you simply appeared drunk from the sedative, but you were able to also disembark from the plane and board the next."

"Why don't I remember any of this?" Jakob asked.

"The sedative I gave you is specifically designed to erase memory."

"So what happened next?" He prodded the Professor to continue.

"Jakob, I'm not going to tell you exactly how we came to be in this place," he waved his arms around and tilted his head down, "because that would defeat the purpose of concealing the journey from you in the first place, but I will continue with more generalities instead of specifics.

"So in the Falklands, we boarded a seaplane, which can of course land on water. From there we flew further until we hit a land mass with a hidden entrance way. By this point you were completely passed out but it really didn't matter in the end because they were expecting us. There were plenty of people to assist me with your dead weight when we arrived," the Professor let a smile slip to try and soften the mood due to his poor choice of words. "And from there we traveled underground until we arrived here."

Jakob finally managed the will power to turn his head from the awesome scene below and simply said,

"I'm still apprehensive about this whole thing, Professor, but I'm going to go with it for now, ok."

"I appreciate your understanding on this matter Jakob. I really do. Just try to keep in mind that I'm the same Professor Briarton that I was before this incident occurred, ok? How about I show you around your room and all that? We've still got to get you settled in." And with that he followed the Professor off the balcony and back down the corridor from which they came.

* * *

‖ 19 ‖

After Professor Briarton showed Jakob where he would be staying, the pair walked side by side down a warmly lit corridor near his apartment. Jakob looked to the right, and while moving, noticed that the light strip coming from the wall seemed to be the same type of glow that was in the main 'dome'. "Where is this light coming from?" he asked the Professor.

"I knew you'd have a lot of questions Jakob, I just did think you'd start with that one," the Professor looked over at him with a smile. "As you've already discovered we're inside a hollowed out mountain, a mountain of enormous proportions. It is bigger than Mt. Everest and Mt. Blanc combined. And like those mountains it is also part of a range that spans hundreds of miles and all of which is inhabited by us.

"The lights are a product of a highly sophisticated series of mirrors which utilize the available light to their maximum efficiency. When there is no natural illumination we also have artificial means to ensure our bodies collect the proper amount of ultraviolet radiation"

"Are we still of Earth Professor?" Jakob immediately asked. This question stopped the Professor in his tracks and the two men faced each other.

"What do *you* think, Jakob?"

"Well I'm asking because if this mountain is so big and scientists have never heard of it before, then we must not be on Earth, right?"

"Your first mistake is believing that scientists know everything. Be careful not to limit your perception of the world around you. These so called 'scientists' used to say the world was flat, they used to say man could not fly, they used to call fusion fueled, hot stars heaven, and they're easily bought by politicians and other influential people who systematically ignore reason and logic. Jakob, I realize that you've had a lot to handle in the last few months, but would you do me a favor?" The Professor placed both of his hands on Jakob's upper arms to soften the implications of what he was about to say.

"Yeah Professor. What is it?" he said with air of seriousness in his voice.

"Your mind has been conditioned to react to that place – way back there," he pointed in a random direction, "but now you're here in a new place filled with unknown possibilities that neither you, *nor I*, can fully perceive. What I need you to do is to filter out all of the older paradigms by which you used to live – science, political systems, economics, and so on – and put them to the back of your mind. Because Jakob, the vast, *vast* majority of those idea are built on a faulty foundation of lies and deceit. You can start by preemptively examining what you say *before* you say it. Does that sound about right?

"Yeah, I see what you're saying professor. I need to try and 're-wire' my brain, basically. That's what you mean, right?"

"Jakob, that's exactly what I mean," the Professor grinned as he put a hand on his pupil's shoulder. "To answer your question about where we are, well. . . . this place here is called. . . . Arkonos, but I just call it 'home' for short," the Professor said with a particularly warm smile.

"Alright then. . . I'm in Arkonos," Jakob replied, halfway in a daze of excitement.

"Good. Let's get going, there's a man I want you to meet."

"What's his name?"

"His name is Kralsich, and I know he's going to want to meet you as well."

The pair kept walking down the hallway until they came upon what appeared to be an elevator. The Professor pushed a button, as one would have anywhere in New York City, and the door gingerly slid open. They entered the circular lift and the entire apparatus bounced a little up and down as though it were suspended on air. The Professor could see the anxiety on Jakob's face in reaction to what seemed to be an unstable piece of equipment.

"Jakob," the Professor spoke to his pupil, "do you know how many human beings die in car accidents every year?"

"Umm, can't say that I do actually, but I'm sure it's gotta be a lot."

"I'm sure you've known several people who've been killed personally. It's rather unbelievable but almost 1.2 million people die world wide in vehicle accidents. 1.2 million *per* year. And even still, everyday people get into their cars and drive along like nothing happened, even though yesterday 3287 people lost their lives in those repugnant machines. Jakob?"[10]

"Yeah."

"No one has ever died in this machine. *Ever*. And yet despite what I've just said your fear level will be far higher riding in this elevator than in the passenger seat of a car with a buddy driving who's probably had a few drinks. Why is that you think?"

"I don't know really," he physically shook his head.

"It's because despite our very complex cerebral cortex, and despite our unique consciousness, do you know who is often times at the wheel of this machine?"

---

[10] Peden M, et al (editors), *World Report on Road Traffic Injury Prevention*, (World Health Organization, 2004).

The Professor's arms motioned toward himself. "A scared little monkey who fears the unknown. Because chances are, our ancestors ran when they heard a dark bush rustle and imagined a tiger inside. It's this same type of fear that's manipulated by politicians and titans of industry for their own benefit. Jakob, we must do all that we can to stymie these animal impulses. . . . . because it weakens us and clouds our thinking."

Jakob nodded at the Professor in a motion of understanding. "You may want to hold onto that rail over there for your first try at this," the Professor said as he reached over to a panel and pressed a button. With a concentrated whooshing of air they descended forty stories within seconds, finally touching the ground softly as a feather would have. Jakob's eyes widened during the rush downward but quickly returned to normal at the end of their descent.

"Thanks for the warning Professor. I'm pretty sure that helped a lot."

"Anytime Jakob, anytime."

They stepped out of the elevator and began to stroll on the ground floor of the interior of the mountain. The sights streaming into Jakob's eyes were not at all what he imagined for such an 'advanced' society or at least his vision thereof. There were green gardens which dotted the mountain floor as far as the eye could see. At various points scattered about the growing vegetables were massive careening oaks, their arms horizontally stretching, stoically frozen in time.

Flocks of the most colorful birds thrust themselves from one tree to the next indiscriminately. Squirrels and chipmunks played among them as well, completely unwary of predators despite the occasion cat lurking about.

Hundreds if not thousands of people were laboring in the gardens, moving dark, rich soil about with their hands! Jakob spied every vegetable imaginable there: beans, cabbage, eggplant, tomatoes, cucumbers, peppers, potatoes, lettuces, watermelons, pumpkins, cantaloupes, zucchini, carrots, turnips and on and so forth. And they did not just come in one color or variety – far from it. The tomatoes, peppers, cucumbers, squashes etc., appeared in every color of the visible spectrum! Jakob had never witnessed so many fruits and vegetable of such great variety in all his existence. Sure, he'd seen hundreds of acres of *one* crop before but never such a daunting selection all in one place.

Walking abreast of one another, the two men continued to stroll through the lush vegetation. The Professor was pleased to see the wonder and joy on Jakob's face and was well aware of what Jakob probably envisioned when he first heard he was in an 'advanced' society. He thought that Jakob had imagined laboratory produced nutritional sources which would have broken men from the bondage of the natural Earth. And like others when they envision the future, he probably thought that people would simply pop a single pill and have all of the nutritional requirements for the week! Nothing could have been so distorted and absolutely false. Even if that were scientifically possible, which due to a number of reasons it is most likely *not*, the social consequences would be catastrophic on an unimaginable scale.

As they walked, the Professor reflected on man, the earth and the scene around them. He gestured with his hands as he spoke, "removing man from Earth, from feeling the soil in his hands and the cracking of leaves underfoot is the single most destructive force of Earth. When removed man begins to forget how inexorably linked he is to the very balanced Earth. Human beings love to believe that they are an organism on their own. This is preposterous. The human body consists of about ten trillion cells of our own material and that's when you consider such disparate system like the endocrine, nervous, immune systems (and so forth) as one unit! The body has ten times the number of bacterial cells in our intestines. Ten times the number![11] They are not parasitic but rather symbiotic. This complex system, which modern medicine typically ignores as evidenced by the over issuance of penicillin (acting like chemotherapy for the digestive system), is vitally important for not only simple digestion, but also for vitamin absorption. There is no doubt that human beings get far more than that from these bacteria, which are most likely excreting various chemicals influencing not only out bodies, but probably our minds as well.

"The truth is doctors' understanding of the functioning of the body is like a mechanic who tries to fix a car but only fiddles with the gas pedal, steering wheel, and brake. The mechanic can adjust those instruments with astounding accuracy, but he meanwhile laments when having to attempt to understand the inner workings of the engine.

"So, yes, the highest form of mankind's existence is not to live *without* nature, quite the contrary in fact. Maintaining a perfect balance of body and Earth is what allows the body as well as the mind to reach its highest potential."

Jakob was indeed beginning to see that too as he wandered throughout the gardens. "This is incredible Professor. It's hard to believe a place like this is even real," he said with eyes wide and filled with childlike excitement.

"I know Jakob. It's very peaceful here isn't it. Do you feel it? The serenity I mean?"

"Yes," the hairs all over Jakob's body began to stand up, "yes, I do."

---

[11] Guarner F, Malagelada JR (February 2003). "Gut flora in health and disease". Lancet 361 (9356): 512–9.

"You've been in nature, I know you told me you like to fish, right? You've been in that perfect place surrounded by Earth's beauty. What is that feeling, Jakob? Why does it happen?"[12]

"I don't know really."

"It happens because what we've been told about nature is untrue. What we've been told about our connection to nature, really mankind's attempt to *disconnect* us from the Earth is wrought with problems. The reality is that our relationship with this planet is far more complex than these very primitive devices can tell us," the Professor motioned toward his own eyes. "Our advanced society has realized this and prospered because of it."

"You're right, I need to take what I used to believe and reexamine *all* of it."

"Remember not to be angry with those who have *unknowingly* lied to you. . . . . most of them are simply doing what they believe to be right."

While looking up at a tree Jakob noticed that his calculation to the top of the inside of the mountain had clearly been off a bit. The ceiling of this place was *definitely* higher than a hundred stories. A towering two hundred perhaps even three hundred stories was more likely the truth.

"How tall *is* this place Professor?"

"I'd thought you'd never ask. You've been staring up at it for a while. Honestly, I've been waiting for you to trip over something! You wouldn't be the first for the record," he said with a slanted smile. "Seriously though, from the bottom to the utmost peak of the dome is about fifteen thousand meters or about three hundred and fifty stories."

---

[12] Thoreau, Henry David., *The Natural History Essays*, (Salt Lake City: Gibbs Smith Publisher, 1980).

"It's incredible. It's truly incredible. How has no one found out about this place?"

"That's complicated Jakob, but we'll definitely get to all of that in due time. For the moment though, we still have much to see and do, but I assure you all of your questions will eventually be answered, ok?"

"That's fine, Professor. For the time being I'm just along for the ride."

"C'mon let's keep making our way; I think Kralsich said he'd be over in that direction." His finger pointed forward as the men continued their journey.

* * *

‖ 20 ‖

"We're all well aware of the truth *here*, in this *place*," Kralsich spoke deep down from the bottom of his diaphragm so that the gathering crowd in the garden could hear. All around him people were putting down their tools and shaking the dirt from their blackened hands coming ever closer to him. He spoke:

"The truth - that the Old World has honed and perfected their nefarious tools of bondage beyond what the Elders had even imagined. Shall we reexamine these, the sharpest weapons in the Old World's arsenal, so that our minds will be become as razors in face of their bluntness? *YES, yes,* we shall," Kralsich called out to the ever growing crowd. He stood atop a three foot tall bed of garlic chives, which made his six foot seven frame tower above the crowd despite his lanky appearance.

"Before the 3rd Exodus of our people began, brought on by the insidious concentration of power in the 1400's and its suppression of reason, liberty and science, the powers attempted to intimidate us with eternal *damnation*. That attempt proved to be fruitless because we knew they had no possession of such power! They then decided they would use earthly means to punish us . . .this attempt was far more brutal to our nervous systems, what with the floggings, torture and public humiliations. After this proved ineffective, Inquisitions began to spread about the land where they tried us in preposterously false courts if we did not deny such despicable things like all manners of science and reason – yes the Earth is round, the Earth. . . . . is round. If we did not recant they simply *burned* us until our *souls* fled from the ensuing terror. Effectively silencing us. . . .or so they *thought*." As Kralsich spoke to the crowd his hands were careening and turning so that all could feel the effects of his body as well as his words.

"The truth is they gave us credence through martyrdom – a stirring inside all of mankind which they had not anticipated. This led to small spurts of progress in the Old World in relation to the freeing of one's mind. Unfortunately, the old mind-encapsulating prisons of old – institutionalized churches, schools, monarchial governments – were soon replaced with *new* churches, *industrial* training schools, and supposedly *democratic* governments. Mankind became somewhat contented, *falsely* believing that they had ushered in change, when in reality their prison had become *taller* and far fiercer than in the past. Those in positions of now supposedly *legitimate* power, proved to be far crueler than their predecessors. For they began to use the sheep to act as sheppards themselves – the ultimate form of control had been instituted.

"Step out of line Mr. Scientist. . . . . I don't need to burn you at the stake. . . . . I can simply ensure that the 'top' scientists are closed minded, memorizing buffoons who are incapable of breaking out of the current paradigm of thought. *They* will be the ones to continue the status quo. *They* will ensure that all new discoveries and inventions are twisted and contorted so that *they* propel the future of weaponry and luxury, rather than being used as tools to open the minds of all those around us to new possibilities. But most *importantly,*" Kralsich's face became contorted with despicable disgust, "*THEY, the scientists themselves, will be the ones who cast the reasoned and logical ASIDE!*" The crowd stirred and whispered among themselves as their energy began to build.

"And today. . . . . hmmm," his voice began to dim down, "what do we have today? More of the same? No, noooo. Not more of the same. It has become exponentially *worse.* The people of today are not only in self-regulating shackles for fear of ostracization, they are now also in a *chemical* prison! Huge industries with massive amounts of toxic waste – unable to know what to do with these poisons – dump them into the water supplies of the Old World and then call them *helpful* and *nutritious!* Even though the people who work in places, from which these chemicals came, are dying as flies would when swimming in hydrochloric acid!!! Pharmaceutical companies through their middle managers called doctors have indulged, very openly I remind you, into the largest pharmacological experiment in mankind's history. Children are bullied into taking these drugs by their own school teachers. Adults voluntarily consume myriad chemicals for an innumerable amount of 'diseases' all the while they try to ignore not only the cause of their calamities but, in addition, the actual effects of the 'medicine'. When sickened by an imbalance brought on by the medication itself, the doctor reluctantly admits there are side effects. These are horrible *lies*. A *real* doctor doesn't simply get to choose which effects he favors and which ones he doesn't!!!! There is no such thing as side effects. . . . . only effects.

"The Old Worlders recognize that these chemicals don't produce the desired effects. So they go back to their doctor and are lulled into believing that the same doctors who made them imbalanced and overflowing with 'side effects', the *very* same doctors, are now telling the truth when the say that the *new* medicine will be much better than the *old* one. This could be the perfect one, they say. . . . . over and over again. Each time the patient is made sicker and the doctor justifies the dispensing of poison by calling his craft 'practicing medicine'. All the while these medicine men ignore the first thing in their own medical books," Kralsich's arm thrust forcefully into the air, "homeostasis. . . . . balance. All living things try to maintain balance! It's in their very own teachings! This is why the introduction of new chemicals in the body, such as steroids, (something even *they* believe) always interferes with the body's natural processes thus flipping the balance upside down. So they learn these things and just as quickly forget them. *And yet,* the supposed experts agree – everything is fine. Everything is just fine.

"As if doctors making patients sicker weren't enough - look at what they call *food!!!* They have a wonderful word for poisoning themselves; they call them preservatives. The vast majority of these chemicals are simply byproducts of gasoline production! They put them in their *foods.* They concoct new, ever more reprehensible artificial sweeteners in order to replace the use of highly refined sugar (an unnatural, addictive poison itself). So you see . . . . . a nastier more poisonous venom replaces the previous one. The Old World, now supposedly at the self-described height of their civilization, is more mentally and physically sick than they've *ever* been.

"The governments of the world, clearly in league with this dastardly situation, create food and drug monitoring institutions to ensure that *all* of the horrible additives will be considered safe. This guarantees the unresearched, rote consumption of the poisons because government 'experts' have said they're healthy!" Kralsich paused for a few moments, took a deep breath while the crowd swelled to the point of people climbing trees so that they could merely glimpse this ballooning spectacle.

"The damage to the physical body is what the Old Worlders would call a 'side effect'. The true goal of this despicable, very calculated poisoning is the prize of all men ravenous for more power – the mind. As it was in the 3rd Exodus and as it is today, these disreputable people wish to enslave all of mankind in the shackles of mental bondage. They've realized that rather than letting man ask the question and then persecuting him. . . . . why not clog his mind so that the question is *never even asked.* Over not just the centuries, but rather the millennia they have continued to hone their diabolical skills to the point where we are today. These new weapons are more lethal than the ones of old because they cause the body to become imbalanced which ultimately suppresses higher mental functions. No need for chains and whips and shackles of *old*!!!! They have aspartame, BHT and pharmaceuticals!!!! No need for inquisition and fire and death!!!! They have the Health Departments, monosodium glutamate, and yellow #6!!!! Kralsich fell silent for fifteen seconds after his crescendoing remarks had been concluded. Then, suddenly, he hoisted his arms above his head; palms open toward the crowd and began to speak again with eyes *wide* open.

"So when all of *you* begin to wonder why *they*, trapped in a cave of their own ridiculousness, cannot seem to crawl *out*. . . . . wonder no more. . . . . wonder *no* more. They are but prisoners in a cell and will fight those to the death who wish to liberate them. But they, like all beings of this planet, still long to be freed, and in the coming months. . . . we shall most definitely *not* forget *that*."

The crowd, now having swelled to hundreds of people, began murmuring in approval of Kralsich who nodded his head quickly down and up again to show his appreciation. He stepped down from his raised garlic chive stand; while most of the crowd began to disperse, some remained to show their satisfaction with the speech.

At that moment Jakob and Professor Briarton began walking up to the gathering, unaware of what had just transpired. "What is all this?" Jakob inquired.

"I'm not sure to honest with you," the Professor replied. And he wasn't just saying that to shield Jakob's ears from something he wasn't ready to hear. Spontaneous public speeches were unheard of in

Arkonos due to several reasons. The human animal was very susceptible to its inherent tribal tendencies and this had proven to be rather dangerous throughout history. Even in the Old World scientists are aware of the dopamine release that occurs when people gather into a group. Just as the dopamine release from sex encourages that activity, this good feeling was meant to encourage early humans to be more tribal – an obvious advantage in their environment. This phenomenon, when perpetrated on a grander scale, becomes especially acute. So in essence leaders like Adolf Hitler, who designed massive parade grounds so to maximize this effect, were in actuality administering a large dose of feel good drugs to the crowd simply from the gathering itself. Anyone who has ever attended anything from a concert to a political rally is aware of this phenomenon - even if they don't consciously realize it. Arkonsians were *especially* cognizant of this, so typically any large gatherings were viewed as a ploy to falsely influence people. Why Kralsich had suddenly indulged in this technique was beyond Professor Briarton's knowledge.

"Kralsich my good friend! It's been too long," Professor Briarton said to him as the two men approached each other with exuberant faces. As the crowd thinned Jakob finally managed to catch a glimpse of the speech giver. The moment he caught sight of the large man, Jakob's surprise became evident. It seemed to him that Kralsich's forehead protruded out of his head far beyond what a normal mans should. His skin was neither white nor brown, but rather, grayish, and he lacked two thirds of the hair that a normal person should have. His thinness enticed the protruding bony features of his head to stand out more than they should. Jakob looked around at the crowd and noticed some of the same features in other people as well – although none were as pronounced as Kralsich's.

"Hello Phillip. Did you have a successful journey into the Old World?" Kralsich said in calm, soothing voice. Professor Briarton nodded and then immediately motioned toward Jakob, who began to wonder why he all of the sudden felt so important.

"Hello," Jakob said extending his arm for an obligatory hand shake, "it's nice to meet you." It was all Jakob could do not to show his surprise over Kralsich's odd appearance, but unfortunately to no avail. Kralsich understood the younger man's obvious facial expression, and extended a hand to him.

"*Very* nice to meet you too Mr. Jakob Vanden. I've heard many *magnanimous* things about you." This was technically true; however the source was definitely *not* Professor Briarton. "I have been awaiting your arrival."

"*Awaiting*?" Jakob objected.

Kralsich was quick to fill in the gaps. "*Expecting* your arrival rather. I knew that a young man of *your* intellect, when shown the reasoned truth, could only make one decision. . . . . .to accept this wonderful place you now see around you!" Kralsich threw his gangly arms toward the top of the mountain. He knew that the truth was far more complicated than he had just let on, but at the same time, he was also aware that Jakob could only handle so much in one serving. *The mind is weak, and it is at its weakest when asked to absorb large amounts of change*, Kralsich thought.

"Phillip?" From the dispersing crowd, a stocky man with raven colored beard and hair called out inquisitively.

"Sergei Ingistov! I can't believe it's you!" Professor Briarton and Sergei firmly shook hands and smiled at one another. "Wow, I haven't seen you in a while."

"Yes, yes," he spoke with a think Russian accent. "Not zince ofer a decade have ve laid eyes upon one another. Are you still a Professor zhese days?" The Russian scientist asked him.

"Well, it looks like I may be on sabbatical for a little while. Um," Professor Briarton was quick to change the subject as there was no need to worry Jakob about leaving, "what about you? I can't believe you're working on nuclear energy here in Arkonos?"

"Ha ha," he let out a guttural laugh, "no, zhis is not necessary here. Ve haff a virtually unlimited power supply due to the geo-zhermal energy. I haff been *very* pleased working on harnessing itz *poten-ti-al*," with the excitement for his favorite subject evident, the scientist squeezed his fist tightly.

"I'm just glad you managed to get here in one piece. It wasn't easy coordinating your escape from Moscow."

"And becauze of zhat, I am forever in your debt. You risked your life for mine . . . and one day I hope to do zhe zame for you." Sergei said sincerely while Jakob and Kralsich watched the scene unfold with admiration.

"Sergei, let's hope the day does *not* come when I must redeem your debt. Yet I have no reservations about your ability to keep your promises. Ahh. . . . . so," the Professor again switched the subject, "have you been pleased with your decision to immigrate to Arkonos?"

"Vords cannot dezcribe the vonder of zhis place. It zeems that I'm free to be who I vish without fear of irrational rejection, or haffing to always look over my shoulder. Zhe openness of the people haz truly astounded me. I'm fery grateful to be here." The two man locked eyes in mutual esteem. "It vas fery good to zee you again Phillip, but I must be on my vay. . . .my vork is fery zens-i-tive."

"By all means," Professor Briarton replied and they shook hands before Sergei departed.

Jakob suddenly began to feel uneasy in his new surroundings and wondered if this was some strange dream. His head was spinning and cracks of paranoia had begun to shake and move his mind. Unable to think clearly and consistently, only the most devious thoughts pertaining to those around him were able to surface to his conscious mind. When a man dropped a shovel a few meters away, Jakob jumped in momentary panic.

Kralsich looked over at Professor Briarton and the two men were perfectly aware of Jakob's condition – culture shock. The Professor put his hand on Jakob's back and said, "Maybe we should get going, it's been quite a day thus far. How's that sound Jakob?"

"Yeah, I am kind of tired I guess," Jakob slowly replied.

"Sleep allows the mind to *assess* and *realize* its true potential for the coming day," Kralsich affirmed, tapping a gangly finger repeatedly on his gray temple.

Professor Briarton led Jakob back up the elevator and to his apartment. After exchanging parting pleasantries Jakob found his way to the bedroom. Lying down on his new bed, Jakob wondered if this all was just a dream. . . .*what a shame, if it is.* He soon lost consciousness.

* * *

‖ **21** ‖

Chairman Gorshial tapped a frantic finger repeatedly on the seething silver desk. "Frankly I don't know how you stand be around them. Look how they treat one another?! Categories upon senseless categories, with every possible division exacerbated to the maximum degree. It's truly amazing they exist in the relative social peace they do. Of course the anger and disdain is *omni*present, it courses like a slithering snake under a lid just *waiting* for the pressure to have built up and . . . . . *pop!*" His fist hit the desk and a thud reverberated through the room sending his assistant, Hickel, into a surprised spasm. "It comes out. . . .the riot, the war. . . .the famine.

"Take racism. How have they not grown out of that man made mental contraption? Dogs don't even behave in this manner! A sire will always mount a bitch – irrespective of the breed. How did they learn this *ridiculous* behavior knowing that *all* children are born without racist tendencies? They teach each other. . .that's how! Generation after generation - it goes on and on," the Chairman quickly leaned forward from the backrest of the chair and for the first time looked Hickel, a younger man with a slight red beard, directly in the eyes

"You see," the Chairman continued, "when a child first goes into the house of someone of a different race he'll notice that things are, of course, quite different than his own residence. Think of your childhood if you can, although it is quite unusual that an adult can actually *recall* this time of his life. It's what makes undoing adolescent conditioning particularly difficult – one does not even know it happened.

"Like I was saying, back in those days you may have noticed that some of the furniture and decorations of someone of a different race were perhaps different, but that doesn't *really* enter your mind because *all* of your friends have different decorations in some form. No, no. . . . what will *maybe* get your attention is the smell of a different breed of human!! A poodle certainly does *not* smell like a Beagle and humans are not exempt from that fact either. So when do the children begin to change, hmmm? When does it all take place? They have to learn it from others. . . . . pure and simple. Otherwise the various smells of people don't mean anything. Oh, but wait until adulthood! Eventually the adults associate the smell with the skin color, which they were *taught* to be suspicious of by those around them. This is also the reason that multicultural societies attempt to hide their smell through the use of deodorants and anti-perspirants. The truth is, if you take a child and raise him around different races and that child *never* comes in contact with racist thoughts he/she will simply not have them.

"Even in the face of this Darwinist *dis*advantage that racism wroughts; they still maintain this ridiculous behavior! This prejudice separates races into competing smaller units which don't work together as a community – whole cities, states, and countries utterly divided. It's beyond me Hickel, *completely* beyond me," he waved his arms from side to side in frustration. "And if they were to meet me?" The Chairman dragged his hand down the length of his gray-skinned, almost hairless head. "They would kill me on site! That much is obvious.

"We've lived in this place for years without racism. Even during the times of the Elders we *only* had problems when receiving a large influx of Old Worlders. And then the problems were extinguished quite rapidly when the study of sociology was applied. It only took a generation or less for the last vestiges of these racist tendencies to finish melting away. It's a reasoned, majority thought process versus an unreasoned, minority thought process. The former, in a healthy free thinking society, always overwhelms the latter!"

"But we are not speaking of a reasoned, free-thinking society are we Chairman Gorshial?"

"No we must certainly are not Hickel. And in the case they were to discover us *here*. . . . . huh?" His finger continued to tap frantically on his desk. "What do you believe they would think of the ones with gray skin? They probably would despise the mixing more than anything else, you know! We have people from every continent on Earth here. Do you think they would understand that we've adapted quite naturally over the course of *all* this time. Most of them can *barely* even recognize that every human breed's skin color is perfectly suited geographically to receive the proper amount of UV rays from the sun!! How can we deal with these people?!?"

"Or a better question Chairman. . . . . how did they detect us?"

"It really doesn't matter how they did it. They have detected us! Maybe *all* of us."

"Chairman, we don't know that. We only have one incident thus far," Hickel was quick to counter.

"Stop Hickel, *just*. . . . . stop. They have all the technology. We know for certain they detected us with a *local* tracker. They were on to us. This doesn't mean that we're fully exposed yet. No, no. . . . . this place here, we have taken the utmost precautions to ensure that we are all fully shielded. There is simply nothing for them to detect. We've seen *all* of their topography maps. They believe we're a massive plateau – nothing significant. No minerals, no water, nothing of interest for them here. And, due to our damping shield all of our Quantum

Bursts are completely blocked from upward movement." He breathed deep and his back crashed into the chair, while fingers continued their incessant taping. Silence momentarily filled the room.

"They may not find us here but they will undoubtedly find all of our Travelers, Enlighteners, and Monitors, that much is certain. Time is *not* on our side Hickel. We must enact Section 7b."

"Chairman Gorshial. . . . . that will certainly *stop* all the progress we've made! Not to mention the ramifications of removing the *only* thing that lends any sanity whatsoever to that awful place out there. And you *know* what else it will do!"

"You think I don't know the ramifications of my own actions? How do you think I got to be Chairman? *Damn it!*" This time both of his fists pounded the table sending Hickel again jumping from his seat in fright. The Chairman ran his wispy gray fingers over his forehead and down the back of his protruding skull and let out a sigh. "Never before in our history have we had to evacuate almost *all* of our people from the Old World. *Never*. Is this how I'll be remembered?"

He knew the thought was egotistical. Thinking about himself and his irrelevant legacy when *so many* of their people could be captured, or even worse their entire civilization could be discovered and *destroyed*. Chairman Gorshial had to act and he knew it.

"You know you're effectively signing away your own job if you do this?"

"Yes *Hickel*. I'm well aware of *that*." The Chairman replied. He had heard from his sources that Kralsich had predicted that their people in the Old World would be detected. If he was indeed accurate, which he almost always was, then that would be *another* perfect Prognostication by the unprecedently successful man, moving him that much closer to the Chairmanship. By enacting Section 7b Chairman Gorshial was effectively taking a step toward handing Kralsich the keys to his own position.

"We have no choice, Hickel. Our people's lives, as well as our entire civilization are at stake. We must enact Section 7b immediately – we don't have much time."

"Chairman I implore you, isn't there some other option?"

"Hickel," Chairman Gorshial turned toward his assistant, "you are familiar with the way the law is initiated, are you not? I'm sure one of my *top* advisors is intrinsically acquainted with the rules of the game. Shall we canvas the simplicity? Hmm? Let us," he said coldly.

"The Prognosticators make their predictions, which then go to the Council of Many for evaluation. They formulate Plans of Action for *all* of the Prognostications, some in secret and some with the consultation of me, the Chairman. Then various private and public entities, depending on who is best suited for the task, program the Plans of Actions into concise, executable systems. In the event that a prediction is correct then the Plan of Action most be executed as instructed. The physical act of execution of the Plan falls to me, the Chairman. And *that* is why, Hickel, we are headed to the Hall of Many to initiate the Plan."

In a desperate attempt to change his mind Hickel blurted out, "you know he made a public speech today."

"He *what*!?"

"Kralsich just stood up in the gardens and delivered a speech. Just like that. Done."

"This is spinning out of control *very* quickly, but it doesn't matter anyway." He shook his head in what appeared to be defeat. "We have our duty! We're enacting 7b."

"But Chairman, we could wait and. . . . . "

"*NO!*" He shouted in a rage. "I'm going now, and you're coming with me."

"Yes sir. Whatever you say," he said through clinched teeth. The two men reluctantly shuffled out of the room in trepidation to carry out their mandate.

* * *

‖ 22 ‖

Within a few hours Jakob awoke and was momentarily startled by his unfamiliar surroundings. After realizing again where he actually was, his mind raced with excited curiosity about the things yet to be discovered in this unbelievable place. He decided at that point, due to the jet lag *of course*, that there was no need to even waste his time trying to sleep any longer.

He got out of bed, walked over to the window and pulled up the blinds to look out. The "sun" had set by this time of the day. Jakob saw lights coming from the gardens below as well as from people's apartments across the mountain, contrasting the darkness of the night.

Even from forty stories up he was still able to notice a fairly large gathering taking place in a building situated about a mile away in what appeared to be a dense forest. Turning his head, he looked at his bed and then his suitcase. Within seconds he reached into his carry-on and found a 'stylish', collared shirt to wear with some jeans. He looked in the mirror long enough to think, *how do I know this is even 'fashionable' here.* He brushed the thought expediently aside.

While walking out of his apartment, he quietly slid the door closed behind him. Jakob did not think he was necessarily doing anything *wrong* by exploring Arkonos unassisted. Even still, there was clearly no need to draw suspicion to himself by making a huge racket when leaving, so he walked softly down the corridor toward the elevator.

Upon entering the air powered contraption, he could not help but feel like he had entered the tube system that they use at banks for drive-through customers. He closed his eyes as he pushed the 'Ground' button, sending a loud *whooshing* noise through the extremely fast moving cylinder. A momentary feeling of nausea poured over him but quickly subsided when the feeling of weightlessness dissipated. Within *seconds* Jakob was on the ground floor, lying in front of him were dimly lit gardens and forests as far as the eye could see.

    Again he, like a tourist staring at skyscrapers, looked straight up toward the pinnacle of the mountain. On the sides of the sheer cliffs were millions of lights shining out from the apartments within. Shaking the surreal scene out of his head, Jakob looked straight ahead and began making his way toward the dense forest where it looked like quite a gathering of some kind was taking place.

    After about ten minutes of walking through the vast and varied gardens, his path led him to the edge of the forest. Even from where Jakob was he could begin to hear the subtle sound of voices and music. He turned his head and looked into the darkness before him. While there were running lights visible along the path through what appeared to be enormous elm, oak and chestnut trees, he was still instinctively hesitant to walk through a dark place at night.

    His curiosity overwhelmed fear and after hurriedly shuffling through the wooded area he came upon a clearing. Immediately the building in the middle of the forest he had spied from his apartment became visible with well over a hundred people enjoying each other's company in addition to their drinks.

    Not wanting to be seen hovering around the edge of a scene, Jakob instinctively walked among the people, making eye contact and smiling when the situation warranted it. The crowd was mixed with respect to age and gender. Their dress was very casual with most people's clothes fitting rather loosely and unassumingly, however some of the younger women did not hesitate to show off their newly blossoming figures. These young females wore a similar style of clothes as the others, only theirs were a few sizes reduced. Some people also randomly donned bright colors and had styled hair.

He looked over toward the bar and noticed one of these women walking toward *him*. She was wearing a striped, rather snug-fitting gray and red dress. At first Jakob thought she was going to briskly walk past him, but instead she turned to him. Their eyes met, with his cobalt piercing into her silver-green irises.

She stood *right* in front of him, her height only slightly less than Jakob's which accentuated her presence in the crowd. She shook his hand and spoke, "Jakob Vanden, I presume." His face had the look of shocked surprise as she was clearly aware of whom he was. He replied defensively.

"How'd you know my name?" He asked with a tinge of paranoia.

"Well, it isn't exactly a state secret or anything, but I know it through Kralsich, a friend of mine. Jakob. . . . . relax. . . . . how about I buy you a beer?"

"Alright. . . . . let's start there I guess. How 'bout you tell me *your* name?" Jakob's surprise melted away into a smile as he nodded, accepted the situation and began to follow her through the crowd toward the bar.

"I'm Terra," she said and offered a slight handshake while still navigating forward.

Jakob noticed her skin was slightly gray yet still glowing in appearance. Her facial features seemed to combine all the people of the world into one structure – Caucasian, African, and Asian all converging. Jakob had seen this in other gray skinned people here as well, but this particular combination had a more pleasant overtone to it. He happily tailed her to the bar.

"Silim, nanga def," she said to the group standing in line to grab some drinks, who were obviously acquaintances. The exact language was unrecognizable to Jakob.

"How's a beer sound?" She asked, handing it to him at the same time.

"Good. Thanks."

"To new beginnings," she said loud enough to be fully understood over the echoing music. Both of them raised their glasses where they lightly clanked together. Their eyes hovered slightly above the rims and stayed locked until even after the first taste of the beverages.

"So, this is really cool, this place I mean," Jakob said in her ear and noticed the gathering crowd who were still arriving on foot and bicycle.

"Well, you know, it's just home to me, but I'm sure it seems very strange to you right now."

"Yeah I'm still getting used to everything . . . . . but umm, actually, I wanted to ask you. . . . . what language *was* that you were speaking back there?" Jakob was trying to keep the conversation light yet at the same time sound intelligent, and this was the best he could seem to do.

"Ohh, yeah," she smiled and twisted her hair, momentarily forgetting the gaping holes in Jakob's knowledge about Arkonos. "Hey, let's move that way," she pointed toward some benches near a vibrant, dark green chestnut tree, "so it's not so loud."

"Lead the way," Jakob called out motioning his hand forward. They walked together out of the noisy crowd and went over to the benches where the sound was unobtrusively ambient.

"So that's a mix of languages, huh?" Jakob said quick to pierce the silence with some sort of noise as they sat on the solid wood benches.

"Actually, *you're* a mix of languages!" She shot back with a smile.

"What do you mean by that?"

"Well. . . . . you heard me speaking that strange sounding tongue which you referred to as *mixed*. Right?"

"*Yeah*, and?"

"How about your language? English?! If I were alive a little over a thousand years ago I would have said the *exact* same thing to you! Now, however, English is established as perhaps *the* standard language internationally and people don't look at it like that."

"Alright," Jakob conceded but was quick to remain guarded, "I know English has some French and German words in it but it's still its own language."

"Oh, absolutely! It's definitely its own language inclusive with all of it own unique dialects spread throughout the world. All the same though, if you had learned all of its component languages at a young age, then you too would see it as I do."

"You learned what?!" Jakob said with a cursory smile.

"Don't look so shocked!" She laid a hand on his shoulder as the two laughed together. "Yeah," she shrugged her shoulders playfully, "they learned that I had a gift for languages at a young age and, so I . . . . . started learning them – one right after the other."

"Wow. How many can you speak?" Jakob said looking over the top of his beer as he took a sip.

"Ohh, I don't know. I guess like thirty or forty, maybe?"

"*Really!*"

"Yeah, but don't get too excited or anything, that doesn't make me a genius. It doesn't work like that with languages. What I mean is that they all inherently possess aspects of one another. So if you learned like, I don't know, five base languages the other ones are mostly just mixes. I'm sure you've noticed that whenever you have to spell something of Francophile origin – something like 'rendezvous' or 'pneumatic', huh?

"The truth is that people tend to look at languages in a very static, unchanging way. Nothing could be further from the truth!" It was obvious to Jakob that Terra had an unquenched thirst for her favorite discipline as she continued vocalizing her passion.

"A language's main purpose is to ensure effective communication and therefore as society changes so too *should* the language. For instance: when Romans began invading the British Isles thousands of years ago, linguistically the end result was that the existing English population added aspects of the Latin vocabulary, which in turn allowed complicated ideas to be distilled down to one word. This in turn allowed local people to better communicate not only with the Romans but also each other.

A more modern example of this would be the use of English words in a host of other languages, which occurs on a global, daily basis. Words like hello, computer, and dude! Another future example will be the incorporation of Spanish words into American English due to the ballooning Hispanic culture in the United States. While often times not viewed as such by the masses, the blending of these languages is essential in order to facilitate communication and more importantly empathy. I mean . . . deny the phenomenon if you'd like, but I bet you'd be hard pressed to find an American that doesn't know what 'loco' means, right?"

"Hmmm, I didn't think of it that way really. So you mean that as cultures naturally combine to create their own unique identity, concurrently so do languages?"

"Exactly," she said, again locking eyes long enough for it to be pleasantly uncomfortable. She hesitantly continued, "the most interesting example of people who have a rather static idea about language is the French. They've arbitrarily decided that their language is now *perfect* and they wish to freeze that perfection in its current form. The result has been a myriad laws and regulations about what people are allowed to print or say publicly when it comes to the French language. Quotas have been set up to ensure that a certain percentage of songs on the radio are French. Their government officials are adamant that no more foreign words should be permitted in their *pure* language. They make all these rules and regulations while completely blind that French itself is a colossal mix of languages. How funny do you think it is to listen to a French official using words derived from another language to not allow any addition languages into his own?!?! Also, by ceasing the development of French they are impeding the ability of their language to change so that communication can be best facilitated. The linguistical arrogance is unprecedented in all of human history!"

"So that's what learning forty some odd languages does to intelligence, huh?" He said obviously impressed.

"Well thanks for that Jakob, but please, it's really," she paused momentarily, smiled and nodded her head up and down in self confirmation, "I should learn to take compliments better anyway. Thank you." They both paused their conversation in order to enjoy some more of their cold drinks.

"Forty languages. Wow, and you're about my age aren't you?"

"Yeah, I'd say we're about the same age, yeah," she said, taking the opportunity to scan his face and body for evidence. "Don't worry though; I won't hold your lack of linguistical skills against you. I just happened to have been born in this place where we have such wonderful opportunities to learn and grow. Looking down on you for not learning a lot of languages would be the same as looking down on someone for any birth related difference like race, social class or nationality. That's just not fair to anyone."

"Yeah, I guess you're right. People *don't* get to decide all these things about themselves and yet we're constantly judging people in my society based upon them."

"Don't forget the other trap in judging people as well – positive judging. This occurs when you see someone of say. . . . . a national origin that's had a perceived tougher time. So as a boss or whatever, you decide that person shouldn't be held to the same standards as other people and you give them a lot of free passes. I'm not talking about cultural differences, oh no. I'm talking about that little sordid impulse which says: his people have had a tougher time because of his race. . . . . he should definitely win the election. Or, the poor man should get the promotion even though his performance is below that of his peers.

That form of preferential treatment is in the end just as destructive as any other form of discrimination. It artificially exalts someone to where they shouldn't be and their potential to fall further increases."

"So I guess I shouldn't look for any preferential treatment from you then, huh?" Jakob joked with an ear to ear grin.

"Well, we're in a slightly different place then I just described. And besides I never said *anything* about not being able to help a friend!"

"I'm glad you at least made some sort of exception for me."

"Anytime," she quickly responded again laying a hand on his shoulder in confirmation.

"Have you ever left Arkonos?" He asked.

"Definitely. I've studied all over the world. Actually I've only been here for about half my life. The other half I lived in China, Thailand, Germany, India, Italy, Portugal, Brazil and even your own United States."

"What," he mocked her playfully, "did you just pack your suitcases and go? Is that how it works here?"

"No. . . . . c'mon, you know better than that! I mostly lived with other Arkonsians. It's kind of like a student exchange, I guess. The Arkonsians that live in the Old World for extended periods of time want their children to enjoy the educational benefits of their homeland. So they send their children here to my parents and I go to theirs. For me it was perfect because I not only got to experience another culture besides my own, but in addition I had the opportunity to explore all of those wonderful languages. Oh. . . . . and I got away from my parents!"

"Wow, that's a nice way to do it. I, on the other hand, was never allowed to do an exchange like I wanted to . . . . . my father was always against it."

"And that's what's so incredible about you Jakob. You've never truly experienced another culture before, and yet you have an air about you like you'd lived abroad most of your life. Some of your conversations have shown incredible insight for monoculturalist."

"What do you mean 'some of my conversations'?" Jakob's demeanor suddenly shifted back into paranoia.

"Umm, well, you're. . . .I mean the conversations we've had." Terra a master of many languages suddenly found herself struggling for the right words.

"Bullshit!" Jakob suddenly jumped up from the bench and looked down at his new *'friend'* both physically as well as metaphorically. "That's not what you meant by that. You better start talking or I'm outta here." He turned as though he were going to leave.

"Ok, ok, ok," Terra grabbed his hand and motioned for him to sit back down. "Look, I'll explain what I meant ok, just *please* . . . . . sit back down." He found the bench again and awaited her explanation. "Alright, you remember your conversations, the ones you've had with Professor Briarton?"

"Of course. . . . . "

"The thing is. . . . . it's not solely at Professor Briarton behest as to whether you were brought here or not. Obviously having someone who's emotionally invested in a situation become the sole decision maker is not a good idea. You can agree with that, right?"

"Alright, I'm listening," he muttered hesitantly, pursing his lips in dissatisfaction.

"Well, with that in mind, a group of people needed to evaluate your conversations with the Professor before we could ascertain your status. I was one of those people."

"What about the black car and that guy in the woods behind my apartment. . . . . who the hell was that? Did you have something to do with it?"

"Oh, that. You saw that, huh? Yeah, we were afraid of that," her face contorted with embarrassment as she continued explaining the odd event. "We became worried that your father was spying on *you* - so we had to find out the truth. That guy was never supposed to be behind your house in the first place. We're still not sure what's wrong with him but for whatever reason he suddenly became erratic and *extremely* paranoid. We think he may have seen something that he shouldn't have and was tortured or something, but we can't be certain yet. Once we realized that he'd pretty much lost it, we sent someone in there to apprehend him."

"Who put you up to it? I mean, who's in charge?" Jakob's paranoia was beginning to dissipate, yet parts were still bubbling to the surface in confusion.

"It's not like somebody 'put me up to it' in the way you're saying it. Jakob do you believe that someone could have altruistic intentions and use spying as a tool toward that goal?"

"I guess. . . . . it's just that I'm skeptical. I feel violated that so many people have probably listened to conversations that I thought were private."

"Yes. . . . . but why did we listen?" She leaned in closer to him, her pupils dilating wider in the semi-darkness which surrounded them. "Was it so that we could harm you? Were we trying to do something nefarious? No! Absolutely not! What *did* happen is that we saw someone special and then we decided whether or not they were *really* special enough to be chosen to come here. That's what we did." She continued looking into his eyes as her face wrenched emotionally.

"I understand, but just give me some time to absorb all of this," he replied to her explanation while finding it difficult to deny her reasoning as well as her smooth symmetrical face and bright eyes. Even still, he felt as though she had said too much and was simply covering her mistake. The truth was she had been dishonest with him and there was nothing stopping her from doing that again.

"Look, Jakob," she laid her hand on his recently grown, stubbly face, "I'm on your side."

"Alright. . . . . you're on my side, huh? Then I think that I deserve to know who gave you the recordings of the Professor and me. That's all I want to know."

"That's fair. The person besides Professor Briarton who has a lot of interest in you is the Professor's old friend – Kralsich."

"Kralsich. . . . . I met him earlier today."

"Did you hear his speech?" She responded excitedly.

"Uhh, no. . . . . but there was a crowd of people leaving right when I got there."

"Well, I'm sure you'll get to hear him eventually. I've been told he's planning at least one more speech *very* soon."

"Hmm, I'm still not sure what I'm doing here, or why it's *me* that's actually been chosen, but I'm not going to ruin a good thing by being paranoid and over analyzing everything."

"I think that's a pretty good attitude to have, Jakob. I think you should also remember that just because someone doesn't think it's the right time to share some information with you, that doesn't *necessarily* mean that they have mal-intentions toward you. I mean, c'mon, I know your parents lied to you about Santa Claus and the Tooth Fairy but they didn't mean any ill will toward you did they?"

"No, I guess you're right. I'm starting to think I've been put on a 'need to know basis'. In this strange place amongst all of these strange people, present company excluded, it's just a little unnerving. . . . . that's all."

"I totally understand. I think anyone living in a foreign place is a little apprehensive about what's going on around them. If you add that to how you got here along with your recorded conversations, then I don't think you're at all off the mark. You're handling your situation far better than almost any of your countrymen would, which is *exactly* why you're in Arkonos."

The crowd was slowly beginning to thin out and the music was now being played at a lower level, prompting even more people to exit the party. Jakob and Terra looked around for a minute, both of them absorbing the revealing conversation in which they had just been involved. While he was coming to terms with having been spied on, she was pondering whether or not Jakob still trusted her.

"I guess this party is just about over," he commented, emptying what was left of his beverage into his mouth.

"C'mon let's grab a beer for the road and I'll walk you home," she said invitingly.

"Yeah, you're probably right. There's no telling what Professor Briarton has planned for me tomorrow."

"I've heard that guy is a real slave driver!" She said in jest.

"Seriously?"

"No. . . . . you're too easy to fool now, what with all that rampant paranoia I can see bubbling inside you." She smiled as the two laughed together which was a much needed respite compared to the tense conversation earlier.

"Look, I just found out that there's a secret society and that it is possibly thousands of years old located somewhere near the south pole. . . . . can you blame me for being a little paranoid?" He said continuing to laugh while he playfully patted her bare leg.

They both stood up, happy that the tension between them had appeared to melt away and made their way to the bar. After grabbing two more beers they set off through the forest in the direction of Jakob's new apartment and kept the conversation about personal things the entire way.

Somewhere along their trip, they had begun to walk closer to each other and although neither one was certain how it happened, by the time they neared the elevator up to Jakob's apartment, they were definitely holding hands.

"I guess this is it," Jakob said with a reluctant smile.

"Only for now," she replied. Terra leaned in a bit closer to Jakob and gave him a huge hug, squeezing all of her curvy figure against his. The two enjoyed the moment for a few seconds before their bodies partially parted and Jakob instinctively gave her a soft kiss.

"Good night," he said.

"Good night Jakob," she sincerely responded.

Their eyes locked briefly before she turned and left for her own home.

* * *

‖ 23 ‖

After a long day of travel and varying degrees of reverse culture shock, Professor Briarton was glad to be in his apartment. It had been over a decade since he was last here and was grateful that not much had changed. Some of the furniture was not in the right places due to whoever had lived here while he was away. Even still, they had positioned all of his personal possessions, which were by no means vast in number, in the approximate places where they resided previously.

As he relaxed on his couch and poured himself a decades old scotch, he began to reflect on the day. As if bringing Jakob here hadn't been enough for him to absorb in one sitting, it had come to Professor Briarton's attention, through the local media, that Chairman Gorshial had enacted Section 7b. The Chairman had no choice, in reality. The Council of Many along with the Prognosticators craft Plans of Action. When certain triggers are "pulled", in this case the detection of his Quantum Communicator, then the Chairman *must* execute that part of the plan. That is the main role of the Chairman.

It was now inevitable that his old friend Kralsich would soon fill that roll and become the new Chairman due to his uncanny Prognostications. Professor Briarton knew this, Chairman Gorshial knew this, and most importantly of all - Kralsich himself knew this as well. And *everyone* knew that this planet was getting ready to do some drastic changing. If nothing else the recall of *so* many Enlighteners would. . . . . and that's when it hit Professor Briarton. The historical significance of this event was incredible. Astounding. He wanted to make sure that no matter what the outcome may be, people would know the truth. . . . . even if it were just a few.

He immediately withdrew a digital recording device from his still unpacked suitcase, took a sip of his scotch, hit record and began talking:

> "Chairman Gorshial's enactment of Section 7b of the 'Alternative Solutions in the Event of a Constrained Time Frame: Goal of Continuity', is already having profound effects within minutes of its initiation. All around the globe Enlighteners, Travelers and Monitors are receiving messages on their Quantum Handhelds with specific instructions on returning to Arkonos. These instructions had already been predetermined so their transmission was as easy as pushing a single button which is located in the Council of the Many.
>
> "The Arkonsians in the Old World could not all leave at the exact same time, that would be *far* too suspicious! And they could not *all* take flights to South America either because that would raise too many flags. Some will fly to South Africa and buy research ships to come back on; others will go to Australia, India, or even Russia. With their ultimate destination being Antarctica, it did not make much sense to sail from the Northern Hemisphere, but with concealment of their journey being paramount many would have to make that long journey.
>
> "The Enlighteners, those who were in positions of academia like Professor Briarton for instance, wouldn't have too difficult a time slipping away. More than likely their departure would be temporarily covered up by a research trip or even

a sabbatical. Likewise Travelers, the Arkonsians equivalent of tourists, also wouldn't draw much attention because, well, tourists travel.

"The most difficult part of enacting 7b was the departure of the Monitors. These Arkonsians have lived in the Old World for so long that they have now assumed roles high into the upper echelons of business and government. Some of them are CEO's with wives and children who were unaware of their true identities. Needless to say 7b stipulated that no children or wives could accompany these individuals; this is an order that was difficult on which to decide but necessary nonetheless. Anyone who attempted to bring unrequested Old Worlder back with them put the entire civilization at risk.

"Some of the Monitors, who constantly updated Arkonos with pertinent information, were *very* high in the ladders of government. Every spy agency in the world had been infiltrated by these individuals! Thousands of Monitors were in diplomatic offices, international organizations, ministries of defense, counter intelligence services, and even in Congresses and Parliaments the world over. One in particular was going to carry the highest level of risk. Senator William Langesé was a high ranking member of the United States Senate and it would be *extremely* difficult for him to depart without being noticed due to his obligatory secret service attaché. Because of this and because someone *so* high up in government could be an indispensable asset, he hadn't been given the evacuation order yet.

"Everyone was aware that these were indeed perilous times. Arkonos had never had to recall *everyone* back from their respective assignments in the Old World. Many here have speculated that the influence of the Enlighteners has been the only stitch holding the entire global fabric together. Those brave educators, which include not only Professors, but in addition, positions where tools of *actual* learning are at their service, all create a vast network of positive influence in the world, injecting their ideas like doctors would a medicine. So when they leave, well, that positive influence will no longer exist. And because that safety net will no longer be in place, the world could certainly enter into a free fall. This only made it more likely that *all* of Kralsich's predictions would come true, and perhaps that's why he was beginning the unprecedented practice of spontaneous public speaking.

"Arkonos had long ago stomped out this crude behavior because it exacerbated the 'Crowd Chemical'. Long before the current era, the Elders had seen this force be used in order to cloud and subsequently confuse the minds of those involved in the sordid spectacle.

"The amazing thing was, in order to get rid of this sort of behavior no law or edict was required – it simply happened. People began to realize that the behavior was a rather unproductive force in society. It occurred much like the manner in which saying "God Bless You" has been mostly phased out. At first it was awkward to be in a room when you heard only silence thereafter, but soon, like the watch on your wrist or an earring in your ear, people did not even notice. So it was with public speaking and clapping. Now. . . . . silence.

"This made it all the more strange that Kralsich had begun teetering near the edge of this cavernous abyss. Why was he going in public and spontaneously drawing large crowds? What did he have planned?"

That was exactly the moment Professor Briarton pushed the stop button as he realized what Kralsich was doing. After once more slowly sipping his peat inspired beverage, he began recording again and spoke softly and profoundly:

"Kralsich is planning the Emerging. He's going to expose us to the World and he's preparing the throngs of people for that *quickly* approaching time."

* * *

|| 24 ||

When Jakob's eyes parted and he realized that the day before had in fact *not* been a dream, he sprang out of bed with renewed vigor. He found that the bathroom facilities were very similar to what he would have found at home minus some water pressure of course. Even his room wasn't much different than he would have expected anywhere else. It was a bit über-modern in some ways but it still had a warm feel to it.

In general Jakob had expected everything to be more technologically advanced, but besides some of the furniture everything was generally low key and earthy. There were no automatic blinds on the windows, nor any automatic cooking apparati of which to speak. The entire interior was fairly barren and in fact, he did not even see a computer screen built into the wall!

At that moment Jakob heard a rhythmic knock on the door. *No doorbells, really?* He thought as he headed to the front of the unsophisticated apartment. The front door did not swing open, but rather, it effortlessly slid inside the wall.

"Professor Briarton, good morning. C'mon in," Jakob said cordially.

"Thanks. You ready for breakfast?"

"There's breakfast here?" He said jokingly and let out a slight chuckle.

"We've even got lattes! Follow me."

"Well thanks. . . right behind you." As Jakob slid the door closed he could not help himself and had to ask the Professor about the low tech décor. "Professor, what's with the simplicity of everything here? I mean, I just expected to see more technology everywhere."

"Is that right?" The Professor asked dryly as the two strolled down the curved, windowed hallway, simultaneously taking in the spectacular view forty stories down toward the lush interior of the mountain.

"Yeah, you know I haven't even seen a computer since I got here."

"We definitely have computers Jakob, don't worry about that. We, however, don't use them all the time. Arkonsians are more likely to only use technology when we need to, whereas you tend to surround yourselves with it. Think about it. Enjoying a night at home and staring at an artificial screen or flipping the crisp pages of a book? The former does not sound nearly as enticing as the latter, that's for sure!"

"Fair enough," Jakob replied.

"We just don't have the need to be so distracted from life like you. Our society, partly out of necessity, has become far more homogenous with its surroundings and that makes differences in mind-sets that you can scarcely imagine," the Professor turned his head and looked Jakob in the eye for just a moment while the two men continued on at a fast pace.

"I can see that. People start to have different priorities. All of the sudden expansion isn't as important as sustainability," Jakob said, looking out the corridor window at the mesmerizing view of gardens and forests on the floor of the mountain.

"Unfortunately Jakob, history tells us that more than likely, a perpetually expanding society has to hit rock bottom before they can recover."

"What do you mean by 'hit rock bottom'?"

"Well, I mean that a society gets accustomed to having certain resources at a certain prices and when there's a change in availability of those resource the price naturally raises. This in turn tests the system in regard to how much it ultimately relies on those raw materials. If the system cannot restructure itself to compensate for the loss before panic, rioting, and social unrest sets in, then we call that rock bottom."

"Ohhh. . . . . I see what you're saying." Jakob now understood how deep the Professor's implications had gone. *You typically have to have social collapse before you can become sustainable*, he thought.

"Jakob, it's kind of like a gluttonous man. He has to actually *have* a heart attack before he'll stop consuming such a dangerous volume of food. But don't be fooled! For many the heart attack isn't enough. They'll continue to eat copious amounts of food just like a smoker with cancer will continue to light up."

"Do you think we're close to the bottom Professor?

"I think we're close and getting much closer by the minute. Remember, this isn't to say that all collapses are inherently bad. Look at the American Revolution. . . . . there's a situation where an extreme imbalance existed and its reconciliation surely wasn't without its heinous moments. No, we must understand there are cycles which nations go through – any historian worth their salt knows that this pattern is recognizable. A small independent republic turns into empire which eventually crumbles under its own weight. Many of us are well aware of this and yet remain powerless to stop it."

After walking for what seemed like about a mile down the long scenic corridor with windows facing the interior of the mountain, the two men reached a lush terrace café complete with a forty story view. Jakob quickly leaned up against the outermost rail, around which were people enjoying their beverages and conversation. From this angle Jakob could see straight across into the interior of the mountain range. Although it was slightly hazy at this distance, he counted the interiors of at least seven distinct smaller mountains, all of which appeared inhabited. Before this point Jakob thought there was only one mountain, but now he realized that the Arkonsians inhabited the entire range.

Beams of light shone down huge cylindered vacancies in the rock directly above the café allowing sizable quantities of sunlight to flood the smaller mountains in the distance. Plants of all varieties stretched out toward the life-giving light and pleasantly draped the café in the process.

As Jakob continued to scan the 'horizon' for more interesting spectacles, he noticed that there were parks, forests, and café's just like this one, clustered all about the inside of the mountain. Some of the café's and parks were easily three hundred stories high, situated near the top of the peak.

The Professor noticed him looking up and spoke. "Now you see why our elevators need to be so fast!" Jakob managed to pull his eyes away from the awesome sight to notice the café in which he was standing.

"Let's sit down and grab some breakfast. I'm hungry."

"Thought you'd never ask," the Professor said happily. They managed to get a table right next to the outermost railing – one of the best views in the café. Within a few minutes a waiter came over and took their order. The two men continued to talk as coffee was brought out.

"So, how does it work here, can you start a business, a café or something. I mean do people earn money? Get rich? What's the. . . . . " Jakob trailed off rather unfocusedly.

"Yes and yes, Jakob, but it's all very much different. Remember when we talked about how living with your surroundings rather than against them produces a different mind-set? Well this is definitely the situation in the Old World as well as in Arkonos. The main difference is that people here live *with* their environment while in contrast, you live *against* yours. In your world each individual is pitted against everyone else to try and snatch up as many resources as possible; this situation is exacerbated by virtually everyone being locked into this competition. Nations prime the pump using inflation to disallow secure savings for most people. This occurs, all the while your easily accessible resources are becoming scarcer, and to compound the problem your population is constantly expanding and requires more and more."

"Why do you think there's a general trend toward unmitigated growth without really the idea of sustainability taking root?" Jakob asked, carefully taking a sip of coffee and immensely enjoying the view.

"The basic structure of the system elicits this response from you. It's simply a manipulated change in environment. Imagine a bear who doesn't know how to catch a wild salmon because he's always lived off campers' leftovers. The bear is reacting to an unnatural change in his environment. These unnatural changes in your environment are all the manipulations such as interest rates, inflation, subsidies and etc.

"Your people, like the bear, can no longer exist without the assistance of 'campers' (manipulators). In fact he cannot even *imagine* that he could catch one of those fast moving fish without assistance. The same phenomenon undoubtedly exists in humans."

"What role does the individual play in all this?"

"Certainly you could look at them as the building blocks, and see what they're doing. Working, paying rent, raising families, and besides all those duties, mostly just trying to escape." The Professor leaned in toward Jakob and spoke in a low voice for emphasis, and said, "You don't need hard drugs to escape. A TV with some rabbit ears will get the job done! Pharmaceuticals seem to be the favored method in your particular part of the world. A lot of people clutch onto religion, which is of course *very* different than spirituality, in order to cope.

The majority of the way that religious texts are interpreted advocate a virtual surrender to the authority of government making that particular escape even more encapsulating. Shopping, movies, trash novels, cable, gossip, sports, celebrities and so on and so forth fill up most people's free time. Of course you have the male and female versions of escapes, like sports for men and celebrity gossip for women. They're truly just two sides of the same coin, one lathered with testosterone and the other with estrogen, respectively.

"Don't get me wrong there are *plenty* of small groups that passionately advocate for this political cause or that *really* important thing here and there, but even the vast majority of these people don't see the true cause of their calamities. These people are bobbing up and down in an ocean and they believe that every time they hit the peak and valley of a wave they have moved. But Jakob they have not moved. . . . . the wave moved *past them*."

"What do you mean by that last part?" He asked, while a curious eyebrow showed his thirst for knowledge.

"Well. . . . . this may be a conversation for a later time. Ummm, where were we?" The Professor asked while his seasoned face scrunched in contemplation.

"Building blocks," Jakob was quick to steer the conversation on its proper course.

"That's right. So, the building blocks, people in our case, are locked into a system in which most of their time is spent on duties and raw escapism. Very few people are actually interested in the way that their own society is run. When most attempt to become politically involved, an overabundance of nationalism compounded with the tribal instinct of crowds, dampens the reason and logic in their minds, thus ensuring they do *not* see problems from a more global as well as individual perspective. This mindset leads to countries competing with each other even more, which in turn trickles down to *every* building block. The end result is an even faster utilization of resources."

"So are the 'building blocks' shaped like they are because of the society or do the blocks make the society?"

"Chicken or the egg, ehhh Jakob? Which came first? In our question it's really who influences whom. The answer is a combination of both. . . . . most of the time." Just then their waiter brought what looked like fresh vegetables and eggs, a plate for each of the hungry men.

"Enjoy," the waiter, in plain clothes with muted colors, announced before turning and checking on some other tables.

Jakob and Professor Briarton began eating the freshly prepared food while taking longer intervals in between talking so as to enjoy their succulent meals.

"So you asked earlier if people here have money, if they can start a business, or if they can get rich, right? The answer is yes but it doesn't happen like that because we've grown to live *with* our environment not against it. Our building blocks have become different."

"I think I know what you mean Professor. How about I try an example on *you*?" Jakob asked, leading the Professor to nod in affirmation.

"I remember years ago," Jakob paused before continuing. "I visited this furniture designer who was making this incredibly complex furniture. . . .I had never seen anything like it before. I immediately thought about helping him expand the small shop into a factory, but the funny thing was when I told him my idea - he seemed uninterested. So I kinda pressed him, you know, and asked if he thought the idea of expanding *could* be successful, and to my surprise he believed it could be *very* successful. Even still. . . . . he was uninterested. Now I realize he was really just content with what he was doing. He didn't want to have a dominating business. It was the craftsmanship that was so important to him."

"Exactly. I bet he had other interests as well Jakob."

"You're right, I think he played music and went hiking with his wife. But this guy was into all sorts of things really. I remember seeing his book shelf and he had read almost everything imaginable."

"You'll find that people who study a variety of subjects tend to be more content with their lives than their narrowly focused peers. The Old World's educational system in general tries to put blinders on people and have them focus primarily on one subject. People become experts in their field; however don't notice the complex interactions between all things. They only know their own subject. This often leads to very profit driven behavior which doesn't have time nor the 'know how' to contemplate all the interconnectedness of life.

"Think about the last major intellectual awakening. The Renaissance. Michelangelo, Erasmus and da Vinci were all men who individually studied a wide variety of subjects with intensity. These open minded individuals invented and discovered things that were wildly advanced and ahead of their time. This is *no coincidence*."

The Professor sat back in his chair, continued properly chewing his food, and admired the still impressive view which radiated tranquility into his being.

"This is delicious. Is all of it grown here?" Jakob asked in between bites.

"One hundred percent grown here, in fact. And just about everyone takes part in its cultivation."

"What do you mean?"

"Gardening is beyond a hobby here. While we have professionals who are dedicated to the planning and growing of our food stocks, the reality is that the majority of the labor is performed by Arkonsians who enjoy both the social facet of working with others and being with nature. Living in a mountain for so long here, we've learned to appreciate the physical participation in plant growth among other things."

Jakob, now done with his meal, sat back in his chair while concurrently taking a gulp of coffee to wash down his food. His eyes scanned the people sitting about and walking around and decided to ask a question that had been nagging him. "Professor," he leaned forward in order to speak softly about the subject, "what's with the grayish skinned, really tall people."

"Oh, you mean, why are they like that?"

"Yeah, pretty much."

"Well Jakob, why are people lighter skinned in places where the ultraviolet radiation is minimal all around the globe? It cannot be a coincidence, right? Excluding the more recent, mass migrations of peoples, all the races are in the optimal place for UV exposure from the sun. Melatonin, the stuff that makes you tan, acts as a regulator to the sun – some people have more than others. The same thing applies here, of course."

"Yeah, but that takes thousands of years to occur and," Jakob stopped mid-sentence. "People have been here that long?"

"That's a bit more complicated but let me give you the short story, ok? People have been living here," the Professor pointed toward the ground underneath him, "in this mountain range for almost 500 years."

"Ok, and for how long before that?"

"We don't know."

"You don't know?" Jakob quickly shot back. "What do you mean you don't *know?*"

"I mean exactly that, we don't know. All of the records that predated that period were destroyed. The history is very fuzzy, but what we do know is that a huge influx of people began leaving Europe and coming here to escape the mental oppression that was taking place at that time in the form of witch hunts, inquisitions, and so forth. While many of the immigrants were fairly enlightened they still managed to bring a lot of their, shall we say, mental baggage with them. This created huge societal problems and our entire system consequently became imbalanced. This is why we carefully select our immigrants now. In the end there was some sort of uprising and all of the historical records were destroyed. Some claim they were purposefully destroyed by the leadership while others say it was the act of a lone perpetrator."

"Interesting. So I guess the gray people's ancestors were here for much longer than yours, huh?"

"Well . . . . at the same time most of us are mixed in some form or another. The traits for the gray people are extremely recessive, even more so than Caucasian, so even if you're half gray you would most likely still look white."

"So you're part. . . . . gray?" Jakob hesitantly inquired.

"I'm a quarter gray and the rest European."

"This is an interesting place Professor. Unbelievable," he said gazing again across the interior of the mountain range.

"Let's say we get going," the Professor prepared to stand up, "Kralsich is waiting to explain some important things to you."

"What does he do exactly?"

"Right now he is a Prognosticator but very soon he'll become the new Chairman. And Jakob. . . . he's *very* interested in you."

"Really? He is, huh?" Jakob sometimes wondered why *he'd* been chosen over so many other people to be here in this place. He was fairly certain that having a reasoned, open mind was the explanation, but even still, he was unsure. Maybe someone like Kralsich could give him some more answers.

"Definitely. We're supposed to go and meet him. We've been invited to his residence. This is most unusual for such a private man."

"Lead the way," Jakob said as they got up from their chairs. The Professor motioned his hand toward the exit and they left.

* * *

‖ 25 ‖

Herschel rolled over in bed to get closer to the phone; consciousness only partially filled his mind.

"Hello?" He said instinctively after pressing the answer button on his cell phone in an attempt, not to talk, but rather simply to shut the blaring ringer off.

"Herschel! Wake up! We've got a situation." Roger matter-of-factly shot backed on the other end.

"What. . . . . what is it?" he replied now sitting up as adrenalin substituted his usual caffeine fix.

"The satellite has gone haywire. . . . . it was like. . . . . at first, the thing lit up like a damn Christmas tree and then all of the sudden. . . . boom. Dead, silence, *nothing*. I don't know what the hell's wrong with it. We need your help. . . . . *now*." The urgency in his voice was beyond obvious.

"Roger. I'm in DC and it's the middle of the night. What the hell do you expect me to do?"

"I expect you to get your ass to the airport. Your flight leaves in less than two hours. It's the redeye."

"Aghhh. Alright," he rubbed his eyes knowing he wasn't going back to bed. "I'm on my way. You bastards at Cosgrove owe me for this one."

"Don't worry. The company sprung for a first class ticket. Just don't drink too much, ok?"

"Roger, you're ridiculous," he hung up the phone and started packing his things.

* * *

26

Professor Briarton stared at the door of Kralsich's apartment which was two floors off the base of the mountain. For some reason both of them were a bit hesitant.

"Well," the Professor said resolutely, "here we are. This is Kralsich's apartment."

"Should I ring the doorbell?" Jakob asked.

"Please do," the Professor gestured his right hand toward the door. Jakob's reached out and pushed the button sending a relaxing, low pitch chiming noise reverberating through the door in front of him. Within three seconds it quickly slid open and a towering, gray silhouette appeared before them.

"Ahh, you've arrived. I've been expecting you . . . . . please. . . . . come in," Kralsich, donning a flowing red and gray robe, turned, leading the two men into his home. The apartment was filled with antiques from all around the world and rather than being modern and svelte like the other Arkonsian places he had seen, Kralsich's home was dimly lit and ancient looking. Of particular interest was the Egyptian, Greek and Babylonian statues as well as the unrecognizable inscriptions which adorned the walls.

Jakob spoke, hoping to sound intelligent, "I see you have a huge selection of statues from various civilizations' mythology." Kralsich continued walking them into the apartment. He turned and met eyes with Jakob as he replied.

"Perhaps in a thousand years people will study your history and religion and call it *myth*. . . ology," Kralsich smiled while Jakob stayed silent, suddenly feeling intimidated with whom he was conversing. The three men made their way to the back of the calming apartment and each took a seat in their own darkly plush, slightly reclining chairs. All surrounding an ancient stone table, Jakob wondered if Kralsich purposely prepared the chairs to form the perfect Pythagorean triangle in which they were currently sitting.

In the far back area of the apartment, was one unfinished wall which appeared to simply be the slanting side of the mountain. Most peculiar was a large jagged crystal jutting out of it. It was about the size of a large dog, and it seemed to be naturally occurring within the rock.

Upon noticing Jakob's interest in it, Kralsich commented.

"It's extraordinary, wouldn't you say?"

"What is it?"

"A few miles below us lay a complex cave system which in its expansiveness stretches on for hundreds of miles. This massive geological wonder, which we call The Great Cavern, consists exclusively of crystals which look exactly like the one on that wall. In fact, Jakob, this is the highest point of the crystal structure – it connects to the entire cave system."

"That's incredible," Jakob was wide eyed with excitement.

"Perhaps we'll travel there one day . . . . together." Kralsich exuded a pleasant demeanor, happy to lock eyes with Jakob in mutual anticipation. Jakob continued to stare at the crystal structure and when he thought he saw a flash of light emanate there from, he quickly spoke in response.

"Did you *see that?!?*" He pointed at the wall. "It lit up for just a second."

"Hahaha, ahh yes Jakob. They're interconnected crystals. Shining a flashlight hundreds of miles away could light up this very crystal here in the room. There are probably several groups touring the caves as we speak, each with their own flashlights. *Incredible* is it not?" Professor Briarton and Jakob shook their heads up in down in affirmation.

"So gentlemen, here we are," Kralsich began, pausing to take a small sip of tea and motioning to the other men to try theirs. Jakob carefully grasped the delicate cup and brought it up to his lips to sample the tea, however the liquid was far too hot to consume at this time. Jakob's mind began to precipitously wonder. *That means he must have just poured the tea at the exact moment before I rang the doorbell. . . . . but we were 15 minutes early; how did he know when we were coming?* Jakob pushed the thought aside for the moment being quite focused on the coming conversation. He placed the tea cup back onto the intricately designed Chinese saucer and met eyes with Kralsich.

"I'm not going to waste your time gentlemen, therefore we're going to move onto the topic at hand and dispense with the normal pleasantries as I'm quite sure you've had a pleasant stay thus far Jakob. Your mind has now acclimated to its new surroundings and I'm certain you must be wondering why you've been brought to this very, *very* special place," Kralsich's arms opened wide somehow motioning not only to his apartment but in addition the entire Arkonsian civilization. "I formally apologize for the manner in which you were brought here. We always find it unpleasant to force individuals to do things; however in your case we believed that you would have chosen this path regardless, thus justifying our actions. Is this a correct assessment?" Professor Briarton and Jakob sat attentive and silent listening to Kralsich's voice, along with his presence, resonate throughout the apartment.

"Yes. I would have come here anyway, but I'm sure there would have been a lot of hesitation. I may have wanted to say good bye to some people or bring a bunch of stuff that I really didn't need anyway. All of that seems like it's a world away from me. I mean. . . . . that stuff that I had. . . . . clothes, shoes, awards, posters, and pictures. . . . . I used to think that they defined who I am. But now. . . . . what I *believe* defines who I am – not the stuff I have," Jakob answered confidently.

"Magnanimous. It seems as though you've traded in your consumerism for intellectualism – something with which I believe will help your soul excel. Jakob," Kralsich leaned forward over the table to bring his hauntingly passionate eyes closer to Jakob's before he spoke, "what I'm about to tell you could shock you, or it could infuriate you, or it could convict you. Before I begin, I'm going to tell you, why *you,* Jakob Vanden, were chosen to be here.

"You may or may not be aware that our civilization has helped myriad scientists, tradesmen, philosophers, sociologists and so on and so forth, escape the clutches of the intellectually isolated Old World in order to come here, to this place." Kralsich's hands were folded in front of him, occasionally motioning during the conversation for effect as he continued.

"The methods we use to verify their supposed legitimacy are not unlike your relationship with the Professor here. Deep conversations, shocking epiphanies, eloquent allegories are all techniques we employ to help your development as well as to test your tolerance for those things with which you may not feel comfortable processing. As you've learned already these techniques are of *vital* importance because of the magnitude of layered lies which your mind perceives, excuse me, *used* to perceive as reality.

"What we rarely do, in fact, is bring college students back to Arkonos - irrespective of their intellectual development. Every once in a great, *great* while, one of our Enlighteners, like Professor Briarton, will come across a legitimate genius. These are your Einsteins, Edisons, Mozarts, Hawkings – you're probably familiar with the type. And you Jakob, as you already know, are not like those people. Your future could be incredible and your achievements more stupendous than those men I just named; however, you are not them. You knew that already – so this comes as no surprise." While Jakob was aware of this, that did not mean he needed Kralsich to tell him in front of his mentor. Jakob tried to shake the feelings of pride out of his mind before he responded but could not accomplish it succinctly.

"So *why did* you bring me here!?" He called out.

"There are a number of converging reasons why you're here Jakob. One of those is that you have a desire and will to understand and contemplate the truth. When you see the world move around in a way which obviously looks unnatural, your mind gravitates to reasoning and truth rather than clutching onto accepted beliefs and propaganda. I'll put it this way: When an apple falls off a tree, we know, due to gravity, it should fall in a straight line to the ground below. In the Old World apples fall constantly but very few actually move straight down. The majority zig and zag and go about unnaturally before finally hitting the dirt. That means that even though we cannot actually *see* the obstacles which are in the *way* of the apple, we still know they exist. When this situation befalls most people they believe that their eyes have played a trick on them! Or they believe that the apple has *always* fallen in a zig-zag pattern!

"You on the other hand, Jakob, you seek out the obstacle, consequently realizing that an invisible hand has been at work behind the scenes. Your critical mind is acutely aware of its purpose, and your senses and intellect are not as dulled from malnutrition and food pollutants which make seemingly intelligent men think zig-zag patterns are straight.

"However, don't misunderstand me – you are not alone. There are many who have open minds when they are younger as you are now, but the enveloping nature of your society, in large part by a neo-feudalistic system which indebts the unborn, leads most of these semi-enlightened to trade what they know to be fact for what they falsely call 'life'. A marriage, mortgage, and few children will soon be the impetus for seemingly rational people to put aside their 'college-aged fantasies' of a better world and trade them in for working at a company which they know is bringing the world system quicker to collapse. Some rationalize the situation by using such wonderful phrases like 'it's just the world we live in', or 'I'm just trying to make ends meet'. Others refuse to acknowledge the truth by erecting barriers which they call nationalism or religion. Many simply escape into sports, celebrities, shopping, hunting or whatever else they can do to obliterate the truth, if even for a few minutes. And yet it remains, the truth, eating them up inside like parasitic protozoan gnawing on the inside lining of the heart, ravenous with hunger. When the pain of the truth again surfaces, most of these people more *ardently* rationalize, descend *deeper* into their escape, or erect *higher* barriers." Kralsich leaned back in his seat and began to speak in a more soothing voice.

"In this current era, it is most evident in veterans of World War I. The men who fought in this pointless conflict are in their nineties and beyond by now. Ripened with age one would believe that with all the things they've seen these men would be like fruit from the tree of knowledge – ripe for the picking! But alas, something else is unfortunately the case. Many of these men still believe that the 'Great War' was not only heroic but also *relevant*. Even though the modern era has exposed the absurdity of not only the start of the war but also the way in which it was fought (calvary marching at machine guns) and wrought with mis/disinformation, these men still maintain they 'served to protect liberty'. They effortlessly regurgitate the same propaganda which was used to roos them into the trench warfare conflict - if they weren't drafted - while men three times their age ruthlessly moved them around like pieces on a board game. Why is this? Why haven't these men reflected upon the meaning of life, central bank funded war and Machiavellian governments?

"The reason, Jakob, is that these men are no different than the hoards of black suits out there that will not admit that something is amiss!!" Kralsich threw is arms in the air and his voice was strained with enthusiasm. "These people, when told that a company is involved in heinous activities simply say – consciously or *un* - 'shhhh, I've got stock in that company through my 401k'! Or they quickly realize how interdependent their place of employment is to the possibly evil firm. *They* begin to shudder to think of their lives without all of their 'stuff' and methods of escape. The reality is that they wouldn't need all that '*stuff*' and escapes if they had simply confronted the problem rather than slithering away in craven escape! So you see . . . . . this is a perpetual motion machine, which is seemingly perfectly designed to keep any and all people in."

The supposed future Chairman sat straight up in his chair and brought together all eight fingers and two thumbs to his face, just *barely* touching the corresponding digits to each other. After looking over at Professor Briarton, Kralsich then stared at Jakob and waited for a response.

"And that's only the educated," Jakob agreed. "The uneducated and poor are kept so busy trying to feed and cloth themselves in this. . . . . what was it that you said. . . . . neo-feudalistic system, that they never have the time to think about anything else."

"A good point. Could you give an example of what you mean?" Kralsich quickly responded in an effort to test the young man.

"Well," Jakob contemplated his answer, ". . . . . it's like a lot of these people have taxes imposed upon them or have governmental debt incurred before they were even born! In essence this was one of the main grievances against the British during the Revolutionary War – no taxation without representation. Do my parents or grandparents count as representation? I think not. The poor falsely believe that they don't have to pay taxes. Many of the lowest wage earners even believe that they receive money from the government. *Nothing* could be further from the truth.

"For example: when people rent an apartment or house they believe that they don't pay property tax, but the truth is vastly different. A land owner naturally includes any property tax into the price of the rent, just as a soft drink manufacturer also transfers the corporate tax onto the consumer. Even still most people are blindly fooled when they see the 7% sales tax on an item and believe that is full amount of the tax. The reality is tax collectors *love* it when companies transfer it onto the people! What I mean is that it's a percentage tax attached to a pre-existing tax you don't see. *It's a tax on a tax.* This unnoticed scam goes into virtually every consumer product on the market.

"Inflation is another rather insidious way to tax the unsuspecting citizen. Who would vote for a politician that vowed to raise taxes on the poor??!? On the other hand a politician, who vows to increase social programs and welfare benefits, would garner huge favor from their electorate. Nevertheless, because government cannot create real wealth, they must print and borrow the money to pay for the new social extravagances. As they do so a larger amount of money will begin to chase the same amount of real things thus leading to what most economists call inflation. Prices will rise and when they do rise who will pay the most? For those who don't earn much income, a 10% increase in the price of food, for instance, would be devastating. On the other hand, a middle or upper class person may not even notice the increases, because when looked at in proportion to their income, the amount is too small.[13]

"So while you talked about college students who realize the truth but put it aside for various reasons, I'm talking about the other side of the equation – the poor. Because of the nastiness of inflation and taxes (really one in the same) they don't have the time to take a deep breath and view the world for what it really is." Letting out a sigh and feeling confident Jakob awaited Kralsich's response. A few moments went by while the imposing, gray skinned man waited for the precise timing to deliver his comments.

"Magnanimous, Jakob. I've heard from my colleague, Professor Briarton that you were brilliant as well as sharp, and both of those wonderful traits have subsumed your intellect. Wouldn't you agree Professor Briarton?" He turned to the Professor who had thus far remained in silence, hoping, with mental fingers crossed that Jakob would impress.

"I would have to agree. Although it's really no surprise, Jakob was my most open minded student in all of my years of teaching. He has a natural contrarian spirit, which of course initiates the process of critical thinking. For many with a contrarian nature, they find the most difficulty in turning it off. Even when truth and reason are in front of them they instantly react against the issue, unaware that this is simply a personality

---

[13] Hazlitt, Henry, *Economics in One Lesson: The Shortest and Surest Way to Understand Basic Economics*. (New York: Three Rivers Press, New York, New York, 1962).

impulse. Jakob did not have any problems turning this mental mechanism off when he was presented with truth. That was my one concern with him, and it has slowly been alleviated as far as I can tell." Jakob felt his endorphins surge on such solid praise from his mentor.

"Well then Jakob," Kralsich continued, "back to the topic at hand. While your open-mindedness was a prerequisite to you coming to this place it was not by any means the only reason we chose you. As you may or may not be aware your father, Roger Vanden, works for a company called Cosgrove Strategies. Were you aware of that Jakob?" He asked the question calculatedly and awaited a precise response.

"Umm. . . . . well I knew he did some kind of government work tracking terrorists and criminals, but I didn't know the name of the company because he never told me," he made quick eye contact with Professor Briarton before again locking pupils with Kralsich.

"Alright, well Jakob let me tell you something about that company . . . . . they have one directive - find us," he leaned toward the younger man, "and *destroy* us. You see . . . . . from their perspective, they too have noticed that the apple is not falling in a straight line to the ground but rather in an odd zig-zag pattern. What's causing the apple's odd movements? We are, *Arkonos*," he folded his arms and raised an eyebrow. "We've been seeking to positively influence the world throughout the centuries, albeit with limited results.

"Nonetheless, they have noticed us. They've noticed the occasional people who simply stopped whatever work it is that they were doing and disappeared; they've seen writers, musicians, scientists, workers and all people influenced by our teachings; and they've tracked us down like dogs. . . . . and killed us." Kralsich's face grew cold and serious.

"I didn't know he was involved in anything like that. He always said he wasn't allowed to tell us . . . . . and now I see why," he cradled his chin in concern.

"Don't misunderstand me Jakob, I'm not trying to say that your father is mal-intentioned – quite the contrary in fact. Your father, and others like him, believes he is saving the world and protecting the innocent. He doesn't realize that the very people he has been tracking down the majority of his life are actually trying to help him. Jakob, do you believe if he knew what we were doing here . . . . . that he would embrace us?" Kralsich asked Jakob as Professor Briarton turned his head and looked at his pupil.

"I think he'd never believe you. Even if you brought him here and *showed* him this incredible place he would still think that you were simply trying to deceive him, and wonder what your ulterior motives were."

"Can't teach an old dog new tricks," Professor Briarton said and smiled trying to lighten the room up a bit.

"Understood," Kralsich said and forced a smile before he continued, "once the mind is closed so tightly it is difficult to reopen, that part of your expression I agree with. However, a mind that has never been closed to new possibilities and thoughts can be quite old, and I assure you they *can* learn new tricks!" Kralsich attempted his own wit in reciprocation of his old friend, and all three men chuckled, clearing a pessimistic mood from the conversation.

"Yeah, but seriously I think my father may be unreachable. The only people he'll take any advice from are his colleagues at Cosgrove, and you see what they've got him doing! If I told him what I was doing right now he'd probably have me committed." Jakob reached forward and lifted his cup off the saucer to try his tea again.

"That is what I assumed you'd say unfortunately," Kralsich commented.

"The only other person who could reach him would be my mom or little brother, but the truth is he's encouraged them to pharmaceutically escape, rendering my own mother unreachable. Rather than becoming upset with what she knows is going on around her, she's become even more content in her situation."

"Your father has erected quite a few of his own mental barriers as well, I'm sure. He's is completely encapsulated, Jakob. . . . . completely." Kralsich slowly folded his arms across his chest, making eye contact with the other two gentlemen as well as the crystal jutting out of his back wall before continuing.

"Jakob, if the situation would arise where we would need you to contact your father. . . . . would you be inclined to do so?"

"I think so. . . . . what exactly do you want me to ask him?"

"The truth is, you are about to have to make some very difficult decisions in the near future. These decisions will surely change the course of your entire life because their consequences cannot be reversed. Will you do so only tepidly? Will you take a piece meal approach by only making *some* of the fractious decisions while leaving others to languish until they ultimately are made through the expiration of time? *OR*," Kralsich jumped up from his chair and looked down at Jakob as he spoke forcefully, *"will you ACT on your convictions and DO what you know will support truth and reason!"* He sat down again, regaining his composure after what was definitely an unusual outburst for a man of Kralsich's stature. Professor Briarton looked over at him in surprise and waited for Jakob to reply.

"You want me to be a spy *don't you*? You want me to deceive my own father in order to further whatever it is you're planning on doing. Well. . . . . I'll use your own reasoning against you, *Kralsich*," Jakob leaned forward and pointed his finger around the room as he went on. "Before I'll commit to doing *anything* for *anybody* I want to know what hell is going on here. What are you planning to do?!?" Jakob was tired of sitting on the sidelines just happy to be here. He'd slowly become aware that this wasn't some kind of vacation – he had been brought to this place for a reason and it was time to find out what that was.

"That is a reasonable enough request. Let's start with saying that the world is about to change."

"What's about to change?" He asked questioningly.

"Everything." Kralsich said succinctly looking off to the side at a clock on the wall. "I'll explain much of what you want to know in two hours. Will you meet me at Rosario's Café then?" Professor Briarton and Jakob looked at each other, puzzled at the sudden abruptness from Kralsich.

"Sure, that sounds good. . . . . two hours in that case," Jakob quickly replied. Kralsich stood up and the other men quickly followed suit.

"Till then, gentlemen," Kralsich said, remaining in the apartment while the other men exited. With the door closed Kralsich lumbered over to his back wall where the impressive crystal was exposed from the rocky surface. His gaze penetrated the opaque structure and he laid all of his wispy gray fingers on its smooth surface. He slowly closed his eyes and waited.

* * *

‖ 27 ‖

"Sir," Agent Roger Vanden's phone blared, "there's a Dr. Herschel Bohr here to see you."

"It's about damn time . . . . . send him in," he replied hastily.

Within moments Herschel craned his head around Roger's half-opened door and obligatorily knocked.

"Herschel, nice to see you could grace us with your presence."

"Roger, it's 8:45 a.m. and I've already flown from my warm bed in DC to here. I had men in black suits escorting me to the airport. What the hell is going on?" Herschel managed to squeeze a smile in for his old friend while still remaining visibly agitated.

"I'll explain everything in just a second, would ya close the damn door before you go all ape-shit on me!"

"Yeah, yeah," he apologetically nodded his head as he reached for it, "didn't mean anything. Sorry about that." The solid oak door quietly latched shut.

"It's fine, please have a seat. You want some coffee or anything before we go into this? I didn't mean to rush you, but we do have a *bit* of a situation on our hands, that's all." Roger slowly took a deep breath and just as slowly let it out, calming his nerves.

"No, I'm fine. Had some on the plane actually . . . . . let's get down to business."

"Alright, Herschel - listen up. The word is that a *lot* of people in DC have been briefed on what is going on with our Quantum Detectors. We've got huge ownership in this gadget and this is one *hell* of an oddity. What have you heard so far?"

"What have I *heard*?" Herschel shook his head in curiosity of the question. "I've only heard what *you've* told me. Why would you ask that?"

"I didn't know if you had an extrinsic source briefing you on the matter."

"*Extrinsic source?!?* Roger, I'm a scientist. I'm really not sure what's going on here, so could *you* do *me* a favor and explain exactly where we're at right now with this thing." His eyes widened to proportions which were only dwarfed by the mystery of the situation.

"Alright," Roger shook his head up and down, again realizing that Herschel was not familiar with active, operational missions like he was. He continued in the framework of a typical briefing, although the content was anything but *typical*. "Here's what happened. Yesterday morning it looked like your quantum detecting satellite went on the blink. Quite unexpectedly within minutes of each other *all* of the Quantum Bursts we had detected disappeared. Poof. Nada. Just like that they were all gone. What you have to realize Herschel, is how many eyes have been watching that data. Ever since the cat has been out of the bag on this thing, a *lot* of intelligence insiders have been enthralled with that little shoe box sized piece of equipment floating around. There's no doubt that defense analysts are producing papers, at *this* very moment, that are linking these Quantum Bursts with every unexplained event that's happened in the last seventy or so years."

"So basically," Herschel paused for a moment as the scale of his invention was beginning to come into full view, "they're looking at this thing like it could be the puzzle piece that makes *all* of these disparate events suddenly make sense."

"Exactly. So, out of the blue, when the screen went blank, my phone started ringing off the hook. Hell, just to give you an idea how big this thing has become some big shot general put all of our nukes on *standby*. Do you hear what I'm saying?!?"

"Yeah, yeah. . . . . ok. I got it." Herschel sat up a little straighter and stiffened his posture, now realizing the seriousness of the situation.

"The strange thing was that after the screen went black we detected two other signals. The first signal would pop on and off momentarily in DC. Sometime in the afternoon we detected a second signal in Athens, Georgia."

"Did you ever detect these two signals at the same time?" Herschel quickly asked.

"No, we did not."

"So, the only two signals which have appeared since the others stopped emitting have *not* occurred at the same time?"

"Right, exactly." Roger replied slightly frustrated.

"Sorry, I was just making sure that's what you meant. In that case I would presume that these two separate signals are being produced by the same device."

"How can you be so sure?"

"Because Roger, I believe that whoever these people are, they know they've been detected. Think about it. If you designed a secret communication device that *no* one else should be able to detect or hack into, you would want to know when someone else has actually detected you, right?"

"I guess. . . . . yeah. . . . . you're right."

"I'm guessing because my satellite detector was so low powered and far away that we didn't trip any of *their* internal detection devices. No, no," he looked around the room as if he could simply pull the answers to this puzzle from the walls, "they didn't know then. *That's it!* Think about it. . . . . within twenty-four hours of you detecting Professor Briarton, virtually the whole thing shuts down, right?"

"Yeah. . . . . I'm listening."

"So, let's examine this for a second, ok?" Herschel frantically looked around, his brow arching with inquisitiveness, and quickly arose from his seat, shuffling toward the dry-erase board. He hastily sketched out a rough timeline.

"Alright. Let's start this out with you detecting Professor Briarton, ok, now directly afterwards he suddenly goes AWOL – with your son I might add."

"I'm *aware* of *that*," veins on Roger's forehead pulsated and his knuckles grew white as he growled through clinched teeth.

"So," Herschel continued, "after you detected him he skips the country. Gone. Disappeared. That's obviously no coincidence right?" Herschel continued drawing on the board as he passionately summarized the situation to Roger. "And," he literally drew a line connecting the dots on the dry erase board, "it's also no coincidence that within twenty-four hours after originally detecting the Professor, almost all the Quantum Bursts disappeared."

"Except for the signals in DC and now Athens, Georgia, right. Go on," he said.

"Roger, this reeks of some kind of huge conspiratorial network of individuals. Think about it . . . . . in a web of spies like this you'd be damn sure that they've also got somebody way high up in the government. That person, whoever they are, would be much more likely to communicate with their home base than some lower level lackey who on the other hand could easily disappear."

"I see what you're saying," Roger said as he picked up his phone and punched a button. "Denise?"

"Yes sir," her soft voice blared through the speaker phone.

"I need you to do a check on any high profile figures that have recently flown from Washington DC to Athens, Georgia."

"Sir. . . . . I don't need to do a check for that. Senator Langesé is speaking about the Stakz epidemic there later this afternoon. It's so horrible about all those kids. . . . . just horrible."

"Senator Langesé. Ok. Thanks Denise," Roger punched a button on the phone to end the conversation and nodded his head up and down. "First mystery solved, huh Herschel?"

"I would say so. Senator Langesé has been the token DC contrarian for years now, and although I must admit his ideas make sense, it's clear that this country has grown into something else under his nose. Yes. . . . . I'd say there is a high likelihood that he could be the spy. That means, of course, if we catch him unexpectedly we just may be able to snatch his Quantum Communicator." Herschel's face lit up with the glow of child anticipating a new toy, causing his eyebrows to dance about on his forehead.

"We're not going to be able to just walk up and accuse the Senator of being a spy Herschel! It just doesn't work like that, and besides all we have right now is a coincidence. It doesn't exactly count as evidence." Roger spoke knowing that there was also another element already working against Senator Langesé. He had heard from a friend of a friend in typical DC fashion that the Stakz problem was not at all what it seemed. While his friend did not know exactly who was behind it, he was aware of what it was intended to do. Namely it is supposed to shock the people of this country into a reinvigorated drug war and expose all of those as dangerous frauds who tried to oppose the use of any new government powers. At the same time Roger was skeptical about this blatant manipulation, but understood it as possibly a necessary evil in order to rid this nation of the scourge of drugs. He did not, however, believe that Herschel was ready for this sort of knowledge and therefore concealed the truth from him.

What Roger did not need right now is the foremost quantum scientist in the world to start to question the intentions of his own government – that was for sure.

"Roger, do you know what else we haven't seen yet?"

"What?"

"If these people are receiving and sending all of these communications, why isn't their home base lit up as bright as a Christmas tree?"

"Hmmm, that's a good point. Could they be dampening the signal somehow?"

"Yeah," Herschel said, looking off into the distance in deep thought for a moment while he gently stroked his cleanly shaven chin. "They'd have to have some sort of way to block the detection of the signal without disturbing its actual transmission." Herschel's eyes got wide as an idea had just sparked in his head. "I've got it! Roger, can you pull up the satellite feed on your computer real quick?"

"I've got you one better. Flip that dry erase board over and I'll use this projector so we can *both* see it." Herschel twisted the dry erase board over and Roger quickly got the projector into position. The board lit up with a map of the world showing no Quantum Bursts whatsoever. As the map rotated around North America and then westward to Russia, Herschel noticed something in the Arctic Circle.

"What's that?" Herschel said, leaning in closer. "Can you rotate the map up toward the Arctic circle," the map rotated and there appeared to be a discoloration of some sort. "Is that coming from the projector?"

"No. . . . . I don't think so. It's definitely picking up something over there, but it doesn't look like any of the other signals we've seen. Wow. This thing is huge! It's covering almost the entire Arctic Circle and it's incredibly faint. Herschel, this must be some kind of interference or something, right? Why didn't we see this before?"

"Hmm, not sure really. Wait a second," Herschel said, stroking his chin in contemplation, "ok, I know why we didn't see this before! Roger, do you have a flashlight in your desk?"

"What?! What are you talking about," he curiously replied.

"Do you have a flashlight?!" Herschel repeated.

"Ok, ok," he reached in his bottom drawer and pulled out an elongated, black flashlight. Herschel snatched it from his hand and tested the brightness, which he found to be sufficient for his theory.

"Alright, you see this light," Herschel stood about six feet away from Roger and shone his dimly lit keychain light into his friend's eyes.

"Yeah I can see it, ok," He replied skeptically with a slanted smile.

"Ok, how about now," Herschel pointed the powerful flashlight into Roger's eyes while keeping the weaker, keychain light on as well.

"Damn that's bright. Turn it off. What the hell's your point?" Roger said frustratedly blinded.

"You noticed that whenever I turned on the much brighter light you were unable to even see my little keychain light, huh?"

"Ahhhhh. . . . . I get it. That's why we couldn't see the 'dim' Arctic Circle Quantum Burst until all of the much brighter signals had stopped emitting."

"Exactly. Now we need to figure out why there is this huge, albeit extremely weak signal covering almost the entire Arctic Circle. How are all the much brighter, regular Quantum Bursts connected to this one?"

"Maybe that's where they're being emitted from? Whoever's in charge could have some kind of base up there!"

"Yeah, but that's the thing. . . . . it should be brighter and more powerful, not weaker."

"Herschel," Roger spoke and stroked his salt and pepper, bearded face for a moment, "how does the satellite detector work. . . . . I mean what does it actually look for. And please, keep it in English, alright?"

"I'll do my best," he jokingly cleared his throat before continuing. "Basically it looks for a special electro-magnetic pulse emitted when a quantum communication is initiated. Do you remember when I explained this device to you?"

"Yeah, sure. . . . . at the bar that time."

"Good memory Roger! For a meat-head field agent. . . . . you always surprise me. Umm, well remember that you can set two atoms to be a pair, right? Then once they're paired you can take one as far away as you want, I think I said Ottawa and New York if I'm not mistaken."

"Nope. No, no, no. . . . . I remember - you said Winnipeg!" Roger was quick to point out for a victory over his old friend.

"Well, whatever. . . . . immaterial," Herschel physically shook his head at the irrelevant, if not well remembered, detail. "The paired atoms, despite the distance, can then be set to 'on' or 'off' or 'both'. Think of it in computer terms - like not only '1' and '0' but also '2', or something like that.

"What I postulated is that theoretically the device which *creates* the Quantum Communication would emit a special electro-magnetic field that is easily detectable. Quite ingenious really."

"So you're not actually 'catching the carrier pigeon, huh?" Roger asked, confident that he had reduced the thought into a manageable expression.

"Wait. . . . . what? Oh! You mean that I'm not actually detecting the quantum 'message'. . . . . I see. Yeah that's right. It's kind of like. . . . . imagine they were communicating with tin cans with strings tied to them. The difference here in the quantum world is, however, there *are* no strings attached to the cans. There's nothing to intercept – at least in our world! Remember these signals move faster than the speed of light not because they're actually traveling in the way a string travels from one tin can to the other – no, no. They move that fast because, well, frankly we don't know where they go. But we know where they end up, and that's all that's really necessary to use this technology."

"You're losing me a bit, but I think I got the gist of it anyway. Alright. So we're only detecting the energy signature of the devices."

"Yes, they emit a specific frequency that we can detect. That's right."

"And you were saying earlier that like a radio station the 'main tower' would probably be using a much stronger power source than the handheld units. Hmmm. . . . . yet, all we have is this huge blob in the Arctic Circle which is clearly much weaker than the other signals."

Herschel turned his head and looked at Roger enthusiastically in the eyes. "If this thing is really as big as it looks . . . . .I mean if this organization has thousands of operatives using advanced technology that even *we* don't know about. Then they must have an operations center and more than likely they have some sort of dampening field so that we can't detect them. Think about it!"

"You could be right Herschel, but at the same time you just named another technology we don't have – a dampening field. What are the chances that this organization has broken two technological barriers?"

"The truth is," both men's faces were cemented with seriousness, "we don't know *who* we're dealing with. But if I'm right and they are dampening their signal, then that's exactly what this could be." Herschel pointed at the massive blob of green spread out over the entirety of the Arctic Circle.

"Do you think that the dampening field is bouncing the signal from somewhere? But from where? And if they're dampening everything how is their signal getting through?"

"You really don't listen do you!? There are no strings attached to the tin cans . . . . . remember? We're only detecting the firing up of the machine that sends the signals, that's all. That signal goes somewhere (many say to another dimension) and instantly changes the atom on the other side. So in this rare case, because we're detecting the device and *not* the signal itself, you can dampen the electro-magnetic signal while causing no adverse effects to the sending of it."

"Ok, I got it this time. I still don't see how this shit *really* works . . . . . but I see the process."

"Well, good, that means you understand as much as we do!" The pair both let out a chuckle at the terrible joke which acted as at least a momentary respite from their difficult situation.

Herschel walked up to the projected image of the signal covering the top portion of the Earth like a baseball hat. He scratched his scalp in contemplation and snapped his fingers as an idea sparked through his head. "Look at how even this signal is compared to the other ones we've seen. Put the pictures side by side; I want to check something." Roger immediately began moving the pictures around and amazingly had them up within seconds. "There," he said upon completion.

"Look how the individual signals fan out like waves, much like you'd expect electro-magnetic fields to act since everything from light, radio and electricity are all just waves. Now look here," he pointed to the evenly dispersed blob in the Arctic Circle, "it's diffused, it's completely even. It doesn't look like a wave but rather simply a flat emission of energy." He paused for a second and again scratched his head.

"Why are they so different looking?" Roger inquired.

"Hmm. . . . . that's it!" Herschel clapped his hands loud enough to make Roger momentarily jump out of his seat. "If you had a single light bulb in a room, and you thought that the light was too intensely bright what would you do?"

"I'd buy a lamp shade I guess."

"Exactly! And then the light would disperse evenly throughout the room after the light went *through* the shade."

"Ahhhh. . . . . I see what you're saying. You think that the energy signature is going *through* something and is then getting dispersed evenly thus creating this huge blob."

"Right," Herschel walked over to his old friend's desk and picked up a globe.

"Careful with that – I've had it since I was a kid!"

"Don't worry, I wouldn't dare drop it," he said motioning toward the North Pole with his hand. "If the dispersed signal is emanating from here, then the material it's going through must be the solid rock of the Earth making it very likely that the original signal is being produced down *here*," Herschel's finger struck Antarctica making a slight tapping noise in the process.

"Seriously. Their base is in Antarctica?! Oh, they're going to *love* this in DC!"

"There's no other rational explanation." He used his finger to track the signal through the globe, "The electromagnetic field they're using is probably going up, then bouncing off their damping shield, and then is somehow getting kicked through the entire planet until finally coming out into a dispersed pattern in the Arctic Circle. The truth is, whoever is behind this wouldn't have even *known* they were emitting this pattern over the Arctic Circle. Because of what I call the 'flashlight effect' there would have been virtually no way to detect the Arctic signal until the other more powerful Quantum Bursts were no longer emitting. When you think about it, we were definitely in the right place at the right time."

"You are aware this is going to be a hard sell, right?"

"That's not my job. I'm just here to figure out the science – you can handle the rest!"

"Wonderful. . .well. . .I'll get the ball rolling on tracing travel activity toward South America, South Africa and Australia, the easiest ways to get to Antarctica. What I need you to do is to write a report about everything we came up with here. Can you do that for me Herschel?"

"Not a problem. I'll make sure and use a lot of diagrams, you know, to make it easier for the field agents and all that."

"You know we appreciate it," Roger replied thankfully.

"Give me a few hours and I'll have it ready. And Roger," Herschel said in earnest. . . . .

"Yeah," Roger replied and swiveled his chair to face toward his old friend.

"We'll find Jakob, ok."

"I hope so. I really do."

* * *

‖ 28 ‖

Knowing that Rosario's Café was only about a ten minute walk from Kralsich's apartment, Professor Briarton decided to take Jakob on the scenic route in order to clear his head a little before what was sure to be an intense afternoon. They had taken the stairs a few flights down and had now begun to mingle amongst the gardens and their accompanying horticulturalists. In one area on this part of the mountain base, two smaller streams merged into one. The Professor and Jakob stopped on a large pedestrian bridge overlooking the rushing blue stream and didn't talk for several minutes.

Both men shared a common interest in silent meditation and did not feel the need to fill the air with useless conversation when so many thoughts within their heads needed pondering and reconciliation. Jakob looked over at the entrance of bridge and saw a rather attractive girl about his age approach them. Initially he thought she was simply going to walk by the two of them but then he noticed her familiar silver-green irises approaching.

"Terra? Nice seeing you here in this beautiful place today," Jakob said excitedly as the pair hugged each other. Professor Briarton suddenly looked puzzled as to how the two of them were acquainted

"Have you guys heard about Kralsich's speech?" She said in an excited, soft voice.

"Kralsich's speech?" Jakob inquired, his face looking bewildered in response.

"Yeah, it starts in about two hours and it's over that way," she responded and quickly turned her body and pointed, the moment not being lost on Jakob.

"Really?!?" Professor Briarton chimed in.

"Yeah, *really*." She handed him a flyer with all the details. "There's a map on there if you can't find your way," she said jokingly laying her slender hand on Jakob's chest and momentarily meeting eyes before smiling and going on her way. "See you there," she called back at him.

"How do you know her?" The Professor asked.

"Ahh, don't worry about it. . . . . I met her the other day," he replied. The Professor was acutely aware of their schedule thus far, but who was he to keep two young people apart. Besides that he realized that he had done quite enough spying on Jakob. He therefore moved the discussion forward.

"So that's why Kralsich sent us away so quickly," Professor Briarton muttered and brushed his hand across his forehead in contemplation. He still could not believe that Kralsich was not only giving speeches but in addition, mobilizing people to advertise for it. All of this was *extremely* unprecedented, which is what assured him that this was no ordinary speech he was about to give.

"Professor," Jakob asked after observing the worried look on his mentor's face, "what exactly do you think is going on?"

"A *lot*. A hell of a lot is going on. How 'bout we see what he has to say." The two men confidently strolled through the gardens, and steadily made their way to the destination.

Knowing that they had some time to spare before the speech, Professor Briarton took Jakob to the Old Hemlock Bar and Grill which was situated just off the walking path in a grove of trees near the river. They quickly found a table and ordered a few drinks, and both the men were happy to momentarily shut their brains down by escaping into the bar's flat panel TV showing the news.

The news woman on the screen appeared quite normal, like you'd see on any newscast. Sure, her simple, yet elegant light brown blouse was slightly casual. Even still the studio, set up, and production content were about the same. It was naturally told from the Arkonsian perspective which made Jakob feel strangely uncomfortable. Instinctively it seemed to him that the news casters were not on his side – whatever *that* meant. *What side AM I on? Why are there sides?* His mind raced as he momentarily felt his body panic. He soon shook the feeling and focused instead on the TV with the newscaster speaking:

"In alarming news, almost a thousand children have died over the last three days from ingesting the drug known as Stakz. According to classified memos, which our news organization has obtained through Observers, this drug was created by a convergence of government officials in order to increase the waning public support for the drug war which in turn will cease job cuts in their departments. We've obtained information from several sources substantiating that undercover government officials purposefully distributed the drug through dealers targeting primary and secondary schools.

"We now turn our attention to our correspondent in Athens, Georgia who is about to attend a press conference given by Senator Langesé. The Senator has come under *heavy* scrutiny lately due to his stance on personal liberty in relation to the school searches. Throughout the inception of the Stakz epidemic he has continued to advocate, and was successful in a multitude of states that the searches were illegal, in violation of individual liberty, and therefore must stopped. Unfortunately, the states where the Senator's arguments prevailed have more than seventy percent of the children's deaths despite their much lower per capita population.

"According to official documents those involved in the spread of Stakz were aware that only two or three doses of the drug would ultimately prove fatal to the unsuspecting user. The difference between this over dose and other drugs is that it takes a total of two to three months for the user's internal organs to completely shut down. Consequently, the first children who took Stakz a full *twelve weeks ago* are now dying.

"This has been politically damaging to say the least for Senator Langesé, and he has consequently called a press conference in an attempt to explain himself to his constituency," the screen flashed to another correspondent who was standing in a high school gymnasium. A livid crowd gathered and news anchor woman Kristen Eskandar asked, "Mark what *is* the mood there at this moment?"

"Well Kristen, one word – angry. The school gym in this small town is filled beyond capacity with hundreds of furious parents, many of whom have personally lost sons and daughters in this horrendous situation. Athens, Georgia was one of the worst hit so far and with almost two hundred children having died in the last few days here. Many are now calling it the epicenter of the Stakz epidemic. Umm," he turned his head to the side toward some men with dark suits entering the gym. "Ahh. . . . . ok, it looks like the Senator is making his way to the podium to speak. Let's listen as he begins." The boos and derogatory words were ubiquitous in the echo chamber of a gym. The stoic Secret Service agents closely flanked both sides of Senator Langesé as he ascended the speedily constructed stage and addressed the crowd.

"Ladies and Gentlemen I come before you in the direst of times. Only a few short days ago hundreds of bright, wonderful children have succumbed to the ravages of this *horrible* drug." The Senator continued to speak; his passion was felt by all in the huge gym, even still, some of the infuriated parent hurled comments at him.

"You're a murderer," a middle aged women with puffy, red eyes yelled from the back.

"You son of a bitch. . . . . you killed my boy," an auto mechanic still in his oil laden jump suit screamed at the top of his lungs. Senator Langesé vainly attempted to address the outbursts.

"Look," he faced his palms toward the crowd in an effort to calm his constituency, "I know these are very emotional times and it's normal to try and blame someone even if that means *irrationally* doing so." Now even the silent members of the crowd had begun to murmur.

"You shouldn't forget that it is whoever *created and distributed* this despicable substance that should bear the guilt. We should never indulge in placing blame on those who try to end the unconstitutional menace known as the drug war." Senator Langesé had become aware only a few days ago that the rumors were indeed true. The creation and distribution of this drug was a false flag operation (the government posing as unscrupulous drug dealers). The operation was designed at the highest levels of government to illicit three nefarious results: First, it acts as a Public Relations campaign ensuring that waning public support for the drug war is strengthened. Secondly, government and private officials who resisted law enforcement officers further encroaching on civil liberties were now made to look like fools as the body count began to *stack* up. And lastly this new, horrifying drug would be used to further justify the erosion of privacy laws in not just schools but places all over the country. The government created the problem, stoked the reaction, and would provide the solution, destroying political enemies and amassing new powers along the way.

Senator Langesé, knowing that he couldn't expose the truth about the origins of the drug, simply tried to calm the hearts and minds of the crowd. He continued to speak.

"We are *aware* of the devastation that these synthetically concocted drugs have caused. They probably would never have been developed if the now illegal, naturally occurring drugs were not prohibited in the *first place*," he threw his right arm into the air while grasping the podium with his left for effect. The Senator was aware that his comment was dangerously close to the truth and was quite purposeful in its dual meaning. He hoped that his constituency which had heard about the truth - namely that this drug was in fact part of a classified government operation - would understand what he was really trying to say. He continued when the murmurs in the crowd had subsided to a bearable level.

"These are trying times for all of us. A rapacious monster has been released on our streets and is hunting down our precious, innocent children. It's having *devastating* effects on not just our families, but how we view the place of government in our society." He paused a few moments for effect before more forcefully continuing.

"*We* must take responsibility for our children *no matter what* the circumstances. First of all we must talk to our children! Then, if their bags or rooms need to be searched, *we* must accomplish that task. *We* should be the ones going to their school unexpectedly on our lunch breaks and exposing the contents of their lockers, not some armed government agent. I know right now it seems like a good idea to cede your rights away for temporary protection from this monster, but I implore you to understand the long-term consequences of your actions. Whenever you give up your rights to another entity – you *never* get them back. But most importantly, the only ones who can truly solve a community's problem is each individual of the community doing whatever is necessary to fix it. We *will* work together to defeat this. I can promise you that. . . . . " he stopped as something jumped in his peripheral vision.

Before he could even react a bottle hurled through the air and struck him on the right shoulder. One of the two Secret Service agents valiantly dove at the perpetrator before he could toss another one. Immediately the crowd erupted in fury, their faces red and vainly with anger, they again hurled insults at the Senator while surging forward. Senator Langesé was momentarily protected by the small stage, however, even that began to give way as the angry parents were being pressed against it by the surging crowd.

Inside as well as outside the gym, crowds had gathered to the tune of thousands of people. In the parking lot Sheriffs Deputies were being overwhelmed by upset parents who weren't given access to the gym due to strictly enforced fire codes. Many of the parents had found ways to sneak in anyway, and now the gym was fifty percent *over* capacity.

As the Deputies noticed that the Senator was quickly becoming surrounded, they tried to make their way through the angry mob but to no avail. With such an extensive amount of pressure building up on the makeshift stage, it couldn't hold out for much longer.

"You lying *bastard*. . . . . my little girl is dead 'cause a *you*." A red faced frantic woman cried out.

"You ain't gettin' away with this *you piece a shit*!" Her husband in jeans and an old t-shirt angrily declared.

The other Secret Service Agent sensed the situation was rapidly spiraling out of control and signaled to the Senator that it was time to go. Senator Langesé made one last attempt to calm the crowd, "Please, ladies and gentlemen, try to maintain order. After everything else that's happened, we don't want anyone else to get needlessly hurt. *PLEASE*," just as he finished, the shrill, crisp sound of a beam of wood buckling, cracked throughout the high school gym. Senator Langesé's stage violently lurched to the side, sending him careening toward the ground and crushing some of the angry parents underneath it. Their piercing screams pumped more fuel into the rage of the crowd and several berserk fathers found themselves in sudden, close proximity to the dazed, fallen Senator.

Langesé had fallen on top of the microphone which was now jutting into his back and blaring horrible screeching noises that sounded like the metal teeth of a rake on concrete. He wobbled in an attempt to regain his footing but it was difficult because of the crowd surging back and forth. As he tried to steady himself, his eyes met those of a man with a long, dark beard whose face was red and puffy from sobbing. Upon seeing the Senator enfeebled on the ground his look of sorrow began to turn to agitation and then to full, fiery rage. Senator Langesé noticed he was clutching a picture of a child in his shaking, white-knuckled right hand. In a flash his rage exploded as his fist violently descended on the helpless Senator sending blood streaming out of his mangled face which doused the crowd around him. Another man, his anger now turning into frenzy upon the sight of the crimson liquid, stomped the Senator's face with his steel-toed work boot, rending his body limp with unconsciousness. All the while the ghastly cries of the Senator were being amplified through the speakers for all to hear.

The camera angle from the bleachers made it difficult to say what happened next. It appeared that a few people attempted to bring order to the situation by trying to protect the injured Senator but they too felt the brunt of the mobs fury. Soon a few gunshots were heard in an attempt by the Sheriff's deputies to disperse the crowd. Although they did in fact begin to run frantically away from the scene of the crime, leaving three or four bloody corpses in their wake, the damage was already done.

Jakob, Professor Briarton and a quickly gathering crowd, stared at the screen in unmitigated horror.

"Oh my God," Jakob said as sheer revulsion and shock cemented into his expression. Whispers and gasps wafted around the Old Hemlock Bar, while all conversations and enjoyment abruptly ceased as the scene unfolded.

By this time the Arkonsian reporter and his camera man were beginning to panic too as the infuriated mob was running around attacking everything in sight like angry ants that had just gotten their mound kicked. Undoubtedly every Old World network had cut to commercial as the gruesome public spectacle took place. The news here was different. Apparently they showed all the violence and grisly scenes which play out on the stages of politics and war. The mindset was that reality should shock you more than fiction in order to have a proper effect, and there was no doubt that had worked.

"He's dead isn't he?" Jakob turned to the Professor and asked.

"Yeah," he turned and looked at his pupil empathically, "there's no doubt about that."

* * *

"Jakob," Professor Briarton twisted his neck in order to face the young man, "there's something I have to tell you." Neither Jakob nor Professor Briarton were sure why they were walking at such a fast pace through the hemlock forest. As Jakob said nothing in response to the Professor's statement, a small flock of dull brown birds with bright orange markings fluttered by overhead.

"Look, Jakob. Hey! Slow down for a second." He reached his arm forward and grabbed Jakob's shoulder in an effort to impede his pace. "Hey . . . . . let's stop for a second, ok?" He finally succumb to the Professor's wishes and managed to get his flight response in check long enough to slow down.

"I. . . . . I just can't believe they just mobbed him like that," he said slowly, shaking his head in disgusted outrage.

"Jakob," Professor Briarton forcefully grabbed the sides of his shoulders, physically shaking the impressionable man out of his daze, "there's *more*. Look I haven't always been that forth coming with you about everything."

Jakob whipped his head back quickly, conveying some of the emotion from the dastardly act he had just witnessed.

"*Hey*, this isn't a joke. Listen up. . . . . I don't always have moments of absolute candor but this is one of them. He was. . . . . " the Professor's voice trailed off.

"He was what?" Jakob inquired, his face rumpled with concern.

"Senator Langesé. . . . . . he was my brother."

"I'm so sorry," he said softly.

"It doesn't matter now anyway – I'll never get to pay him back for saving me." Professor Briarton's eyes welled up with tears at the thought of their Amazonian crash landing.

"I had no idea you were brothers."

"How could you have? We kept it secret so that nothing would happen to the other one in case somebody got caught. I just can't believe he's gone," he placed his palm on his forehead and closed his eyes. Both men stood there in the peaceful forest for a few moments of contemplation before Professor Briarton finally broke the silence.

"Jakob,"

"Yeah,"

"There's more I have to tell you. Look. . . . I know you understand our methods aren't always perfect. I did not want to drug you or record our conversations for inspection. Yes we've kept secrets from you; that's for sure. But we've always had altruistic intentions and done the best we could. You *know* that don't you!?" Even though the Professor was asking a question a small sliver of his voice was also pleading for forgiveness.

"Yeah, I guess." He said seriously enough to be believed without adding anything extra. The truth was Jakob's mind was overloaded by not only the haunting attack on Senator Langesé but also the revealingly strange morning spent with Kralsich. He tried to get his thoughts in order before the Professor continued.

"Jakob, as you already know, Kralsich is a Prognosticator which means he regularly predicts the future. You may or may not know that his predictions have been *incredibly* accurate. He predicted that our Quantum Communicators would be detected and that you would be ready to come here. Those are only a few of his astounding Prognostications whose accuracy seems to defy what we thought was a random reality. "

"Oh my God, that's it! That's why the tea was already so scolding hot. He knew we were coming!"

"No. . . . . it doesn't work like that. He's not a psychic or anything like you mean. He works in probabilities . . . . . it's his proficiency in a multitude of subjects that makes him able to Prognosticate."

"Professor," he spoke more confidently with coinciding candor, "my mom has been making me hot tea for a *very* long time. So I *know* how long tea stays hot enough to burn your tongue like that. How did Kralsich know to pour it *right* before we came? We were fifteen minutes early!"

"It could just be a coincidence. Maybe he was getting everything ready for us and he poured the tea early so it would be cool enough for us to drink," the Professor debated back.

"Maybe..." His word trailed off.

"Well, either way you choose to believe is up to you, we don't have the time to debate this. But one thing is for sure . . . he's definitely not done with his predictions."

"Really? What do you mean?

"You need to understand that some Prognostications that he makes aren't public. Without going *über* -political on you, the Council of Many deems some of these as, well, I guess you would call it 'top-secret'. Normally I wouldn't ever hear about any of these but we are not in normal times, so some people have begun to talk. Kralsich has only been wrong *twice* in his entire life. Both of his False Prognostications occurred in the first year of his career and both were about trivial matters relative to the high level on which he works today. This means that he hasn't been wrong in over a decade . . . . . in over a *decade* Jakob."

"So do you know some of these . . . . . *Prognostications*?"

"I've heard a few things from a few old friends I knew from my youth. And I have to level with you Jakob . . . . I really don't know where to start with all of this."

"Just say it Professor . . . . look around you! If I've been able to deal with all of this," he waved his hand toward the peaks of the mountains, "then I'm sure whatever you've got can't be that bad."

"Alight," the Professor nodded his head up and down in contemplation, "here goes: Kralsich has predicted that everyone in Arkonos will be annihilated if we don't act."

"Annihilated?!? By who?"

"By the Old World."

"Why would they do that?"

"Jakob, they've already detected us! What do you think they'll do when they find out we've had spies among them for centuries?!?! Think back over everything you've learned in the last few months; do you seriously think they'll just give us a free pass, or do you think they'll want to try out some of their new fancy weapons on us? Because I can gauran-fucking-teeya you Jakob," his face was flush red with anger, "I *WILL NOT* be taken captive by those people . . . . . you don't even want to know what they really do to you." Professor Briarton was shaking with fright; his mind was clearly off in some old, horrible place.

"Ok, what else did he predict? What was that part about 'if we don't act'?" Jakob responded with his composure in far better condition than his supposed mentor.

"In reality Kralsich's Prognostications are a call to action. You see, after a respected Prognosticator makes a prediction, they join the Council of Many and the Chairman to craft a Plan of Action. If his Prognostication proves to be true than the Chairman is required by law to carry-out this so called Plan of Action.

"Well, what happens next?"

"Once a 'top-secret' Prognostication proves correct, the *corresponding* top-secret Plan of Action must be released for all to see. Through what I've gathered from my old friends one of Kralsich's latest Prognostications has just come true."

"Which one?" Jakob asked with concern.

"Nine years ago he predicted that Senator Langesé would be murdered in the exact month and year in which it happened."

"That is *extremely* accurate Professor. You really think he could have done that by chance?"

"What exactly are you implying?"

"I'm not sure to be honest with you. . . .I just don't think he's relying strictly on probabilities to do what he's doing . . . . . *that's* all," Jakob finished with his face locked in a hardened stare.

"Well, however he's doing it now there's a Plan of Action that he must release. I've heard rumors about what he's planning . . . . . it's just," he hesitated for a second and immediately turned away, breaking their steadfast eye contact.

"What have you *heard*?" Now it was Jakob who was confronting the enfeebled Professor, reaching down to grab his shoulders.

"*Fine*," the Professor strafed his sturdy frame from Jakob's entanglement. "Look, I just don't know . . . . Kralsich is never wrong. . . . and this prediction . . . . . it's just," he muttered while shaking his head and staring at the ground before him.

"*Just* say it, please!" Jakob's face turned fiery red as his voice level was elevated to an emotional shout.

"*Ok, ok*. . . . " Professor Briarton met eyes with his pupil in front of him and said, "All the governments of the world will be toppled . . . . . and you're the one who's going to do it."

* * *

‖ 29 ‖

Still in shock from what they had just witnessed on the news and in conversation, the two men nevertheless continued toward their destination. Rosario's Café was on the third floor above the mountain base and was slightly jutted into a corner. This forced Jakob and Professor Briarton to make their way through the quickly funneling crowd. To the Professor's surprise thousands of people had already gathered and were murmuring with anticipation.

After climbing the stairs to the third floor, they walked down a windowed corridor giving them better a vantage point from which to view the swelling number of people here to see Kralsich's speech. The Professor had been extremely inaccurate at gauging the mass of people. He thought when he was on the ground floor, that the crowd was limited to those directly around him. It was now five minutes before Kralsich was supposed to speak and as far as the eye could see out into the gardens, people were pushing, rather orderly, closer and closer. The crowd was beginning to stack up like snowflakes in a winter storm. Tens of thousands if not hundreds of thousands of people had come to this place. It was incredible.

The long windowed corridor finally led out to Rosario's Café. The café was similar to the one at which Jakob had just eaten breakfast. The main difference was that this balcony section was enormous and also the perfect vantage point for viewing the colossal crowd. Three stories up was enough to be observable to all, but not far enough away to seem distant.

Upon moving further toward Rosario's Café, the two men noticed that the entrance was completely roped off and guarded by several uniformed men. This was strange in of itself because security was fairly unusual in any public place. These men were clearly not letting anyone into Rosario's and a crowd had already built up around the barrier. Jakob led the Professor politely through the throngs of people to one of the security guards. Immediately upon making eye contact the guard called out, "Jakob Vanden?"

"Yes?" Jakob responded with surprise.

"You and Professor Briarton can come this way." The security guard detached the rope and the two men left the confines of the crowd, and let out a sigh of relief as they crossed over into open territory. The other security guard approached the men, pointed toward the podium and spoke.

"Welcome, gentlemen, we've been expecting you. There are two chairs right over there near the podium . . . . . if you'd like to have a seat of course."

"Thanks," the two men uttered at the same time. They both took their chairs and looked around noting quite nervously that they appeared to be the only two people seated next to where Kralsich was to speak.

Moments later Kralsich, who now donned a longer more impressive gray and red robe, emerged from inside Rosario's and walked toward Professor Briarton and Jakob, looking straight at the gargantuan crowd of people before him. Their murmur quieted the closer he got to the lonely podium. As he stepped up to it, hundred of thousand of eyes converged on him, and only the bird chirps in the background could be heard. He paused and then spoke with proud conviction into the microphone:

"For those who are unaware of the brutal act of violence which has been perpetrated on

Senator Langesé, I bring you ghastly news. A mob of Old Worlders has savagely murdered him less than an hour ago."

The crowd murmured as the unaware people were commenting to their friends. Kralsich used the opportunity to greet Jakob and the Professor, turning away from the microphone before saying to Professor Briarton, "Hello old friend," he then turned to Jakob, "I'm *very* contented to see you by my side today . . . . . we have much to discuss after this engagement." Jakob nodded in acknowledgement and Kralsich turned again toward the ever expanding crowd and spoke:

"We are *well* aware that after the recall of *so* many Travelers, Enlighteners, and Monitors that Senator Langesé was the last one of us still engaged in his duties. Now he has perished for that duty and resides alongside all the other great men and women who died for their noble causes." With reverence cemented onto his face, he paused for a moment in remembrance of the Senator.

"One shouldn't underestimate the effect that we've had in that other world, there," his long, outstretched arm pointed with conviction directly behind him.

"How many of you have directly participated in the Old World revealing to them the wickedness of their encapsulated system? Please a show of hands . . . . . you deserve to be recognized!" Well over ninety percent of the people exuberantly raised their hands for all to see, and congratulatory murmurs spread through the growing crowd which now numbered in the hundreds of thousands.

"We have toiled and labored to make a difference with them, to affect even a modicum of change in their society. We acted as a safety net and now that safety net has been retracted. Alas, the circus must go on, only this time there are no second chances. There will not be a Monitor who will leak a story about a sordid scheme by a corrupt government trying to drag a country into war. They will not have the benefit of an Enlightener consulting with a former pupil, who now wields immense power, about the right decision to make. And they certainly *will not* have Travelers who have been advising unsuspecting people for hundreds of years. Why is *this*?!!? Because they've detected us and we need to realize *that we CANNOT go back to the way things USED TO BE.*" His voice was loud and booming making it effortless to hear from even miles away.

"Those days are behind us, but we can not hide like turtles in our warm, comfortable shells, believing that no one will *ever* discover us. That is naïve as well as imprudent and would ultimately led to our destruction. *Don't* think for a *second* they would have compassion on the likes of *us*! We look at ourselves as a stabilizing force of reason and empathy hiding near the South Pole because those who need us cannot recognize the good force that we are. They, however, view us as deceptive, dangerous cockroaches that hide and spy and *deserve to be SQUASHED*." His fist rapped the podium and the effect reverberated through the speakers and subsequently into the crowd.

"And I *assure* you they wouldn't hesitate for a *second* to destroy what they don't understand. They would have no qualms about stealing our technology and then assimilating us to their unsustainable society. They have done this to every group of native, harmonious peoples they've discovered. Why would this pattern cease to continue?

"We've discussed the reasons why the small percentage of open minded, aware individuals cannot penetrate the thick veneer of those who remain comatose to what transpires in the World. One must realize that they have *invisible* prisons with ever encroaching, ever enclosing walls all around," his hands began to rise skyward leaving his wide sleeved cloak dangling down from his arms. "Whether it be the physical barriers to *formulative thinking* as with prescription pills, food additives/mal-nutrition, industrial waste voluntarily put in the water; or it be monetary barriers as with insurance, taxes, subsidies, inflation; or it be the social barriers starting with what they call 'education' (AKA indoctrination into a world of unsustainability) and living on a planet where legitimate scientific thought can get you *blacklisted.*

"In combination the end result is the same – most people live in an unsustainable artificial system yet do not see it as such. They have not the time, ability, nor *permission* to ponder why their society is out of balance with everything around it. If allowed to run its course, their demise would come when natural resources become so scarce that war simply must ensue like a village with only one loaf of bread. Due to their barbarous nature, evidenced by the ferocious amount money spent on weapons which clearly favor entropy over syntropy, this would eventually lead to a cataclysmic destruction of their world, and would have dire consequences on not only themselves but also us.

"In practice though, this is a moot point. Their society will not continue till it implodes. . . . it must be systematically demolished *floor by floor!*" The crowd erupted with fearful curiosity at what Kralsich had just bellowed. Most people were now aware that Kralsich was no ordinary Prognosticator as word of his uncanny ability to predict the future spread. The majority of the people had also keenly recognized that they were in fact listening to their future Chairman.

"What are we to do!? You are wholly aware that they've detected us! You know that they will not stop until they find us . . . . . and I think we know *DAMN* well what happens then. We've seen their brutality in action . . . . . I cannot imagine what would happen if we attempted to defend ourselves from their onslaught with our meager missile defense systems. No, no, *NO* . . . . . we *cannot ALLOW* our own destruction to simply *HAPPEN*!

"Yet I do not delude myself in to thinking that we have an inkling of a chance militarily against them, and nor do I believe our foe is the type that would ever surrender even if they faced assured destruction. This is so because these invisible walls of which I speak are being continually constructed by the central powers that be.

"This is nothing new! During World War II Japanese soldiers would commit suicide before being captured. Why? We now view it as insanely preposterous but I assure YOU," he stopped for a moment and vibrantly pointed at the bulging crowd with both hands and then continued, "if you believed that your Emperor was a demi-god you would have gladly killed yourself in devotion to him. No. . . . we cannot face them in an open conflict that much is for *certain*.

"But when the Japanese people saw their *defeated* emperor they realized with their own eyes that he was no *real* demi-god. He was simply a liar! Much in the same way today, the people of the world must realize the strangling grip that the powers have over them. If *all* the peoples of the world were to simultaneously have *all* of the hidden information of *all* the governments, businesses, and powerful people on EARTH. . . . . what do you think the result *would be*?

"There would be waves of questions, anger, and fury as people discovered the *true* extent to which they've been *lied*. Being aware of history I know that we've attempted this before with individual countries in an effort to find a safe haven among the Old World nations. I'm acutely aware that we failed in those efforts many years ago. Most importantly though, I recognize why we failed and know how to correct it.

"So what happened during those perilous times in the past? Can you all remember? We released damning information on the corrupt practices of the leadership and what was the end result? A bloodless coup, much as we anticipated, took place and through our direction a much more benevolent, balanced group of leaders took command of the country.

"We *thought* we had accomplished our goal but yet we did not realize the cunning nature of the plethora of international organizations which were pitted against this fledgling nation. International loans were made under the auspices of development, but the truth was far more nefarious. After they manipulated the small nation's currency there was no possible way they could continue to afford making the payments. Now in default and having no other way to get the money needed, they were forced to offer their only natural resources as payment. Even after their parliament nullified the resource deal the international organizations did not care. They simply staged a coup and reinstated those willing to give them what they wanted. So the experiment failed. Why?[14]

"It failed because even though we exposed an individual country's corrupt cronyism, we did not go far enough. We have to expose everything – *simultaneously*. We cannot simply cut a limb off of this insidious dragon and wait . . . . we must *behead* the *beast!*" The crowd groaned

---

[14] Perkins, John., <u>Confessions of an Economic Hitman.</u> (San Francisco: Berrett-Koehler Publishers Inc, 2004).

acceptingly knowing they had no other reasonable choice.

"Chairman Gorshial, The Council of Many and myself, have crafted a Plan of Action stating that we will release all of our covertly gathered, unquestionably damning evidence against the Old World in the event that four of my Prognostications would be satisfied. These predictions were the following: One - our Quantum Communicators would be detected by the Old World. Two – Senator Langesé would be murdered. The third prediction that needed to come true, was not only the immigration of a certain man to Arkonos but also his acceptance of this truly magnificent place," Kralsich's long arms again stretched over his head and allowed his robe to make him appear like a giant gray and red condor.

"The man of whom I speak is seated here. *Jakob Vanden* would you please stand up and be recognized," Jakob turned his head in surprised response that *he* was in one of Kralsich's predictions. He slowly stood up and looked out over the extraordinary size of the crowd. His heart had begun to thump with such force that he could hardly hear. Time seemed to slow down and he noticed upon standing up that the crowd was not only a half million strong directly in front of him but that people were looking out from balconies, apartments and other café's all throughout the interior of mountain range. Jakob turned to face Kralsich and as they shook hands the crowd did something that hadn't been done for centuries in Arkonos – they cheered. They cheered because of the hope that was bestowed upon them from a normal Old Worlder who could accept their ways. They cheered because they wouldn't have to hide what they thought was the brightest light in the world – *themselves*. And they cheered because they themselves possessed everything they needed to accomplish their ambitious goal. After a few minutes of exuberance the crowd finally quieted down again and Kralsich began to speak.

"Jakob, how do you find this wondrous place?" Kralsich asked as he made a space in front of the microphone so that the young man could publicly respond.

"It's been ahh . . . . it's been quite an experience so far. I wouldn't trade it for anything!" He excitedly announced, his voice thunderously reverberating throughout the entire mountain range. With his third Prognostication now furtively accomplished, he motioned for Jakob to sit back down before continuing.

"Only the fourth Prognostication remains before this Plan of Action can be executed. I unfortunately cannot comment on the contents of this due to obvious reasons. But *rest assured*, once the fourth Prognostication is fulfilled the Plan will be enacted with devastating swiftness. Thank you all for your empathy and attentiveness."

Kralsich calculatingly spun around into a one-eighty, made eye contact with Jakob and Professor Briarton, motioned for them to follow and all three men exited the balcony via the café.

* * *

‖ *30* ‖

Within ten hours Roger and Herschel had accomplished more than most entire governmental departments would in a month. After composing his report on the technical reasons why he believed that this secret organization's base was in Antarctica, Herschel quickly started making plans to physically prove his theory. His ultimate goal was the discovery of what could be perhaps the largest secret spy organization on earth.

Immediately after an exhausting brain storming session, the two men concocted a plan to search the notoriously dangerous terrain at the South Pole. They would use a remote controlled Predator Drone especially fitted for the most inhospitable of climates. A few years earlier Herschel had led a team in designing multiple models of these frequently used mini-planes. He was aware that the military was very quickly approaching 90,000 hours of flying a year with these remote controlled devices, and therefore had supreme confidence in the hardy nature of the planes.[15]

Upon Roger's request, within hours a winterized Predator was delivered to Cosgrove Strategies' office and the two men began their retrofitting operation. Utilizing not only his own expertise but also the extensive knowledge of the Cosgrove's on-site staff, Herschel was able to successfully attach the suitcase Quantum Detection Device to the Predator. The idea was that if they were physically close enough to the dampening

---

[15] Axe, David. *War Bots: How US Military Robots are Transforming War in Iraq, Afghanistan, and the Future.* Ann Arbor, MI: Nimble Books LLC, 2008), *pg.* 52.

shield, they would still be able to detect some energy signature leakage.

When it was ready to go, the device was expedited toward the South Pole to the nearest military facility. While in transit Herschel and Roger poured over the terrain of Antarctica in the map room. Herschel suggested they go under two assumptions during the search. The first being that whoever these people are they must be harnessing some type of geo-thermal energy in order to have sufficient power to subdue the terrain into a long term, livable environment. The second suggested assumption was that they should focus their efforts on ridges, mountains and other geological features because that would be the most likely way to conceal their location. Roger agreed and for hours the two men scanned over a plethora of maps near areas with accessible geo-thermal energy and raised terrain.

The two had nearly ruptured a blood vessel in their strained eyes when Roger came across something that looked particularly strange.

"Herschel," he called out, "come take a look at this." The two men looked up at the exceptionally detailed image on the wall sized, flat panel screen. "See right here where this mountain range is?"

"Yeah."

"This range has hot magma close enough to the surface to easily build a geothermal plant, and look. . . . . here." He pointed to where the mountain range tapered off into a plateau.

"That's weird. . . . . geologically I mean," Herschel leaned a bit closer to inspect the image. "This isn't a typical formation you would expect to find in this kind of mountain range. Geology is only a hobby subject for me and *even I* can tell that doesn't look right."

The two men quickly alerted mission control about the target sight and after a few hours a flight plan taking into account terrain, wind and precipitation was devised. Their Flight Plan comprised of five waypoints where the Drone would intricately examine several mountain ranges and ridges around potential geothermal sites. Even though the Drone is programmed to fly and scan on auto pilot Herschel and Roger were now huddled in the Cosgrove Strategy's Remote Flight Room.

They watched the monitors which supplied data from the multiple scanners attached to the drone. In front of them were screens for night vision, thermal scanning, infrared red, Doppler radar, along with four normal sight cameras each with 20x zoom *and* the Quantum Detector that they had just attached. Their eyes darted from one screen to the next, fixated on suspect geological features.

After five hours of complete Antarctic silence the Drone finally approached its fifth and final waypoint – the prime spot picked out by Roger.

"This is it," Herschel nervously commented as he put a hand on Roger's shoulder. "If they're actually down here, this is where they'll be." The small Drone sputtered along and buzzed in between the glacier laden mountain range. Only a few hundred feet of each mountain peak jutted out of the gargantuan glacier. "Hey, can you go up a little higher to get a good read on the thermal scanner."

"Sure," Roger gladly replied, "I'll just take it off of auto pilot and fly the thing myself."

"Are you qualified to do that?"

"Herschel, do you know how many missions I've flown in this very room?" He rhetorically asked with a smile.

"Good! I was hoping you'd say that. I'd much rather have you flying my quantum detector around than some random military suit. At least if you crash I can slap ya around a little bit."

"Well . . . . I usually bring about fifty percent of these little guys back," he said, pushing the button to disengage the auto-pilot and grabbing the controls to fly the Drone.

"Fifty-fifty, huh? Well then it's about the same as you driving a car!" Both men laughed and shook their heads at Herschel's consistently bad comedic timing. Roger continued piloting the Drone.

"Alright I'm about as high as I can go before this thing freezes up. It's summer time down there right now but frankly speaking that doesn't mean much. What do you see on the thermal scan?"

"That's strange . . . . the scan shows that the surface area directly above the best geothermal site is actually slightly *cooler* than the surrounding area. Look at this," his finger tip tapped the monitor, "it's a huge circular pattern where the temperature is *exactly* the same."

"That's gotta be it, then! They must have some kind of temperature dampener." The Drone, still high above the ice, lurched into a nose dive toward the site on Roger's command. He pulled up on the flight stick and swooped around the largest mountain peak, its zenith partially protruding from the enormous ice sheet below.

"Hey, what's your hurry!? You're going to dislodge the Quantum Detector," Hershel protested.

"That's my hurry," he pointed to the fuel gauge. "We just dipped below a half a tank, and I think you know what that means. This bird's not going to fly home . . . . . that's for sure."

"I *knew* you were going to find a way to crash this thing!" Herschel responding jokingly as he often did during tense moments. The Drone buzzed the mountain peak again, but besides the slight temperature variance nothing anomalous had come up on its instruments.

"Ok, I think we need to try a new tactic."

"Yeah what's that?" Herschel replied to the statement, his eyes still fixated on the screens in front of him.

"I think we need to sting them . . . . like a mosquito to see if they try to swat us."

"What are you implying?"

"This," Roger flipped up the clear plastic cover on the primary weapon trigger.

"What are you doing?!? You can't just fire without authorization!"

"We're *WAY* past that! Don't you see how *big* this thing is! There's no telling what these people are planning to do . . . . . *whoever* the *hell* they are! Look," his voice was calm again after taking a few lung fulls of air, "there's the drone. We're running out of time," his voice was now at a whisper, "and they've got Jakob."

"Alright, do what you need to."

"Here we go," Roger's expression changed in such a way that it now resembled a granite mask of seriousness. "I need you to tell me if you detect something strange. Ok?" Roger moved the drone a few hundred meters away from the mountain before pulling the trigger to quickly lunch two missiles. The cameras shook violently as the force of the departing missiles was transferred onto the Drone. They raced toward the side of the mountain leaving a wispy trail of smoke before impacting the stone and exploding into oblivion.

Immediately the Quantum detector lit up like a Christmas tree and just as quickly it went black again. The men scrambled over the monitors and the Drone hovered in a static position.

"Did you see that!?" Herschel called out.

"Yes. That was fast. Hmm . . . . . I bet," he moved his eyes from the screen to clear his head, "I bet, we tripped one of their detection devices and it automatically cut the signal off."

"Then it's official. . . . we found it! We found their operations center!"

"Herschel," Roger turned and looked at him square in the face, "I need you to notify the brass in DC of what we found. They'll probably want to run their own mission to confirm our findings. I'm going to turn this Drone around and try to get it close enough so it can get picked up by one of our 'copters. With the fuel that's left though it isn't going be easy. I really don't have the time to get another Quantum Detector built . . . . it could really come in handy."

Suddenly the 'missile detected light' angrily flashed red, and in less than a second Roger's rescue plan had come to an abrupt end before it had ever gotten started. Just as he finished his sentence both men's heads jerked toward the screen prompted by the sudden flash of light. Within moments all of the communications from the small Drone had been replaced by static.

* * *

‖ 31 ‖

After Kralsich and Professor Briarton excused themselves for a few moments following the speech, Jakob suddenly found himself surrounded by strangers in the bustling Rosario's Café. He thought that the crowd was amazingly subdued after witnessing such a pivotal moment. He couldn't tell if they were hopeful or frightened.

In a search for the bathrooms Jakob wandered further inside the Café where it was reasonably empty and quiet. Some of the private rooms for patrons were simply cut out of the solid rock of the mountain. The place had a cellar like dampness to it despite the efficient ventilation. He suddenly heard a voice coming from inside one of the quasi echo chambers that he recognized. Grabbing the side of the wall for support while slowly crouching, he ever so inaudibly inched toward it. He stopped and listened to Kralsich's booming diaphragm:

"*Don't* think for a second that the Orwellian word games will not continue!! They'll still call a heinous, violent invasion of another sovereign nation a 'mission of freedom', yet concurrently they will name a complete loss of their own citizen's natural rights a 'war on' this or that.

"The truth is, there is a high probability that the world will soon erupt into a quagmire of dictatorships and warring nations each purporting to possess the divine right to rule in some form or another. I'm *aware* of this, truly, I am. It will most likely be a wretched mess and the risk of nuclear catastrophe is great.

"I know this isn't the best solution, simply dumping all the world's sordid secrets so *very* suddenly for all to see. However, one must remember that even as destructive as forest fires are, afterwards the soil is fertile and ripe for planting."

"The consequences could be *far beyond* catastrophic!" Chairman Gorshial defiantly interjected.

"Even still . . . . it must be done," Kralsich continued, "for two important reasons. The first is that we have been discovered. That is an inescapable *fact*. How long do you personally believe it'll take for them to put the whole story together?? It is *inevitable* that we will indeed be found . . . . that much is certain gentlemen.

"The second reason this must be done is simply put. . . . it is the *law*! We have deliberated, voted, formulated and Prognosticated to bring ourselves to this point. Is it simply a coincidence that multiple issues are coalescing at the proper moment? No, of course *not*! This isn't a coincidence; it's a symptom of a perfectly functioning system. And this system *must* be allowed to continue.

"I am *aware* that we've never done anything in these paradigm shifting proportions, nevertheless, it *is* ultimately our responsibility and duty. Most importantly, though, it's the *right* thing to do."

"He's right you know," Professor Briarton's voice bounced about the rocks and landed on Jakob's eavesdropping ears. "I hate to say it, but this is the best solution that we have."

Jakob almost shrieked in terrorized surprise when his unsuspecting ribs were skewered by a stiff finger. His head snapped around to see who it was when a voice chimed in, "who are we spying on?" Terra whispered, crouched down behind him.

"Shhhhhhhh," Jakob's stomach fluttered at the sight of her. He responded and was reassured by a mutual smile, "come on let's get outta here." As they began to steadily sneak out of the cavernous hall they could still hear the men talking.

"Professor Briarton would you mind bringing this. . . . . Jakob Vanden to us. There are a few questions I wouldn't mind asking him, actually," Chairman Gorshial flatly inquired.

"Absolutely, let me go see if I can find him. Gentlemen," he made eye contact with both Chairman Gorshial and Kralsich before getting up.

"Go, go, hurry up," Jakob called out to Terra in a frantic whisper. They stayed low until they were out of view and turned the first corner they could.

"That was close," Terra commented jovially. "Look's like we must be rubbing off on you . . . now you're spying too!"

With Professor Briarton searching Rosario's Café for Jakob, Chairman Gorshial found himself purposefully alone in a room with Kralsich; he was decidedly quick in seizing the opportunity.

"How did you do it? How did you. . . . . in *all* your 'infinite' wisdom almost perfectly predict this exact set of events!?!" His soft featured face belched out with a tinge of aristocratic anger.

"Ahhh, Chairman," Kralsich responded belligerently confident, "it's simply a matter of probabilities viewed through synergistic frameworks. When one realizes the potential," he was cut off by an infuriated Chairman Gorshial, who clumsily kicked the table as he got up and immediately turned toward Kralsich to bellow.

"Don't *give* me that *BULLSHIT* about probabilities! I think we *both* know that we are WAY *BEYOND that*," Gorshial stared down the younger man and continued. "You want to know what I've heard?"

"Yes, what's that?" Kralsich said very calmly and precisely as Chairman Gorshial paced around the cavernous room.

"I heard you went though *extraordinary* lengths to get that room of yours with the crystal sticking out of the wall," Chairman Gorshial uttered confidently, knowing that he had extensively snooped in Kralsich's records. "How many *months* total have you spent in the Great Caverns below us, huh? Maybe it's not months, but rather years! Do you enjoy being around them *so very much* . . . . that you," his finger pointed at the man accusatively, "that you had to have one in your room as well!?"

"How do you know all of this?!"

"Fine! I'll tell you something Kralsich," Gorshial's gray face became flushed as he began to loose control. "I've spied on you and looked through all of your personal data and do you want to know what I found, other than you being a little opinionated? NOTHING. No nasty habits or inappropriate relationships . . . . *nothing* except for a rather peculiar obsession with those crystals. So what is it with those things? I deserve to know that much at least since you'll soon be occupying my Chair."

"Very well. I'll tell you what I know, although to be honest with you, it isn't much. One time when I spent a few months in the Great Caverns, I came across some ancient texts which I haven't yet completely deciphered. From what I could piece together, the documents described the crystals in a very strange way. Specifically it said that power in the form of focus could be collected from them."

"What the hell does that mean?" The Chairman's face shifted in protest, "power can be collected. Is this a *joke!?*"

"*No*, but at the same time I have no idea if this power even exists. All I know is that I simply lay my hands on the crystal and mediate. I believe it focuses my thoughts." Kralsich's response was sincere; even still the Chairman's disbelief intensified.

"So either you're a genius who can see the future through sophisticatedly constructed matrixes, or you're sucking some sort of physic energy from a fancy rock? Do I have that right?" The Chairman pragmatically grumbled while gesturing his hand toward Kralsich.

"Believe what you wish! But understand this Chairman, *it's over*. My last Prognostication will soon come true, and *you* will no longer be Chairman thereafter."

"*What*?!?" Chairman Gorshial uttered through a low chuckle. "You actually believe that . . . . . that . . . . *boy*, will destroy his entire civilization. A world he has been without for only a matter of days! I was beginning to wonder why you predicted it that way in the first place!" He slowly shook his head and waited for a response from the much younger man.

"Because Chairman Gorshial," he stood up, towering over him and flaring his nostrils as he spoke, "that's exactly what's going to happen."

* * *

Jakob did not really know why he and Terra were fleeing from Professor Briarton, weaving through the crowd at the Café recklessly. He found a quiet spot around a corner and sat down at a secluded table.

"I'm really not running, I mean I," Jakob tried to say, mixing up the words on the way out. "I just need a minute to think about everything . . . . . that's all."

"I understand," she said empathetically. Her compassion was evident through her beautiful smile. "To be honest with you it's exhilarating to be here, right now at this moment. Think about it Jakob," she leaned in closer to him, "every citizen of Arkonos knew that we could not stay hidden for eternity. It was inevitable that we would eventually be discovered. Our Emergence will irrevocably change the world forever and *our* actions in this pivotal moment will be amplified throughout the ages." Their eyes stayed fixated on one another in the dimly lit corner.

"So you're on board with Kralsich. . . .is that right?" He asked flatly.

"Is there another solution to this *impossible* situation? And more importantly," she clasped his hand in her own, "do you think it's a coincidence that you're *here*, in this incredible place, in this incredible time and it just happens to be your Father who's trying to hunt us down?"

Unanticipatedly the table, which lay between them, shook seemingly without cause. Another heavy jolt sent a huge dollop of rock crashing down onto the crowd beside them. A thundering echo reverberated through the interior of the mountain paralyzing virtually everyone with angst. Although they were sitting, the two grappled onto each other to stay balanced.

"Was that an earthquake?" Terra naively asked as a final shock wave reverberated through the mountain range.

"That was definitely *not* an earthquake. . . . . I know that much for certain," his eyes scanned the Arkonsian unrest all around them.

"Jakob," Professor Briarton called out from about five tables down. As the Professor approached them the couple realized that there was no need to keep their arms clasped and promptly stood up to greet the Professor. He nimbly cut his way through throngs of the frantic people. Finally arriving he said, "hello," his attention turned respectfully toward Terra, "nice to see *you* again."

"What *was* that Professor?"

"I'm not sure. We'll figure it out shortly, but for now," he said concisely, "Jakob can you come with me? Chairman Gorshial has requested your attendance."

At that same moment a voice from an intercom on the wall called out to the Professor. "Professor Briarton . . . are you zhere?" He dashed over to the wall about fifteen yards away, pushed a red button and answered.

"Sergei? Is everything ok?"

"Vell, no not vreally. I haff just gotten vord zhat a mis-zile has hit us and zhat it vas fired from a Pvredator Drone! Geo-Zhermal energy iz a bit touchy as you can imagine. Ve cannot take many more of zhose attacks. Ve haff destroyed zhe small plane, but vhere zhere is one, uzually more follow.

"However, rest assured that I vill never evacuate zhe Geo-Zhermal Plant. I vill die to zafe you so zhat you can accomplish vhat you must."

"Understood Sergei, understood. Briarton out," the Professor pushed a button on the wall and tried to stymie the flood of pouring emotion that had begun to make his chin quiver. The thought of someone else in his life dying was more than he could handle right now.

He turned back toward Jakob and Terra, catching sight of them across the room embroiled in what appeared to be a rather emotional moment. He slowly made his way in their direction, navigating through the dense, distraught crowd.

"Hey," Terra said to Jakob, her smiling face wilted into foreboding concern, "whatever it is that you have to do with them . . . . . *whatever* it may be. Your decision has to be grounded in what you believe to be right and *just*," her voice cracked with emotion and likewise her eyes swelled with water. "Don't let anyone pressure you into doing something that *you* don't think you ought to be doing. Do you understand me?" His hand brushed a tear off her cheek the instant it dove like a single drop off a waterfall.

"What's wrong? What's going on?" His square jaw crinkled with concern.

By this point word had begun to spread throughout the entirety of Arkonos. The few people who were privy to Kralsich's fourth Prognostication were mentally weakened by the endorphins pulsating through their minds. Arkonsians are not as accustomed to the Crowd Effect and therefore are influenced much easier than other people. State secret or not, it did not take much for a few of them to leak the contents of the ominous last prediction. The information spread like a virulent disease, and now the better part of the population had heard bits and pieces of the Prognostication which was typically reserved for only the upper echelons of government.

When Jakob realized that the Café's volume had leveled off to an ambient whisper, he turned to face the mass of people who were huddled for safety behind him. Eerily, hundreds of sets of eyes were focused directly on him. He stared back in stunned silence; the serene moment was eventually interrupted by the approach of Professor Briarton.

"*I think*," the Professor momentarily took in the scene around him, "we need to go. Are you ready?" He said unequivocally to his pupil pointing out the expectant crowd with his eyes.

Jakob turned once more toward Terra where their blue and green eyes reflected off one another like the Atlantic and Caribbean, respectively. Time seemed to crawl on as a puffy white cloud, on a sunny day straddling the divide of those great bodies of water.

"Now I understand," he strained to say to her. After a brief, warm hug the two parted ways and Jakob, a part of his soul still with Terra, followed Professor Briarton down the corridor and out of Rosario's Café while an innumerable quantity of curious onlookers traced Jakob's every step. His eyes remained locked with hers until they could no longer.

* * *

"Where are we going?" Jakob called out to the quick footed professor after they were alone in the corridor.

"Jakob, there's a lot going on right now that even I don't understand," he said hurriedly moving toward their new destination. Professor Briarton had a good idea where he could find Kralsich and Chairman Gorshial; he knew after what just happened that they were definitely *not* still in Rosario's Café. "You know those loud noises you heard a few moments ago?"

"Yeah?"

"Those were two air-to-surface missiles fired by what we believe to be a modified Predator Drone. Coincidentally or ironically, whatever you choose to believe, we are almost certain that it was your father, Roger Vanden, who actually fired the shots."

"Why would he *do that*?"

"C'mon Jakob! It's really no time to bury your head in the sand and shield yourself from the truth. Your father's mind is in a state of paralysis. If he were shown what we truly represent here, he would still not believe us. He could be given hard evidence and he'd still deny the truth. Why?"

He struggled to keep up with the nimble stride of the Professor and became purposefully distracted by the panoramic view of Arkonos out of the corridor window to his right. His mind drifted off to the simplistic nature of his blissfully ignorant, childhood days when he believed his Father was a hero and would naturally do anything to protect his first born son.

"He's locked into his allegiances," Jakob announced with a forehead that looked like a washboard. "It's like Kralsich says . . . it clouds the mind . . . it stops him from being able to reason things out correctly. It's like all the new information that flows into his mind . . . right . . . it *has* to pass through this very narrow filter of his *already* pledged allegiances before he can accept it. And let me assure you," he swiveled his head toward the Professor as they continued down the corridor, "hardly anything at *all* makes it past *that* filter!"

"Right, so we're not going to even bother trying to reason with your father. It's probably of no use," the Professor said bluntly.

"Well, wait a second," Jakob suddenly felt like it may have been a little unfair not to even attempt it. "Maybe we should at least try to get through to him . . . . . there's a chance at least."

"You're right there is a *chance*. That chance is very low unfortunately as we've just established. What would you give it, huh? Five percent? Maybe ten? However, now that we've been detected, in order to contact him we would have to utilize a direct tap into the Old World's communications system. There is a sizable risk that under such a high security threat we would be detected and our last direct line to the Old World could be cut. Would you be willing to risk *all of this*," his arm gestured to the view, "for a plan that has *such* a high probability of failure?" The Professor was in the process of weaning his fledging student off of his guidance and needed to jump start the intrinsically motivated part of Jakob's brain.

"No, I wouldn't. You're right Professor . . . . . that's not an option," he admitted.

Just as Jakob was coming to terms with the reality before of him, he also came to the end of the corridor. Because he had been gazing out of the third story windows lining the corridor, he did not notice that the entire walkway now opened up into a massive stone hall, which traveled to the left . . . . directly through the thick granite of the mountain.

The men were now at the stairs which led down three stories to the cylinder shaped hall and switched their gaze from the right hand side, which showed lush gardens and the interior of a mountain range, to the left hand side. The view down the forty storey tall, gigantic cylinder was astounding. Rather than being decorated with the solid stone of the mountain from which it were cut, every inch of the colossal tunnel was covered with sizable bricks which were sandy in appearance with a tinge of orange. Small cut-outs for light down the length of the tunnel, allowed hundreds of thin beams to criss-cross through the hazy air.

When Jakob switched his view from the massive tunnel to the treacherous stairs in front of him, he noticed something in his peripheral vision. Turning his head he saw that a group of people were now standing behind him, watching the two men. Even though the very existence of their civilization was being threatened, there they were, encouragingly smiling at them. But it wasn't just the small group directly behind! From his three-storey perch Jakob could see a crowd gathering down below.

"I'm guessing we're going down the stairs and into that gargantuan tunnel where all the people are, right?"

"I'd say that's a correct assumption, yes," the Professor replied as he put a hand reassuringly on his pupil's back.

As the pair descended the multi-platform stairs, which were lavishly decorated with colorful plants and fountains, a multitude of people congregated all down the tunnel to the left of them. After descending to the bottom, he placed his shoe on a sandy brick at the bottom of the stairs. As he stood looking squarely down the gigantic passageway, Jakob noticed that it was descending into the depths of the mountain by at least a slope of ten degrees.

Beams of light blindingly lit the hazy air, obscuring from view the shadowy structure that lay at its end. By now, so many thousands of people had flooded to the interior of the hall, that they left only a path about four feet wide down its length.

Jakob took a few steps forward and then instinctively stopped quite suddenly. Looking directly behind him he realized that Professor Briarton had not walked with him, but in fact, stayed behind at the foot of the stairs. He walked back to him and confronted his older, wiser mentor.

"What are you doing standing there?" He said, shaking his head. "Let's get going."

"Jakob, you have been my student and I your teacher for a while now. Contrary to what you believe, this relationship has benefited me perhaps greater than it has you. I've discovered a youthful flame in myself which I feared had long been extinguished, and I thank you for that.

"Where you are going now," Professor Briarton paused and motioned down the hall with his eyes, "you must make the decisions, Jakob. In order to accomplish that task, you must now become your own counsel. That act . . . . that act of unlocking your intrinsic reasoning skills . . . . *well* . . . it means that this pupil - mentor relationship, Jakob," Professor Briarton smiled reaffirmingly at the young man, "can now end and turn into something different. And that is precisely the reason that you must go . . . . . on your *own*." Professor Briarton extended a hand to his former pupil and Jakob grabbed it and shook it firmly. "Jakob, remember to stay focused on what you truly believe in," the Professor uttered plainly with a clenched jaw.

"Thank you Professor," Jakob nodded simply, turned and started down the crowded hall. The truth is he wasn't sure what was in front of him, or what he was about to do. But one thing was for certain, he'd much rather do it on his own accord than have his mentor influencing him, this way Jakob would know that the decision was his own.

After a few minutes of thousands of people laying their hands on his back as well as serenely smiling at him, Jakob could finally see the actual structure at the end of the tunnel. Although still slightly hazy from the dust and sheer *height* of its enormous size, from his current vantage point it was clear that the hall opened up into a perfectly carved dome that must have been over a hundred stories tall. Inside this dome a structure that resembled a combination of an Egyptian style Pyramid and a Meso-American Ziggurat soared to about seventy *massive* stories. The stone used to build the Pyramid was the same sandy color as the interior of the hall. Jakob noted that this was not a typical mineral that exists in the mountains of Antarctica but rather in a desert somewhere.

Now nearing the gaping, arched entrance to the Pyramid, Jakob had discerned from the path formed by the crowd that the interior was his obvious destination. People continued to lay their hands on him and passionately smiled as he entered the ancient looking structure.

The interior was certainly *not* solid with tight corridors as Jakob had heard the other Pyramids were; on the contrary, the inside here resembled an impossibly large parliament building. A tremendous amount of occupied stadium seating throughout the building all faced a four foot tall, stone structure in the middle of the main floor.

"Well," a hand suddenly grasped his left shoulder, "very nice to see you Mr. Jakob Vanden." Kralsich said as brightly as he could muster.

"What *is all* this?" Jakob trepidatiously asked as he examined the detailed craftsmanship throughout the towering Pyramid.

"Ahh, yes," Chairman Gorshial slyly cut in front of Kralsich and addressed Jakob, "I welcome you to the Council of the Many."

"It functions similar to what you know as a 'parliament'," Kralsich piped in, "but with different duties and spheres of influences. All of these people are like members of your Congress. Jakob, could you follow us? There is something that I'd like for you to see."

"Alright," he said soberly.

The three men descended down the steep steps toward the center of the Pyramid. They went down about four floors and could see thousands of members of the Council of Many. While encircling the small stone structure, concurrently the murmur of anticipation dissipated off into silence.

Jakob hesitantly peered at the Chairman and Kralsich who were to his left and right respectively. Situated in the center was the structure made of rough stone yet, nonetheless, possessed several computer panels and a smooth red button at its four foot peak.

"What lies in front of us," Kralsich's arms opened toward the empty air above him, "is the culmination of a plethora of precise calculations, purposeful work, and wondrous Prognostications. Jakob," his voice was now subtly being amplified through the Pyramid, "this is the location where a Plan of Action is physically initiated. You see . . . . . hundreds of these Plans are regularly pre-programmed into our system and must be initiated whenever a corresponding Prognostication proves true."

"Why . . . . . why," he hesitated for a second as thousands upon thousands of eyes pressed upon him, "why are you telling me this!?"

"Because Jakob, the Plan of Action I talked about during my speech is being initiated today."

"What? You mean the plan that will release all of the world's dirty secrets which you've been gathering for eons? Wait . . . . . you can't do that yet. You said that there was one more Prognostication . . . . . the fourth one, which has to take place before that can happen!! Has it?" Jakob said, a brow turning upwards in an effort to coax an answer. Even though he knew that the Arkonsians had no other choice, he still instinctively tried to postpone the inevitable and clutch onto his old thought process.

"No," Kralsich coldly replied, "it has still not occurred."

A momentary silence was broken by a thud and accompanying shockwave which roared through the brick structure. Dust poured down from the shifting ceiling, enveloping hundreds in its blinding haze and causing the Council people to murmur and move about. Two more loud blasts again bombarded their ears and the floor bounced with an even sturdier rumble than the last.

"It's alright," Kralsich called out, "they are randomly striking the mountains above us - we should be fine here for a while at least. They are simply confirming their findings." What should have calmed the crowd seemed to make the Council people even more unnerved. Many of them clamored about in panic.

"Then what are you waiting for!!!" Jakob called out to Kralsich and Gorshial, trying to fight the feeling of twisted panic that seemed to envelope him. "Initiate the Plan of Action! You know that all of those sordid secrets will immediately distract the nations and they will destroy each other before you!"

"As you pointed out Jakob . . . . the fourth Prognostication has not yet occurred."

"Then will you just wait here!?!! Bomb after bomb going off . . . . . you *know* they'll find you. They *WILL* destroy you Kralsich, and all you have built here," he pleaded, his voice turning from exasperated to stoically focused. "You can't *let* them do that to you . . . . prediction or no prediction. Your plan is the only way to at least postpone it."

"Would you initiate the Plan of Action, if you could? Could you simply push the button?" Kralsich asked peacefully in contrast to the chaos all around him.

"What? Me?? Who am I to decide this?" He skittishly backpedaled away from the structure in momentary panic.

"You, Jakob Vanden . . . . *YOU are the last Prognostication!* You are the only thing left. I have predicted that you will initiate this Plan of Action – and thus fulfill the fourth Prognostication."

His eyes grew wide open to proportions only dwarfed in size by the Pyramid in which he stood. It seemed that the red button had slowly grown brighter and Jakob couldn't tell if the change resided in the physical world or simply his mind. Without speaking he stepped forward to edge of the raged, rock structure in the center of the Council of the Many. He swiveled his head toward the top of the Pyramid and all of the gawking, frightened irises around him.

Another air strike shook the building, sending plumes of dust lurching off of the walls and ceiling. Colossal stones fell from above, ripping apart into thousands of pieces upon impacting devastatingly below. And even though noise would have obviously accompanied the disorder, Jakob did not hear it. His focus had also filtered out the clamorous stirring of Council people and everything else suddenly deemed unimportant to the decision he must make.

Jakob quickly flashed back to random conversations he'd had with Professor Briarton, Megan, his Father, Terra and Senator Langesé. He thought about doctors making people sicker, educators making people dumber, food scientists making people malnourished, news people making people more apathetic, law makers passing unconstitutional laws, and worst of all – central banks changing human behaviors so slyly through their sophisticatedly engineered boom/bust cycles, that most people still don't even recognize the ubiquitous manipulation, nor the societal shift.

Conversing about these topics was a recipe for disaster. Nearly every time people were told the truth they simply recoiled in fear and wound up attacking the messenger before even examining the arguments. *They are in a type of prison, and will fight anyone who tries to free them to the death.*

He thought about the people like his father who cloak reality with a façade of belief systems and who are so sincerely warped by this fantasy that they are willing to pharmaceutically 'fix' those who are unhappy with it. Both parties, those willing to accept being drugged, and those doing the drugging, know that something is terribly wrong, nevertheless they either give, or take, their 'medication' in order to placate the truth.

How can it change? How can the closed ears of people listen? There is only one way . . . . the liars must be exposed for what they truly are. In order for people to stop believing a lie they must hear the truth.

He looked up at Kralsich, Chairman Gorshial and the ensuing, yet silent chaos all around one last time before ultimately reaching his decision. He knew that the 4th of April would forever be known as the day the world heard the truth. Thus, Jakob fulfilled the fourth Prognostication and transmitted *all* of the world's sordid secrets as he lowered his hand onto the ominous red button.

A New Era Begins – Are You Ready?

Appendix A

Arkonos Government

In Arkonos, public policy is far more encompassing than is typical of most western representative democracies. Long ago, the Elders realized that in the long run most western democracies begin to consolidate power producing two bloated political parties. The strong two party system at first brings renewed hope as polarizingly ambitious individuals take the reins and march the country in a 'new' direction. The people eventually realize that these two parties are actually one, and that the 'new' direction they march toward every election or two, actually compliment one another. The cycle is exacerbated by higher taxation, money printing (also functions like a tax), and more government bureaucrats. When the government seeks to expand but lacks the public approval to do so by taxation they simply borrow the money and have the people eventually pay for it anyway. When they can no longer find any lenders from which to borrow the money, the government simply begins to debase their currency by printing the money in order to expand the government. At this point the holders of the government debt become concerned that the value of their investment is disappearing through inflation they try to sell the government security only to find out that everyone else is trying to do the same thing, thus making the sale rather difficult. Soon thereafter, the entire system begins to unravel as the currency becomes increasingly worthless.

In order to prevent that sort of negative feed back cycle from developing, the Elders decided that far more time should be spent by ordinary citizens on governance.

While that statement is seemingly easy to implement, several prerequisites must first be in place.

First, if people spend more time concentrating on governance that means they're spending less time on other things. That having been said, it is a necessity that the added benefit of more time spent on governance must produce less time being spent on other activities in order for the equation to be balanced. An example of this in Western Society would be if, say, the majority of a community collectively decided on a new traffic system. Granted it would take some time for the citizens to study all the traffic systems so they could find the most appropriate one, however; in the end the time saved navigating the city would more than make up for the time lost on research.

Second, the citizens must be intelligent enough to make informed decisions. In Western Societies the 'educational system' is designed to produce the best factory workers the world has ever known. By and large the people accept orders willingly without any questions however, they lack critical thinking skills. While perfect as factory workers, when it comes to decision making on a political stage the results are *very* different. The willingness to accept orders leads to a *groupthink* mentality on which slippery career politicians thrive. Many of these politicians openly announce their goal of increasing the budget of 'education' knowing that it will swell their electorates. The Elders were aware that a system like this would destroy all the good they wanted to accomplish and lead society marching toward incentives that reward the deceitful and weak. They decided that education must be first and foremost about teaching children how to critically think rather than filling their heads with facts and figures memorized without reason.

Citizen participation in government must also allow the very best of the participants to actually have a commanding role in government. This will dissuade the purely opportunistic career politician from ever even entering this field. How do you create a political system that actually judges participants based on their performance? In Western Societies politicians are rewarded or punished based mostly upon factors which have little to do with what they've actually done, because most effects of systemic changes aren't felt till long after they've been enacted.

The Elders realized that they needed to somehow be able to rate and judge not outside career politicians, but on the contrary, their own citizens. If their own citizens would participate enough to somehow be rated, than those people could rise up and replace the career politician forever. This is *exactly* what they did.

The most cumbersome part of the plan lied in how the citizens should be rated. To simply rate them on hours of participation would be a colossal failure prima facia. No, no, the Elders knew that they had to judge them on actual performance, not just whether or not they showed up to 'work'. To do this they decided that the most understanding, intelligent individuals would be able to prove their knowledge based upon their ability to be able to predict the future. They could Prognosticate about various economic forecasts, project completion dates, outcomes of various policies, etc. After performing in a higher percentile relative to their peers by better predicting outcomes, certain citizens would than be asked to move further up into governmental positions. The Ascension process higher and higher up the power chain typically does not move with expediency. This was not the case with Kralsich however. He has been the greatest of all prognosticators since records began. At a very young age he now directly advises the Chairman on policy decisions.

More importantly though is how he is perceived by the public. No one can remember a time when one individual had so intellectually out shone his fellow citizens in such a gross array of subjects. Because of this, he was favored by many to be the next Chairman, while at the same time he caused a growing angst in others who feared the imbalance he could impart on their society.

Being elected Chairman surely garners the highest amount of prestige of any elected office. Accomplishing this feat is not, as all who are asked will agree, a venture for the feeble minded. Those citizens, who finish in the highest percentile of prognosticators thus showing all around them that they have the proper clarity to predict events, are solely responsible for choosing a Chairman. One should be aware that the vast majority of Prognosticators remain anonymous. This means that there is virtually no chance of special interests electing a Chairman.

Prognosticators always have the right to reveal their identities if they choose to do so. Many rather unsuccessful ones, in the lower percentile, do have all of their information completely public. The higher percentile ones on the other hand, typically choose not to have their identities revealed because the public spectacle and scrutiny that exists makes it exceedingly difficult to make predictions in the public eye. Most higher percentile Prognosticators tend to reveal their identities at the same time they make their move into government. The timing is essential.

Only Prognosticators can become Chairman, and only the high percentile prognosticators nominate who can run and ultimately become Chairman. This process has been designed with one thing in mind: The Chairman must be able to comfortably predict the future in order to execute proper policy.

The process begins with the Prognosticators nominating other Prognosticators for the Chairmanship. Prognosticators cannot nominate themselves and most of the nominations go to the top ten Prognosticators. Some particularly successful Prognosticators who have already revealed their identities and hold government jobs are almost assured a nomination providing that they have continued prognosticating regularly.

It is not always the case that the top Prognosticators are nominated. During times of economic calamity, for instance, a Prognosticator who has a higher percentage of economic predictions correct may receive the nomination over someone who is more balanced.

Once the nominees are chosen they then are permitted to submit a Goal of Continuity, which is essentially the nominees' platform for their term in office and beyond. The Prognosticators evaluate the nominees' plans and vote for the one they like the best, knowing they can eventually modify the plan with their own Prognostications.

At the end of process it becomes evident that the most intelligent people in society become Prognosticators, who then chose the most intelligent people from among themselves, and then choose the smartest person from among even that upper tier. In conclusion, the participants in this system are the best of the best beyond a doubt. This makes it all the more astounding that as it stands now, Kralsich may not only become the youngest nominee for Chairman in history, but most believe due to his genius level prognosticative performance, that his ascension is imminent.

* * *

Insurance

When Professor Briarton had awoken from a momentary nap in his calming office, he had a thought which his dreams stirred inside him. Having spent so much time as a professor around so much information he would wake suddenly with an idea from time to time. He knew that eventually these thoughts would amount to something and did not hesitate to record them for later examination. He pressed the record button on his digital device and began speaking:

"In this system people tend to always try to protect themselves from various calamities. This is a natural impulse is it not? Birds build nests to protect their young from predators; rabbits live in holes, just as we live in houses to shields ourselves from the outside elements. This animal impulse that protects us is due to natural selection. Birds who did not build nests have their young eaten, rabbits that don't live in holes get chased down by wolves, and people who don't find shelter run a fever and eventually die. Just as sex fills the role for propagation of the species, likewise is the pursuit of shelter and protection for the role of ensured survival.

So if a bird discovered that nest insurance existed, she would surely buy it; would she not? One could easily hear the advertisement: for only one percent of the worms you gather per season we'll come and build you a new nest if yours gets damaged in any manner! Sounds like a good deal doesn't it? Well it is a good deal, but only during the first season in which it's available. The first season in which all the birds buy the insurance almost all the nests have already been built. The next year when even more birds have the insurance they most likely will change their behavior because of this new safety net which has been established. So, for instance, when a bird goes to build a nest, she may choose a branch that is a *little* shakier than one would have chosen before she bought insurance. She does this because she is well aware that if the branch gives way and the nest is damaged, it will be paid for by the insurance agent.

The birds would have never collectively entered into this scheme if they realized they would end up not only subsidizing bad behavior but actually creating it! After many, many seasons the birds have become so accustomed to building nests in the wrong location and with shoddy materials (what's the point of meticulously gathering strong twigs – they'll rebuild for fee) that eventually they don't even *remember how* to build proper nests in suitable locations.

This mechanism plays out with *ALL* forms of insurance. People buy automobiles that cost more money than they make in a *year*. Do they drive as carefully as they should? No. Why should they? If the vehicle becomes damaged due to a collision they don't have to pay - the insurance takes care of it! Because of this they are far more likely to engage in dangerous behavior like turning without signaling, speeding, talking on the phone, eating, and the worst of all offenses . . . . tail gating. There was no significant financial burden placed on them and because and of that, they will simply pay a deductible and perhaps a small increase in their monthly payments, which amount to minor inconveniences at most.

When most natural systems are unbalanced, the resulting correction often involves entities which had nothing to due with the problem, but whom are nevertheless along for the ride. For instance: Deer eat the leaves of young trees. If too many of these trees exist due to artificial foresting, then their will be an overabundance of deer. This overabundance leads to a disease which decimates the deer population. Who wins? You could say the trees because now they will not get eaten. Who loses? The mountain lions will starve being that they eat large game like deer which makes up the bulk of their diets.

So when a devastating hurricane destroys houses which were shoddily constructed on sand, what then?

The insurance companies who were supposed to cover such catastrophes can not possibly afford to pay out all of those claims at one time. At this point the government steps and gives money to either the insurance companies themselves or to the people with the damaged houses. Eventually the government will force the companies to provide insurance for a whole host of idiotic decisions. So in the end, people who choose not to participate in the insurance scheme because they realize that it *increases* riskier, unwanted behavior, are forced to pay for it eventually through taxes. The mountain lion had nothing to do with the clear cutting of the forest and its subsequent over abundance of saplings. Just the same, the non-insurance payer had nothing to do with those people who live in an unstable area. Both the non-insurance payer and the mountain lion are simply bystanders – the mountain lion had the imbalance of too many young trees in the forest – while the non-insurance payer had too many people who lived in unsafe areas due to the moral hazard of insurance. When both systems are put out of balance they both affect bystanders. The Bystander Effect is one of the worst parts of insurance because it forces non-participants to also become involved.

    The next, most insidious part of insurance is the Rising Prices Effect. This happens because the people buying the products have little incentive to find a competitive price. Let's say all of the sudden that the government decided to provide computer insurance. This Computer Insurance stipulates that every American has the right to own a computer, and the government would cover the cost for people who don't have enough money to afford the devices. Seems like a great election campaign idea! We'll just assume the law passes and then all of the sudden the government starts cutting checks. There would obviously be more people with broken laptops because they could get them replaced for free, but even worse than that, people wouldn't care about the cost. This would lead to businesses charging more because price has now become irrelevant.

This phenomenon is evident when people attempt to fix their cars after a minor fender bender. Sure the insurance companies (or government depending on the situation) try in vain to 'cap' the expense. In our case for instance, the insurance company will pay a maximum of five hundred dollars for a fender to be replaced. This unfortunately will have the *undesired* effect of letting the people who charged *below* $500 use the higher price as their guideline. Thus prices not only rise more consistently across the board, but in addition the government decides when the price should rise. In reality this is a form of price fixing, and the only place people should see price fixing is in a command economy.

So it is no surprise *at all*, that the industries with the most government involvement have the highest rate of inflation. In industries like medicine, education, or even real estate, the subsidies and price fixing through *whatever* method, leads to imbalances, the Bystander Effect, the Rising Prices Effect and eventually creshendoing crashes.

When people have insurance they are encouraged *not* to *think* before they make decisions because they know any consequences from a bad decision will be covered by the insurance companies themselves. This same phenomenon plays out in different areas as well. When the government provides regulatory bodies to ensure the safety of certain products there is therefore a decrease in the knowledge about the product. For instance: when a government agency that monitors drug and food quality claims that something is safe, the consumer of that product is far less likely to do the proper research to ensure that the product is in fact safe.

The same is true for something completely socialized like insurance for your bank account in the event of a bank insolvency. How many people research a bank to see if it is a good manager of money, or do they blindly open an account because they're aware that there's deposit insurance?

All of these institutions and companies raise the specter of a full blown systemic crash as people perform less and less of their own due diligence. By not performing their own research the people also loose part of their own da Vincian well roundedness and become consequently more narrowly focused. It's a good thing for people to learn how banks really work, isn't it? However people rarely examine this subject. Why would they? They don't receive a benefit from doing so because the deposit insurance covers their bank deposits. One begins to wonder if the lack of an inspectful, consumer eye was the point of these insurance institutions all along!

**Appendix B
Sources:**

Axe, David. *War Bots: How US Military Robots are Transforming War in Iraq, Afghanistan, and the Future*. Ann Arbor, MI: Nimble Books LLC, 2008), *pg.* 52.

Bernanke, Benjamin. "I couldn't agree with you more that inflation is a tax". July 16, 2008. Congressional Testimony. United States House of Representatives.
See Also:
http://www.pbs.org/newshour/news_summaries/2008/07/summary_16.html
Video:
http://www.youtube.com/watch?v=D4yBrxmEOkY

Gatto, John Taylor, *Dumbing Us Down*, (Canada: New Society Publishers, 2005).

Guarner F, Malagelada JR (February 2003). "Gut flora in health and disease". Lancet 361 (9356): 512–9.

von Hayek, Friedrich, *Monetary Theory and the Trade Cycle,* (London: Jonathan Cape 1929).

Hazlitt, Henry, *Economics in One Lesson: The Shortest and Surest Way to Understand Basic Economics*. (New York: Three Rivers Press, New York, New York, 1962).

Hülsmann, Jörg Guido, *The Ethics of Money Production,* (Auburn Alabama: Ludwig von Mises Institute, 2008).

Paine, Thomas. *Common Sense*, (Philadelphia: printed and sold by W. and T. Bradford [1776]; Bartleby.com, 1999).

Peden M, et al (editors), *World Report on Road Traffic Injury Prevention*, (World Health Organization, 2004).

Perkins, John., <u>Confessions of an Economic Hitman.</u> (San Francisco: Berrett-Koehler Publishers Inc, 2004).

Pollan, Michael, *In Defense of Food*. (New York: Penguin Books, 2009).

D. Salart, A. Baas, C. Branciard, N. Gisin, and H. Zbinden, "Testing spooky action at a distance," Group of Applied Physics, University of Geneva, 20, Rue de l'Ecole de M_edecine, CH-1211 Geneva 4, Switzerland.
For more information search: *Quantum Entanglement*.

Shorrock, Tim, *Spies for Hire: The Secret World of Intelligence Outsourcing*, (New York: Simon and Schuster, 2008). *ALSO: from the Office of the Director of National Intelligence 2006.

Thompson, Earl (2007), "The tulipmania: Fact or artifact?" (PDF), *Public Choice* **130** (1–2): 99–114, doi:10.1007/s11127-006-9074-4

Thoreau, Henry David., *The Natural History Essays*, (Salt Lake City: Gibbs Smith Publisher, 1980).

Made in the USA
Charleston, SC
14 May 2011